the rest of your natural life. *Big German
girls with thighs of steel to crush a man to
his smiling death . . . and the Swedes! . . . .
the Swedes. Sun tanned angels with long
white hair and wondrous lips . . .*" His voice
had taken on a hushed reverence. "*And of
course the little English roses . . . and the
Irish, Scots and Welsh. They all have their lovely
moments. They come here in their thousands – a
vast multitude of provocation thirsting for sun
and sand and sea and sex. This is four-S country,
for sure. It's enough to drive you blind.*"

Attaboy, Russ Tobin!

The Courier

Stanley Morgan

Mayflower

Granada Publishing Limited
First published in 1971 by Mayflower Books Ltd
3 Upper James Street, London W1R 4BP
Reprinted 1971 (twice) 1972

Copyright © Stanley Morgan 1971
Made and printed in Great Britain by
C. Nicholls & Company Ltd
The Philips Park Press, Manchester
Set in Intertype Times

The Courier

CHAPTER ONE

The Kum Kum Club is probably the last place in London you'd chose to discuss anything of great importance in, mainly because there's more noise going on in here than in a dried pea factory working bonus overtime. But it's not only the noise. The place is downright weird. In fact it has to be seen and heard to be disbelieved.

In a room not much larger than the average bathroom eighteen million kids are blowing their mini minds to re-corded mayhem and wallowing in personal freak-outs amidst monstrous flashing lights that spin and whirl and flicker and flash to the beat of the hideous, ear-splitting jungle music. The effect of this stroboscopia is nightmarishly remarkable for in it you see human movement as in every third frame of a film – with the two intervening frames removed, hence a gyrating, arm-flinging, hair-swirling dolly appears to move in great flickering leaps, one moment jerkily bending, the next reaching upwards to grab the low matt-black ceiling, the next straining towards a lurid, psychedelic wall. The brain of both dancer and observer whirls, the eyes are baffled and the heart pounds unnaturally resenting the environment, and if you didn't know better you'd think you were on some form of kinky, drugless trip – which is undoubtedly what is intended and what this kooky discotheque business is all about.

It is half past nine on a Thursday evening, a week before Christmas and what, you may be asking yourself, am I doing in this dump if I hate it so much.

Russ Tobin is the name. Sitting across the square metal table from me in a state of semi-shock is my good and close amigo Tony Dane – handsome, dark, and curly-haired fellow actor in television commercials and all-round good egg.

For six months now, ever since I joined Tony in London to seek my fame and fortune in the Smoke, it has been a policy of ours, Tony's and mine, to "get to know London better" – a programme of social research based on the mutual belief that one's doorstep should be intimately investigated before venturing further afield. And so, last June, we started with the strip-clubs, drinking clubs and discotheques, preferring to leave the art galleries, museums, historical sites and ancient

7

buildings until later in our young lives. So far we've done two or three clubs a week – some sixty in all – and have not yet moved out of central London. And at the rate the new dumps, like the Kum Kum, are opening up we shall both be four hundred and thirty before we get a squint at our first Rembrandt. Wey hey!

As I say, this is no place in which to discuss anything of import and yet I am currently in the throes of discussing with Tony – or rather attempting to discuss against the battering barrage of cacophony emanating from four giant loudspeakers each the size of a tractor crate – the amazing turn of events which in the past four weeks has completely upended my life, fragmented my plans and caused me to do some very hard thinking and decision making. It really has been the most remarkable month and before proceeding to other matters I had better fill you, if you'll pardon the phrase, in.

You may recall how, after an interesting year up North selling sewing machines on the switch method and a further enlightening period of debt collecting for Karefree Kredit Inkorporated, I met up with Tony Dane in Bootle General Hospital in Liverpool, having torn all the ligaments in my leg while attempting to collect a debt from a purple-faced ape named Nutting, Tony having all but removed his knee-cap on the ticket bin of a tramcar he was riding on in the course of shooting a television commercial.

In the ten days we spent together in hospital we became very good friends and at the end of that time I, being fed up with my job and life in the provinces, leapt at Tony's invitation to try my luck in London and in commercials.

Well, since June I've been down here and doing very nicely. To give you an idea of just how nicely, at the moment I've got three commercials going out national for Christmas. I'm playing a suave party-guest in the Glamour Soap ad; a young father in the Klippit construction Kit ad; and a do-it-yourself fanatic up a ladder scaling rust off the house guttering on Christmas morning with a Gusto electric drill. In financial terms this means a very happy Christmas indeed for Russell who should (when the ad agencies get around to paying me) be something like four hundred pounds better off than if he'd stayed in bed.

Add to these a dozen or so other commercials which between last June and this December, having received a plentiful airing right across the country, have paid for a substantial wardrobe of very natty suits, the rent of a bachelor flat in Maida Vale and a two-year-old Lotus Elan and you will see that my sojourn in the south has not been entirely in vain. Put another way, for a twenty-four year old village-born kid from Cheshire with a scant grammar school education and training in nothing but dumb acceptance of fate and station, we are doing all right.

What then has happened in the past month to upset this comfy applecart? Strange to relate it is success itself that has presented me with a very tacky problem – it being: what am I going to do with the next twelve months of my life?

This is how it happened.

A month ago, through my theatrical agent, Mike Spiring, I was approached by Croxleys advertising agency to do some street interviews for a brand of potato crisps. Croxleys told me they were after the highly lucrative Crunchums account and were making a test reel of street interviews for presentation to Crunchums in the hope of pinching the account from a rival agency.

I'd never done this sort of work before but somehow I fancied it and said I'd do it. Well, I spent an hilarious couple of days with a small camera team in the freezing streets of London, stopping people to ask them what they thought of Crunchums and of course doing my best to get favourable replies, and despite the blistering north winds and the snow and sleet I managed to get them laughing and telling me the most outrageous fibs about how they wouldn't have a crisp in the house except Crunchums and how crisp and fresh and tasty and heavenly and inspiring and uplifting they were. (Take the general public by surprise with a camera and a microphone and they'll tell you anything you want to hear).

Then towards the end of the second day we were working our way along Knightsbridge. I'd just interviewed a dear old soul about a hundred and thirty years old and as mad as all get out who had told me she just adored Crunchums but always ate them in the bath and did I know of a way to stop the steam making them soggy, when we happened upon a large hole in the road. Down in the depths was a huge Irish navvy, hacking away at a lump of concrete with a pickaxe and singing "The Rose of Tralee" to himself in rich Irish baritone. I approached the edge of the hole and held my mike down to him.

"Excuse me, sir."

9

He stopped bashing the concrete and looked up. "Yhes-sirr?"

"Sorry to trouble you – but could you tell me what you think of Crunchums potato crisps?"

"Paterta crisps?" he said thoughtfully. "Be Gob, I nhever touch the fuckers!"

I almost fell in the hole laughing. The camera crew was in pleats. "Marvellous ... marvellous!" cried the director. "We'll end the film with this one."

And they did. And they got the Crunchums account. The managing director, an Irishman, by all accounts nearly died of laughing apoplexy when the reel was shown to him and he bought the project on the spot.

Success breeding itself as it proverbially does, Tobin's name flashed around Croxleys as the greatest street interviewer ever to poke a microphone up the public's nose and within the month they were on the phone to my agent with a very, very attractive but also deadly dangerous proposition. Would I be prepared to do a series of twelve street-interview commercials for White Marvel?

Now White Marvel is a detergent and detergent is a dirty word in the commercial world, more artistes having committed professional suicide by presenting soap powders on telly than any other ten products lumped together. I personally know of two fellows who, a couple of years back, presented soap powders for a period of twelve months and the poor devils haven't worked since. At least not in television. One is now a floor-walker in Harrods and the other files bits of paper for the Income Tax people. They were pitifully over-exposed, you see, so much so that half the housewives in Britain their faces were more familiar than the faces of their husbands and after the campaigns were over no casting director would touch them.

So, the initial reaction of my agent, Mike Spiring, to Croxleys' proposition was thanks but no thanks and he winked at me over the desk while he was telling them on the phone. But then, in the next instant, his naturally pallid complexion became positive whitewash and his mouth sagged open. "I'll ... have to discuss it with him," he said and put down the phone.

"What's the matter?" I asked.

"The bastards."

"What's the matter?"

"Money," he croaked. "They're offering money."

"Like how much?"

"Like six thousand pounds."

I went ice cold, numb; then hot with rushing flushes. A fortune!

"Good God . . ." was all I could muster.

"Hold on," he said. "Think about it . . . about the consequences. White Marvel could put you out of business for a year. You'd be dead for other commercials."

"Is that all, though – a year? Not permanently?"

He shrugged. "Who can say? But they tell me the campaign is only for this coming summer, not longer. They want to shoot the street interviews early January and transmit the twelve commercials from March to August. That being so . . ." he shrugged again, ". . . six months after the campaign may be enough to reinstate you with the casting people."

"Six thousand . . ." I was musing.

"No, it won't be six, will it? There's ten percent for me and a great chunk for the Income Tax crowd. You'll be lucky to finish with a net three and a half thousand."

"Still, it's a lot of bread, Mike."

"Think about it. Go home and sleep on it. Think what you'll do with yourself for a year if you can't do commercials. Try and get a plan together."

And so, that being yesterday, here I am sitting in the Kum Kum with Tony trying to get a plan together. I'm still not properly over the shock. My mind wanders constantly in soaring flights of fancy. I see myself reclining on a Grecian beach, the proud owner of a superbly-appointed beach bar, surrounded by a bunch of adoring, sun-kissed lovelies, never having to do another stroke of work in my life. Or I see myself driving the Lotus across Europe, staying where I please for as long as I please, living the life I've always yearned for, investigating Paris, Madrid, Rome with a scrumptious-looking angel with long legs and a generous, loving nature. It's all too much for my plebeian soul. I need help.

Tony tore his eyes from the cavorting mass crowding the tiny floor and made a face of terrible discomfort.

"Man . . ." he shouted. "We have hit new low low!"

The effect of the strange lighting on his grimace was a comical collection of single-frame contortions and even his voice seemed to jump. "I think I'm going to be sick!"

11

I waved him down. "Relax! It's a cheap evening! I'm getting tight on light!"

"I need a real drink!" He gestured with disgust to the Coke on the table, the only drink available in this dry, dreary disco.

"Me, too!" I yelled.

I, of course, knew the true root of his discomfiture and it had little to do with either the lighting or the noise in the cellar. Or, for that matter, with the Coke. Due to travel commitments on commercials that had taken us both away from London for a good portion of the last four weeks it had been a barren, nookyless month for the two of us and we were now feeling the disquieting, insistent needs that nature attends upon strong, healthy bucks of twenty four summers. After such a rare, almost unprecedented period of enforced celibacy the birds in the Kum Kum were driving him potty – as they would have done me had I not such pressing problems on my mind. Even so, I found my attention wandering with increasing frequency towards the dance-floor, towards legs and hips and breasts and long, shiny hair and away from the year ahead.

A particular girl caught my eye. Tall and sinuous, she moved with the lithe grace of a ballet dancer, flowing before her fella with a rippling undulation of hips and thighs that had him boggle-eyed and breathless. He stood it for a few beats longer then grabbed her and pulled her hard against him, driving his groin at her. She threw back her head and laughed, relishing the brutal contact. I heard Tony sigh. I laughed and he turned and grinned at being caught in lust.

"It's been a dull month, son," I said.

"Ain't it, though. But there's a couple over there that could undull it."

"Where?"

"At the back, dancing together. They'll be around."

We waited for them and when they came they'd certainly been worth waiting for. One was blonde, the other dark. They were medium tall and slender, about twenty years old, give or take a few minutes either way. They danced separately, moving automatically, immersed in private thought, almost oblivious of the racket going on around them.

"Not bad," I said appreciatively.

"Not bad, he says."

"All right – do something."

"You on?"

"You kidding?"

"Right."

As we got up from the metal folding chairs there was a sudden and deafening silence. The cacophony ceased. The hideous lighting surrendered to good old ordinary stuff. I breathed a sigh of relief and sat down again, realising my ears hurt. I was sweating just sitting there.

"Buggerit," said Tony.

The girls faltered in mid-floor, searching for seats. There were two vacant chairs at our table. Tony swung towards me, elbows on the table.

"It's Chelsea for the cup, no doubt about it."

"Disgusting – the price of elephants. I was only saying the other . . . they're coming."

He grinned satanically. "Of course."

They emerged from the vortex and silently took the seats. I could feel their eyes momentarily upon us but we ignored them. They turned away from us, facing the floor, and we relaxed and began a close inspection.

Both wore trouser suits of some silky material; it may have been silk. The trousers were bell-bottoms, tight on the thigh, flaring below the knee. Under each long-sleeved blouse was evidence of generous breasts. A fascinating material, silk. It clings, reveals; hillock high, crevice deep; and exhudes the texture of cool skin.

The brunette had long jet hair cut square across her shoulders. Dark brown liquid eyes slept in a dusky oval face. Full and well-formed lips spread beneath a small, neat nose. Italian, perhaps. Or Spanish. Au pair? Quite likely.

The blonde was a complete contrast. Her face was firm with high cheek bones, a thin, aloof face with a straight, serious nose and a determined, though full, mouth. Her eyes, perpetuating the image, were cool grey and unsmiling. I noticed her hands particularly with their long tapering fingers and perfect filbert nails. She moved her hands gracefully, frequently touching her shoulder-length hair, the colour of pale honey. Scandinavian, I thought. Also au pair. Quite a pair. I wasn't at all fussy. Either one would do magnificently.

I raised a brow at Tony and he murmured, "You're telling me," from the corner of his mouth.

The blonde delved into a multi-coloured bead handbag and brought out a packet of Stuyvesant and a gold lighter, offered the cigarettes to the Italian and tutted irritably when the

13

lighter refused to ignite. Tony beat me to it by a fiftieth of a second. The Italian nodded thanks as she took his flame and the Swede or whatever she was managed a grunt. Then they turned to look out across the floor, not once looking at us.

Tony snapped his lighter shut and shrugged at me.

"Change your deodorant," I said.

At that moment the records started up again, this time something much more my cup of cocoa – Stevie Wonder with a slow, romantic smooch. Couples drifted onto the darkened floor and began not dancing with each other. Tony cleared his throat, braced himself and in his best Charles Boyer growl murmured to the Italian, "Would you like to dance?"

I winced for him, expecting either stony silence or some annihilating rebuke, but instead she nodded and immediately got up. Tony slid me a bloody superior wink and followed her onto the floor, swaggering exaggeratedly for my benefit, and began gyrating before her with considerable expertise. I'll say one thing for Tony, he's a luvly moover.

Well, I had to do something. "How about you?" I asked Ice Cool Alice.

In reply she smashed her fag into the tin ashtray and stood up.

To say I danced with her for three numbers would be a filthy lie. It was not this one's policy to dance with anyone. What she did was a narcissistic solo for ten minutes, uttering not a syllable, never once looking at me, certainly not touching me. She just oiled around on one spot and gazed at the floor with the forlorn, despairing expression of Joan of Arc watching the faggots being lit. I really don't know why she'd bothered coming out in the cold. She could've stayed at home and had a ball staring at her navel.

At the end of the third tune Tony and his own bundle of joy emerged from the melee and by his expression he'd had the same riotous time I'd had. He pulled a face at me like he'd inadvertently collected a mouthful of worms and was looking for a place to spit them.

As we reached the table he said to the Italian, "Thank you, that was hilarious."

The girls sat down and resumed the same silent aloofness as before, ignoring us, staring across the room. I was fed up with them and decided to end it. I took a final sip of warm Coke and bashed the glass onto the table.

"I want a drink," I said. "A real one."

"Sure," said Tony.

"You won't get one in here," said the blonde. "They don't have a licence."

I looked at her, not sure she was speaking to me because she was still looking out across the floor. I was perplexed – on two counts; firstly because she'd spoken to me at all, and secondly because she'd done it in a Liverpool accent. Scandinavian? The kid was pure Scouse. Not violently but enough for my well-trained ear to detect. The sing-song lilt was unmistakable. My courage soared. I was on home ground.

"I know," I said. "That's why we're drinking this bilge . . ."

Tony jumped in, brightening visibly. "They've got a licence in the pub fifty yards down the road."

"I know," said the blonde.

"You girls fancy one?" I asked.

She looked at the friend, a smirk softening the forbidding firmness of her mouth.

"Don't mind if I do," replied the Italian. Italian? Ha! Birmingham without doubt. A Brownhills buttercup. Just how wrong can you get? I was overwhelmed with relief.

"I'm Russ Tobin," I said. "This is Tony Dane."

"June Everett," said the blonde.

"Eileen Ash," said the Birmingham Italian.

"Let's get out of this madhouse," said I.

We'd been in the pub less than half an hour and already the girls had gulped three large gins. These two could really shift it. Not that we begrudged them a drop, mind you. They were very good company, chatty, relaxed, and with three equally large vodkas inside us they were getting more yummy by the passing minute.

June, the blonde, was sitting close to me. Eileen was platonically rubbing knees with Tony. We'd paired off that way, more by instinct than any design. We all seemed very happy with the arrangement.

They had talked incessantly, telling us about themselves. They'd both been in London a year, trying, with some success, to break into modelling. They shared a flat off the Bayswater road, near Shepherds Bush, which information we had fished for quite early on and had received with just the right degree of circumnavigation – not too readily nor too reticently. But slowly a picture was forming that had my heart thumping like a pump plunger. We had undoubtedly caught a couple of fliers, and if we played it right there was little doubt tonight would see the end of a double fortnight of stick-strangling celibacy. Tony knew it too. Guarded glances told me he was working on a bomb pattern to breach these lovely dams.

About a quarter to eleven, near to closing time, June finally asked the question I knew had been plaguing her since we left the Kum Kum. Looking at us closely, first me then Tony, she said, "You know, I'm sure I've seen you two before somewhere."

"Yes, me too," said her pal. "Funny that."

"That's supposed to be the fella's line," I laughed.

"No, seriously."

Tony nudged my knee under the table. "You probably have. Do you watch much television?"

"Are you on T.V.?" asked June.

Tony smiled. "Did you see 'Heroes Of Our Time' this week?"

The girls shook their heads, puzzled. Well they might be — there's no such blinking programme. What's the lying sod up to, I wondered.

"B.B.C.2," he said gravely. "Very late."

"No," the girls chorused .

Tony faltered. "It's a bit embarrassing really . . ."

"Oh, go on . . . tell us," June urged.

Tony swallowed his drink, paused theatrically, placed his glass on the table. "We had . . . rather a nasty time. Russ and I were making a documentary film in Peru . . . about an ancient and primitive tribe of Indians — a very savage tribe of head-hunters who live deep in the jungle . . ."

"I think I saw that," Eileen said uncertainly.

Tony nodded. "Quite possibly. Well, one day — it's almost a year ago now — flying over the densest jungle imaginable . . . our engine failed. Petrol blockage. Russ, here, made a miraculous landing on a dried-up river bed but slap bang in the middle of this tribe's territory. We were taken prisoner of course . . ."

The girls were looking at us oddly, not knowing whether to believe this rubbish or not. Tony can be very convincing when he tries.

"What happened?" asked June, smiling uncertainly.

Tony looked at me. "Russ, how about another drink before they close?"

"Mm?" He dragged me back abruptly from darkest Peru,

fighting for my life on a dried river bed, poison arrows whistling around me ear-hole and clanging off the fuselage. "Oh, sure."

I gathered the glasses and went to the bar, grinning to myself. The place was crowded, so close to closing time, and I had to wait a few minutes to be served. Every now and then I stole a glance at the table. Tony was hard at it. The girls seemed riveted to every word he was spilling them. Suddenly June looked across at me. I turned quickly away, offering a brave profile as though the memories of Peru were still searingly painful to me.

Finally I collected the drinks and returned to the table. Tony looked up at me. "Well, I've told them, Russ."

I nodded soberly. "Better out than in."

"It must have been *terrible*," said June, laughter showing in her eyes.

"Awful," echoed Eileen.

"Still ..." June's eyes played over me sexily. "... you're obviously no worse for wear."

"Time is a great healer," I said solemnly.

"Yes," said Tony. "A few weeks in Bognor and we were back on our feet again."

Bognor!

The girls looked at each other. June reached for her handbag. "I must go somewhere."

"Me, too," said Eileen.

We watched them go, heading for the loo, a very desirable duo.

"What," I asked, sipping my drink, "did you tell them?"

His eyes widened with preposterous innocence. "Only the truth, son ... that the tribe had never seen white men before and thought we were gods descended from heaven on a big blue bird ..."

"Mm, that sounds reasonable."

"... and, desiring that our deific essence be inculcated into the tribe, they refused to let us go until we had screwed every woman in the village ..."

"Sure," he said seriously.

I exploded.

"How many women were there supposed to be?"

"Eight hundred."

"Eight hundred."

"Four hundred each."

17

"And how long were we at it?"

"Three months. Think about it."

"I'm thinking. That's ninety days . . ."

"I made it a round hundred. Couldn't make it too preposterous."

"Sure. One hundred days into four hundred women . . . four doodles a day . . ."

"We had the nights, too."

"Of course, I was forgetting."

"Well, we couldn't hang around, could we? We had a film to make."

"And d'you think for one split minute these two believe all this cr . . ."

"No, I don't. But it got 'em going. It got the conversation around to the right subject in short time."

"And?"

"And I think we're in for a very interesting evening."

My blood erupted. I have the greatest faith in Tony's instinct in such matters, a faith born of six months impeccable bulls-eye prognoses on his part.

"Yeh?" I exclaimed.

"Trust your uncle. The lovely things became quite breathless at the word-pictures I drew of you and me and the trailing lines of eager brown queuing up for it outside our nuptial hut."

"I can't believe it. It's been a long, long month."

"An eternity, love."

"Wonderful. Well, what's the course?"

"We take them back to their place for a drink. I've got the two halves in the boot." Tony always has two halves of vodka stashed in the boot of his Lotus Plus-two. Ever since the night he missed a sure thing, after closing time, for want of a couple more drinks, he has always kept two halves in the boot.

"Splendid", I said admiringly. What a joy it is to work with a professional. "Now, how do we mingle? As we are?"

He shrugged. "I'm happy – if it suits the girls. And it appears it does. Eileen smells very nice."

"So does June. I do like girls who smell nice."

"A prime consideration. Cleanliness may be next to Godliness but they don't have to be filthy to be fun."

"Here they come . . ."

The girls were squeezing through the considerable crowd around the bar, attracting a lot of lewd attention from the men, smiling at the wisecracks as they passed. They came up to the table looking refreshed and newly groomed. They sat down and sipped their drinks, then June, with a smile, said to Tony, "Of course we don't believe a word of that story ... but we have seen you both on telly, haven't we? On the commercials. Right?"

"Right," said Tony.

Eileen leaned towards me. "You're in the Glamour soap one, aren't you? You're standing with the girl who gets the box of soap from the chap who's throwing the party."

I held up my hands. "You got me."

Tony added, "He's also the father building the criminally misleading forty-feet-long bridge with the ten bob Klippit Construction Kit for his adoring son. And he's also the nut up the ladder with the Gusto electric drill ..."

"And he," I said, cocking my thumb at Tony, "is the smoothy in the velvet smoking-jacket drinking bathtub sherry by candlelight ..."

"Oh, yes!" exclaimed Eileen. "I love that one."

"And the big butch slob sprawled in the punt blowing cigar smoke at the bird in the bikini," I continued.

"Are all those you two?" asked June, impressed beyond doubt.

A noticeable change had come over the girls in the last few minutes. They were both impressed, fluttery, realising they had picked up a couple of fellas who were "different" almost public figures. It was going to be a *very* interesting evening.

At that moment the chap behind the bar called time and flicked the lights on and off several times to make sure we got the message.

"We'll take you home," announced Tony, making it a statement, not an invitation. He stood and helped Eileen on with her mock-fur coat, a fluffy, off-white job with a deep collar. "We'll have to go in twos," he said. "The cars are a bit small. They're just around the corner."

I helped June on with her coat, a nylon-leopard skin with big spots, noting that no objection, either by word or look, had been made to our taking them home.

We exchanged the smokey, beery warmth of the pub for the bleakness of the street and trudged through wet slush to the cars. An icy wind cut through us as we rounded a corner. I put my arm around June and hugged her close, enjoying the slippery sensuousness of the fur sliding over the silk suit. Her waist was very slim; the texture of her body firm but yielding; she had a strong, hard body in, no doubt, the pale-pink of condition.

We walked behind Tony and Eileen who also clung together against the wind. June slipped her arm around me, not sexily but just there, a comforting reassurance that she didn't find me absolute poison.

"What are you doing for Christmas?" I asked her.

"Haven't really thought about it."

"You won't be going home – to Liverpool?"

She looked at me and laughed, as though I was mad. "Good God, no. Wild horses wouldn't get me back."

I felt inexplicably saddened to hear it. I know I'd just deserted Liverpool myself but I'm still fond of the old place. "You don't like it, hm?"

"You wouldn't ask if you knew it," she said bitterly.

"But I do know it. I only came down six months ago."

She frowned at me. "You're no scouse. You don't talk like one, anyway."

"I was born in Cheshire ... but I lived in the Pool for a few years."

"Doing what – television?"

"Heck, no. All sorts of things. I sold sewing machines for a year ... did a spot of debt collecting ... office work. You name it."

"How did you get into commercials then?"

"I met Tony up there. He was in Liverpool making a commercial. He fell down the stairs of a tram and bust his knee. He was in the bed next to mine in Bootle General."

"What were you in for?"

"I fell down a flight of stairs trying to collect somebody's debts."

She laughed. "What a pair. And you came down to London with him?"

"Yes. He was a big help in getting me started. He's a luvly fella."

"Good for you," she said fervently. "I like to hear of someone breaking out. It's not easy. I know." She made it sound like escaping from a top security prison. I would have asked her what her own experience had been but we had reached the cars. They stood alone in that stretch of road, an impressive duo of Lotuses parked one behind the other. Tony's larger

Plus two was bright, flashy yellow; mine, the Elan, was ano-
dized bronze. In the light from a distant street lamp they
looked immaculate, powerful, luxurious. I caught a glance
pass between the girls. Money, it said. The boys are loaded.
We are not with tat tonight.

I opened the passenger door for June. She parked her bottom in then swung her legs in, doubling them to clear the
sill, then stretched out and relaxed in the black-leather upholstery. I saw her expression as she inspected the interior,
the upholstery, the array of dials on the dash. Something
happens to girls when they see a quality sportscar and it
happens twice as hard when they sit in one. June was no exception. She was ga ga.

I closed her door and walked around, shouted "We'll follow
you" to Tony, and got in, closing my door with a solid, satis-
fying, chunky thud.

The engine leapt into life at first touch and I couldn't resist
gunning it for a bit of swank, revelling in the throaty, bub-
bling roar that raspberried out of the pipe.

Tony shot away. I followed him into Berkeley Square,
throwing June into the back of her seat with a burst of accel-
eration that had her gasping. What a difference to poor old
Fred, bless his rusty radiator. Fred was the Hillman Minx
I'd had for two years up North while I was selling sewing
machines and collecting debts. I was around and out of
Berkeley Square and into Davies Street in less time than it
would've taken to start old Fred. I grinned to myself. I'd
never made a girl gasp in Fred – well, not with his accelera-
tion anyway.

"You two do all right for yourselves," June remarked.

"How – oh, the cars? Well, you need something to run
around town in."

"Something that does a hundred and ten?"

"A hundred and twenty-five," I corrected gently.

"Commercials obviously pay well."

"Some do. How about modelling. does that pay well?"

"It can."

"Does it – for you?"

She shrugged. "The competition is enormous."

"You dress very well. I like that suit."

"Thanks."

"Silk is very flattering – on the right figure."

Her coat had fallen open, exposing her legs. Wearing trous-

21

ers she was obviously not too concerned about keeping her legs closed and I got the impression that even in a mini skirt she wouldn't be all that concerned either. It was the way she said, "We try to please."

"You've certainly succeeded. You look very nice."

We zipped across the lights at Marble Arch, howled around the complex of roundabouts where once stood Tyburn Tree, and rasped into Bayswater Road, hot on Tony's tail. As we stopped for a traffic light she asked, "Where do you live?"

"Maida Vale ... in Carlton Hill."

"Mm! Posh. What is it, a flat?"

"Just a one-bedroom job. Very nice though."

"I can imagine. Are you married?"

Her directness made me laugh. "No."

"Girl friend?"

"No," The lights changed. I gunned across the intersection and whipped through the gears. "Does that surprise you?"

"Of course. A man with everything you've got – looks, a flat, this car and no girl friend. You obviously can't be queer or I wouldn't be sitting here."

"Nope, not queer. Would it help if I said I don't *currently* have a girlfriend?"

"It would make more sense."

"Then that is the case. I did have one but I strangled her. I strangle all my girlfriends, then cut them up and stuff them in the boot. It helps keep the rear end down on corners."

She giggled and swished her hair. "Could I have a cigarette, I'm out."

I fished one out for her then held out my lighter. She caught my hand to steady the flame. It was the first time our flesh had touched. Her hands were warm and soft and stayed on mine longer, I thought, than was necessary.

"Thanks," she said, releasing me.

"You're welcome."

"You're nice."

"Thank *you*. Don't you meet many nice men?"

"Not many."

"D'you find London hard going?"

"No harder than the North."

She sounded lost, disillusioned. She must have had some pretty rough experiences somewhere along the way.

Tony's right-hand flicker spurted sudden yellow. I followed him off the main road into a secondary road, down it for a hundred yards, then right again into a sort of yard separating two rows of garages with flats built over the top.

Tony stopped and I drew up beside him. We all got out and followed Eileen up an iron staircase leading to one of the flats. I noted twin bulges in Tony's overcoat pockets. He was carrying both halves.

"Enjoy the drive?" I asked Eileen.

She was fumbling in her handbag for the key. "What drive? I was blind with terror."

"You think that was fast," said Tony. "You ought to be in it when I get it into third gear."

"Ought I?" she smiled.

She opened the door and found a light switch. We followed her into a clean and very tidy kitchen. I was impressed. When two birds live together a tidy kitchen can be a rare event. My experience has been that the rule rather than the exception is stockings, panties and bras hanging up to dry or dumped on the draining board.

"Come in," Eileen said. "Take your coats off."

All very civilised. Chances are on a first date you get a limp handshake, a 'ta very much' and the door in your mush. These two were pleasantly surprising us by the minute. I wondered what other pleasant surprises we could look forward to.

Tony produced one of the halves from his pocket and waved it. "I, er, thought you might like a drink."

Eileen, who was about to go through a doorway to an inner room, stopped and smiled, mocking him. "Did you now? That was thoughtful." She nodded at a wall cupboard. "You'll find glasses in there. Tonics are under the sink."

Both girls went through the door. I stayed with Tony and got a couple of tonics from the cupboard under the sink while he put four glasses on a purple tray and sloshed a good shot of vodka into each.

"Well, what d'you think?" I whispered.

He grinned lasciviously and wiggled his brows Groucho Marx style, singing in a whisper, "Tonight ... tonight ... it's goin' to be all right ..."

"I can't believe it's going so well."

"That's because of the long lay-off, son. It's like being out of work. You get to where you can't believe you'll ever do it again."

"You're pretty sure, though, eh?"

"Sure! She had her hand on me old man all the way home!"

23

"Did she?"

"Didn't yours?"

"No, we talked about commercials."

He looked at me askance. "There are times when I've got distinct doubts about you, Tobin."

"How long are we going to stay? I can't be too late, I've got this Croxley thing at ten. I've got to let them know about White Marvel."

"Ten! I'm shooting Slimfit shirts at eight. Anyway, let's play it by ear. They might boot us out after a couple of drinks." How wrong he was.

"How d'you do it by ear?" I asked.

I tipped some tonic into the drinks and he carried the tray into the other room.

It was the living room, nothing too fancy, the usual sort of furnishing you get for four hundred pounds a week in London. The wallpaper was getting a bit tired and the yellow floral carpet was no chicken either. The furnishing consisted of a radiogram, a dining table and four chairs, an armchair and two two-seater settees. The lighting came from two lamps – a floor lamp this end of the room and a table lamp on the radiogram, but a nice cozy glow also came from a big electric fire in the old tiled fireplace. It was one of those fires that simulate burning coal.

Obviously the girls had been watching home movies because the dining table had been moved to the kitchen end of the room and on it was an 8mm projector, pointing at a screen on a tripod at the far end of the room, and the two settees had been placed one either side of the table, facing the screen.

There was no sign of the girls. They'd obviously gone through the other door to take their coats off.

Tony put the tray down on the table and I picked up a cannister of film. It was labelled: Spain. Beach scenes. Eileen in sand dunes. June swimming etc.

I handed it to Tony who grinned and said, "That'll be worth seeing." I was about to pick up a second cannister when June came in. She'd not only taken off her coat but had changed her clothes as well. In place of the trouser suit she wore a white woollen sweater and an incredibly short brown corduroy skirt that exposed her bare legs almost to their junction. She had, as I'd suspected, very good legs indeed. With her hair cascading over one eye and over one shoulder she

24

posed for us in the doorway, allowing the ensemble to dev-
astate us.

"Wow!" I said.

"Silk gets too hot in here," she said, teasing the sweater
down around her hips, pulling it taut across her breasts,
making it patently obvious she had nothing on underneath.

"I'm glad it does," I said.

"So am I," said Tony. "Here, have a drink. Where's Eileen?"

She padded barefoot to us and took the drink from the tray.
"She's changing too. She won't be a minute." She sipped the
drink and took it to the radiogram, then crouched in front of
the gram to put on an L.P., showing us everything in the pro-
cess. In a moment out poured late-night goo in stereo, violins
and slow, romantic piano, high-fidelity mush, wraparound
moosic-to-scroo-to. She danced back to us, eyes closed.

The door opened again and Eileen came in. She was wearing a short, short little-girl dress in dark red velvet. Contrast-
ing with her tumbling black hair it looked stunning.

Tony held out a drink to her. "You ... look very, very
nice."

"Thank you."

"I do believe I would like to dance with you."

She put down the drink and wrapped her arms around
his neck. I reached for June who needed no prompting. She
melted against me, pressing her body hard, her cheek against
mine. And we were away.

We did a slow, slo..o..o..w circuit of the room, separated from the others. As we passed the lamp on the radiogram I whispered, "It's so *bright* in here."

With a smile she clicked off the lamp. Tony, at the far end
of the room, must have said much the same because next
moment off went the floor lamp. We danced on in the glow
from the fire. After a while she unbuttoned my jacket and
slipped her hands under it, pressing me even closer to her.
Her breathing got a little unsteady. I kissed her ear. She shud-
dered and laughed. "Don't *do* that. It gives me goosebumps."
I did it again and she giggled. "*Stop* it, you don't know what it
does to me!"

I had a damn good idea. Her fingers were probing my spine
and her pelvic bone was trying to push mine through the wall.
The agitation of her thighs became more pronounced, then
suddenly they separated and she began rubbing herself against
my leg. Her fingers trickled into my ear. Then she kissed it and

stuck her tongue down it. I felt a terrible surge coming on and let it come. She felt it instantly and moved against me with a groan. I slipped my hand under her sweater and found naked breast. She moaned softly and bit my ear, whispering imploringly, "Oh, don't . . . don't," meaning do . . . do.

The record came to an end. She left me to flip it over then came back to the same position immediately. I had a squint down the room. Tony and Eileen were hard at it, locked together like Siamese twins. The music started again and we danced like that for the whole of that side, fondling each other, working each other up to a rare old state.

When the record finished we were down the room by the projector table. While June went to change the music I picked up the cannister of film labelled Spain.

"I'd like to see this."

"It's not very good," June called. "It's not properly edited or anything."

"I'd still like to see it. So would Tony. Wouldn't you, Tony?"

"Mm?" A sleepy sound came from the far end of the room, from the region of Eileen's neck.

"Wouldn't you like to see their film shot in Spain?"

"Oh, sure. Anythin' you say, baby."

June came back to me. "All right. D'you want to see it now?"

"Sure, why not?"

"Sit there, then."

I took my drink and sat on the settee on the right of the table Eileen and Tony came over hand in hand and flopped down out of my sight on the other settee. June threaded the film deftly onto the projector, something I can never manage without spilling film all over the floor.

"When were you in Spain?" I asked her.

"Last summer – in August. It was fabulous."

"Doing what?"

"Just a holiday. Right, ready?"

Tony hadn't said a word since he'd sat down. I wondered whether he'd fallen asleep or just had his mouth full.

The projector rattled into life. A beam of white light hit the screen and changed immediately to a blaze of sunlit colour. June stepped over the back of the settee and settled down beside me with her drink, curling her legs beneath her. She kissed me on the ear and demanded a drag from my cigarette. She exhaled, blowing tumbling smoke through the projector beam and kissed me again on the ear.

This is what I saw on the screen:

The colour was breathtaking; the seascape a sun-drenched reminder of last year's wonderful summer. At first there were just shots of the hotel, an ultra-modern, multi-storey job built right on the edge of the beach. Then there were random shots of the crowded beach, of boats bobbing on the turquoise water, of June (fully clothed in a print dress) waving from the hotel terrace, of Eileen (also fully clothed) paddling in the shallows, carrying her shoes. All very nice but very much amateur home movie stuff, not sufficiently interesting to tear my mind from June's thighs which were disturbingly close. I let my hand drift to her uppermost knee. She caught it and stopped further progress.

"Watch the film," she whispered.

The scenery changed abruptly. Now we were in a quiet, deserted cove – to the right, the sea; to the left, high sand dunes, tufted with waving grass. The camera lingered on this desolate idyll for a moment, then, from behind a sand dune, Eileen in a very brief white bikini walked into frame. This was more like it.

She sauntered towards camera, looking out to sea, occasionally tossing her hair against the breeze, apparently oblivious of the camera. Some five yards from it she stopped and sat down on the sand and raised her face to the sun. I could now see she had been carrying a plastic bottle of suntan oil. After a moment or two she lodged the bottle in the sand, reached behind her and fumbled with her bra strap. The cups relax. Slowly she peels the straps from her shoulders, revealing beautiful, full breasts with large dark roses. I whispered "Wow!" and June chuckled.

Eileen reclines onto the sand, takes up the bottle of oil, pours a little into the palm of her hand and begins a slow, sensuous massage of her breasts. The camera creeps nearer, shaking a little as the operator (June?) negotiates the sand, until it comes to rest over Eileen in perfect focus. For the briefest moment something about the film gnaws at my professional mind but is instantly dispelled by a screenful of Eileen's glistening boobies, the nipples standing up rock-hard and in high relief, the focus so perfect I can see individual grains of sand and the minute hairs around the nipples.

For perhaps a minute she continues to massage and

27

squeeze, tease and knead. Slowly then the camera backs away, until it takes in Eileen's tum and the top edge of her bikini pants. The bottle of oil comes into frame and dribbles a small quantity of oil into the navel. Then her hand appears to scoop out the oil and begin a slow circuit of the belly ... around and around and around ... the circles getting wider and wider. The fingers reach the edge of the pants, tease it, once, twice, then the belly flattens, creating a narrow gap. The fingers disappear inside, a mere inch, then out again ... in again, this time deeper, then the hand disappears entirely. The hand arches, begins easing down the pants. Down ... and down ... and down. The first sprigs of black curly hair pop up between the fingers. The hand moves to one side, revealing for a mere frame or two a thick mattress of black hair, then covers it again. I discover my breath is held and has been held for quite some time. The pulse throbs in my head. My mouth is dry. I am hypnotised by the screen. I can't drag my eyes from it even to reach for my drink in case I miss something.

As the pants descend, the camera is lowered, and the more Eileen shows us the less we see because the camera is now shooting along the plain of her stomach and all that is shown is a mound of black hair that could be a monkey's top-knot. Fine camera work. And now I realise what is troubling me. The camera work is just too good. The movement, the impeccable focus, the framing – they're all highly professional. If June Everett shot this I'm Erle Stanley Gardner.

Anyway, back to the film. The pants are now out of sight, somewhere down around the ankles. The camera begins to slowly rise up and pull back. As more of Eileen is revealed her knee comes up to guard her privacy. The camera moves slowly down the body and moves around towards the feet, there it stops, filming the length of her body. But the knee is still there, shielding her pubescence from its hungry eye. Slowly the knee moves outwards, away from her other thigh. It stops ... falters ... come on, come on! It moves back again ... falters ... the tension is unbearable Will she do it? *Will* she ...? Yes, it's moving again ... by gum, she does do it. Suddenly the legs shoot straight out at camera, wide apart, and there, for a beat of time, in glorious technicolour close-up, is Eileen, naked as a peeled peach. Then – bang. The screen is black. I release a pent-up breath and swallow a good mouthful of vodka as the screen is hit by a new blaze of colour.

The camera is at ground level, pointing along a beach towards the sea. A figure in blue bikini leaps over the camera, drops a white towel on the sand and skips into the water. It is June, her wonderful body shifting muscle entrancingly as she splashes into the shallows. The camera moves, in a cut, to the water's edge. June is now reclining on her elbows, her face turned to the sun, the pale turquoise water lapping between her wide open legs. She rolls around, thrashing her legs, moving towards deeper water. She stands and throws herself headlong into the small waves, surfaces, cavorts around for a moment or two, then runs for the beach.

She picks up the towel and wraps it completely around her. The wet bikini drops to the sand and she begins to dry herself. A glimpse of naked breast is caught in profile and is gone again. Then another, just as quickly gone. She leans forward to dry a knee and offers an overhead shot of twin golden peaks with bursting pink crowns. She stands erect and drops the towel in front of her in a narrow swathe, covering the bare essentials, and proceeds to dry the insides of her thighs without revealing a single glimpse of hair. The suspense is killing. I realise I am now gripping her thigh – the very thigh before me on the screen – here in warm reality. On film she twists and turns, revealing tantalising snatches of naked flesh. Will she do it? She must ... she must! She does. Bingo, the towel drops to the sand and there for a full five seconds it is framed in golden close-up.

The film end rattled through the projector and the screen blazed light that hurt the eyes. June leapt up and switched it. Silence reigned.

"Just a simple home movie," she said with a shrug.

From the far side of the table Tony released a bellowing laugh. "Wonderful! Magnificent! More!"

I got up with some difficulty. "Anyone for a drink?"

"Yes!" laughed Tony. "More drinks and more simple home movies!"

"We haven't got any more," said June.

"What's that, then?" asked Tony, pointing at the other cannister.

"It's not a home movie," said Eileen, leaning across him to get her drink. "Well ..." she smiled at June, "... not really."

"Oh? What is it?"

"Couples," June replied.

"Couples? Friends of yours?"

29

The girls giggled. "No," said June, "just couples."

"*Loving* couples?" asked Tony, grinning suspiciously.

"Very."

He winked at me in the gloom. "So . . . let's see them."

I poured the drinks while June laced up the film. Eileen changed the record, again to something slow and romantic, violins and nostalgic solo trumpet, very stimulato. These girls really knew how to set the stage. But for what? It was happening all the wrong way round. They should be in *our* flats. *We* should be playing the sexy music and showing the sexy films. Still, come what may. I was enjoying myself.

Eileen sat down again with Tony. June clicked on the projector and again stepped over the back of the settee to sit by me.

"Sorry about the quality of the film," she said. "It's a bit scratchy . . . but I think you'll be able to follow it."

The title came on, dim and scratched: One for All and All for One.

What followed had absolutely nothing to do with the Three Musketeers.

The film opens on four people, two young men and two women, sitting in a room, apparently just chatting. Right at the outset the film looks cheap, as though it has been shot in the corner of somebody's grotty flat. A pack of cards is produced and four cards are dealt. The girls look at each other and giggle. Through gestures from the men it is obvious the girls have been drawn to pair off.

Self-consciously they leave the room, smiling at each other.

Cut to: a bedroom containing a double bed and two armchairs. The girls enter and immediately begin undressing. Nothing subtle here, they just whip it all off quick as ink. My heart is banging away so hard I'm sure June can hear it. Here I must admit to a certain naivety – this is my first sex film. Believe it or not, it's the truth. And my reaction to it is the same as my reaction would be to the prospect of going over Niagara Falls in a bathtub. My mouth is as dry as a bucket of old fag ash, my eyes seem ever so slightly out of focus and I am having trouble controlling my facial muscles which for some reason seem to be locked in a silly grin. I need a cigarette. I release June's knee to light one and when I replace my hand she takes it and clamps in between her thighs, half-way between knee and crotch. God, it's warm in there . . .

Back to the film. The two birds are now completely starkers

and big buxom birds they are too, big-breasted and voluptuously hipped and bottomed. They look Italian. One of them sits down on the edge of the bed and leans back until her shoulders touch the wall. The other girl settles by her side and begins trickling her fingers up the first girl's thigh. The first girl suddenly opens wide and the second girl dives in like she's drilling for oil. Whoops! the first girl likes it. She begins rollicking around, throwing her hips at the ceiling, rolling them in a sensuous samba, urging her mate on with soundless mouthing that could've been anything – including "Next time get your bleedin' nails cut". I didn't know whether to laugh, cry or feel embarrassed and before I can decide which, the second girl decides it's time for a snack and plunges in like she's digging for truffels.

Tony calls out, "Save us!"

I'd forgotten about him.

Well, these girls really got stuck into each other for about three minutes before the camera starts a slow pan to the right of the room. And lo and behold, whom do we 'ave 'ere! It's one of the boyfriends, sprawled on his spine in an armchair, watching the girls going at it, his trousers down around his ankles, both hands clamped around what I first take to be a twelve-inch peeled cucumber. I feel June's thighs tighten on my hand and realise then it is not a twelve-inch cucumber, though the lad seems determined to peel it none the less.

"Good God!" Tony gasps and Eileen giggles.

Then we are all laughing. It's just unbelievable.

The camera holds on Cucumber Ken for a moment longer then begins to pan back to the bed. It takes in the girls who are still hard at it, and pans left off the bed to the second lad, Gigantic Jack, who is also sprawled in an armchair giving *him*self a five-knuckle shuffle and trying to outdo Ken in speed, style and determination. You know, I once heard a rumour about an Irish docker who could remove six half-crowns, placed in line, off a table with one sweep of his enormous shillelah and always put it down to public house exaggeration, but by the heck these boys in the film were so endowed they'd have Spud Murphy crying his eyes out and believing himself puny and underdeveloped. I swear they couldn't be real. But real or not they are certainly convincing because June is wriggling on the settee as though the springs have just burst through the cushions. She's in a rare old state.

Anyway, to return to the film. The lads now leave their arm-

31

chairs, kick off their trousers and join the ladies. All hell lets loose. Everybody's going at it hammers and tongues like it'll be out of fashion by midnight. It's one great, bare-faced orgy with big close-ups of the girls in snarling ecstacy, big close-ups of the lads grim with effort, and big, big close-ups of everything else you can imagine.

"Go, baby!" shouts Tony as one fellow nearly falls off the bed. "Pick yourself up ... dust yourself off ... and start all over agaaaaiiiin!"

The lad does so and throws himself back into the affray with renewed determination.

I sneak a glance at June. Her eyes are wide, mouth open, breathing heavy. She's really there, right in the thick of it. Despondency grips me. Am I supposed to compete with *that*! She becomes aware of my glance, looks at me, and bursts into laughter, knowing what I'm thinking.

Then suddenly the film is over. I won't describe the ending, it really was too much. Enough to say that if the company that produced the film wasn't called Klimax Films it damn-well ought to be. Wow!

The film end chattered through the projector. June leapt up to cease its noise. The music was still playing. She took my hand and pulled me up, throwing herself against me with all her former urgency.

"Well?" she murmured.

"It was ... it was ..." I coughed. "... interesting."

She was a millstone, grinding against me, breathing in my ear. I opened an eye and had a squint down the room to see what Tony was up to. It was difficult to tell in the gloom but I think it was his elbow. Those two had really caught the spirit of the occasion.

"I want you," said June. "Now."

She caught my hand and pulled me from the room, across a hallway and into her bedroom. The bedside light was on. Closing the door she launched herself at me. Her mouth fell into mine. Hot, succulent communiques passed between us, urgent and frenzied. Quickly she got bored with just this. Breaking away she ripped her sweater over her head. She was beautiful. Different again from the film. Now they were real, living, three dimensional, firm, full, still palely tanned, their crests dark, hard and protuberant. Swish ... her little skirt hit the floor. White translucent knicks hid nothing. I peeled off my jacket, threw my shirt after it, kicked off the remainder. Then she was hard against me, pressing silky heat down my body, pinking me with her tongue, pushing me towards the bed. I fell, she fell on top, gripped my hair in both hands and wriggled around until she was comfortable. For a fleeting moment I wondered how Tony was making out. I fancied I heard a door close in the next room.

In a low, quavery voice she asked, "Did you enjoy the second film?"

"Sure."

"Did it excite you?"

"Of course."

"How . . . why?"

"Mm?"

"Did you see the girls in the film as Eileen and me?"

"Well . . . no."

"What then? Did you want to screw me when the men were screwing the girls?"

"It did sort of cross my mind . . ."

What was this bird – a sociology student? I had a sudden premonition this conversation was being taken down on tape for replay at some discussion group.

"Russ, would you like all four of us to do what they were doing in the film?" She was still grinding away, slowly, rhythmically. "Is that what you want . . . a foursome? Eileen and I would be willing."

Ye gods, group sex yet. Tony would die laughing. I thought about it. The idea was not without piquancy. Experience, I reminded myself, was a must, an absolute essential. How could I ever call myself complete, knowledgeable, wordly-wise if I'd never participated in an orgy?

I made me decision.

"No," I told her. "I just want to make love to you. There's nothing I could get from an orgy that I can't get from you."

She smiled at me, as though I'd said something nice to her, then the smile changed to one of unadulterated devilment.

"All right . . . you asked for it."

She began at my feet and for thirty incredible minutes worked her way slowly north, using everything – fingers, lips, tongue – even her nose. I throbbed like a pressure hose. Suddenly she whispered urgently, "Russ . . ."

"Mm?"

"I want you. Any way you like!"

She flung herself alongside, pulling me over her, releasing

a gasped "Oh!" at first contact, the sighter. Then ... "OH!" again. All the way home. She stared up at me, no, not at me but at her own galloping climax. Oh! ... and oh! again. Her teeth were clenched in a grimace of delicious agony. Eight filbert nails sought bone. Her strong legs squeezed me vice-like ... her warm insides were chicketting around like bubbles in oil, seeking release. And ... aaaahhhHHHH! The erupting sound of tortured delight, beginning as a muted groan, tearing up into the throat, finally exploded in a full-blooded yell right in my ear, heralding an enormous, shared triumph. It went on and on, a rollicking detonation, for me the release of a month's pent-up frustration, a giant of a job; for her – I knew not what but by heaven she truly blew.

We lay there for some time, stunned, breathing chaotically, drifting into private thought. Her hands dropped from my shoulders, flopped onto the bed, utterly spent. Into our quietness came the energetic, rhythmic thumping from beyond the wall, the faint metallic squeak of bedsprings, the cheerful sound of happy talk. I drew a mental picture and chuckled. June laughed too. In a way we were having our orgy after all.

June said, "I feel sorry for her. It can't be as good as mine."

I kissed her on the nose. "Don't you believe it. Tony's a big and experienced boy."

"Don't care. You were wonderful."

"It takes two to tango."

"You were a rock ... a pen-in-sul-ar!"

"It was all your doing."

The activity next door ceased. I hoped they'd both made it.

"I must go somewhere," she said.

She scrambled out of bed, slipped on a nylon negligee and disappeared through the door. I lay there in this stranger's room listening to the muted murmurings from next door. I felt wonderful, drained, sleepy, happy to stay all night. I checked the time. It was almost two a.m. We'd have to make a move soon if Tony was to make the Slimfit shooting session and me the Croxley interview.

June came back into the room, slipped off the negligee and got into bed, cuddling close. I put my arm around her, hugged her soft warmth to me. The last thing I wanted to do was leave. It would be difficult to tell her I'd have to go very soon without making it sound I couldn't wait to clear off now I'd satisfied my lust. I waited a few minutes, then as I began to speak she started simultaneously and we both laughed.

34

"You first," I said.

"Well, it's difficult."

"Come on, don't be shy."

She sighed despondently. "Well ... I'm in a spot of trouble, Russ ..."

Aye aye!

"What sort of trouble?"

"Money trouble. To be honest we're not doing all that well at modelling. I've got a bit of money coming in but the agencies take an awful long time to pay and ..."

"I know. Tony and I have the same trouble. How can I help?"

"I feel terrible ..."

"No, come on."

"I need ten pounds."

"Is that all?"

"It's for the rent. It's due at the end of the week and I haven't got a thing ..."

"I know the feeling. All right, love, I'll lend you ten."

"Would you really?"

"Sure."

She hugged me hard. "Oh, thank you. It'd be a terrific help. I'll pay you back as soon as I can."

"Sure. That's O.K. Look, I don't want to appear anxious to go but both Tony and I have early calls tomorrow ..."

She kissed me on the cheek. "I understand. Work is work."

"I'd better rouse Tony."

I gave the wall a good thump and called out, "It's two o'clock, Dane! Hands off cocks and on with socks!"

I got a muffled reply that sounded like, "Get stuffed!"

We dressed without haste and at the door I put my arms around her and kissed her. "It sounds wrong to say thanks – but thanks."

"I should thank you."

I pulled out my wallet and handed her a couple of fivers.

"Russ ..."

"Ssh, say no more. I've lost count of the times I've needed a tenner."

"Thanks very much."

We went into the living room and a moment later Tony and Eileen came in.

Tony winced at me. "You look like hell," he had the nerve to say.

"You look divine. You're going to look beautiful in your Slimfit shirt at eight o'clock. Make-up is *really* going to earn his money."

He hugged Eileen and kissed her. "See you, Angel. Be good, now."

The girls waved us off from the kitchen door and with a farewell flash of lights we drove out of the yard towards the Bayswater Road.

Tony's flat is in Stanhope Place, close to Marble Arch. I followed him home, knowing he'd have a cold beer in the fridge. I was parched.

It's a nice one-bedroom pad in a pseudo-Georgian block, comfortably furnished, over-looking the street from the first floor.

He opened the door and went to the kitchen for the beers while I slumped onto a deep sofa in the living room. He came in with two ice-cold Tuborgs two glasses and a very self-satisfied grin. He gave me a beer, fell into the armchair opposite, lit a cigarette, crossed his legs and grinned.

"Well?"

"Well, what?"

He laughed. "Don't be a twot, I heard her screaming through the wall."

"Ai don't know wot you mean, Ai'm sure. Cheers."

"Cheers." He took a long, thirsty swig and wiped his mouth. "Well, some night, eh?"

"Fantastic."

He shook his head wonderingly. "I pegged them for a couple of ravers in the Kum Kum, but by the heck ... I've never met up with that before ... films ... everything laid on. A couple of very unusual birds."

"Unbelievable."

"It was all so damned smooth! No fighting ... no infantile chat like 'What d'you think you're doin', I'm not a girl like that'. Just straight forward, honest-to-God ..."

"Professionalism?"

He looked up at me. "You think so? It did cross my mind. I mean – the holiday film ..."

"Beautiful. Notice the camera work?"

"Of course. That was no home movie, buddy. It would have done Oswalt Kolle credit." He shook his head. "Something very strange there ... the projector all set up ... the

36

films lying around. I've met some grumble-lovers in my time – birds who live for it breakfast, lunch and dinner – but ..." he drank some beer and chuckled. "Tell you something, Eileen offered me a foursome – an orgy."

"So did June."

"Did she?"

"Sure. She started by asking me what I thought of the sex film – whether I wanted to screw her when I saw the lads at it ..."

"So did Eileen." He sat forward in his chair. "Then she asked me if I wanted to make it a foursome like they were at it in the film."

"What did you say to that?"

"I said no, you pillock. I like my joy private."

"That's what I told June."

He grinned. "Must mean something, I suppose. Either were both normal or deadly dull or something."

"What d'you reckon these birds are? D'you think they *are* models?"

"God knows. Whatever they're doing I know Eileen isn't doing so well at it ..."

I knew exactly what he was going to say. It had been on my mind to tell him the same thing but I hadn't quite worked out how to do it without appearing a right dum-dum. I decided to let him make an ass of himself first.

"How d'you know that?" I asked innocently.

"Well, she ... she told me. Said she was in a spot of bother over money. The rent's due at the end of the week and she hasn't a bean. She's got a bit coming in but you know what the agencies are like ... I told her we had the same trouble collecting money ... what're you laughing at?"

"Go on."

"What the hell are you laughing at, Tobin?"

"How much did you cough up?"

"Who said I gave her anything?"

"Tony, how much did she stick you for?"

"Well, the kid's in trouble ..."

"How much, Tony?"

"Aw, lay off ... I mean, how can you refuse a bird you've just grumbled when you're lying there with her hand on your dying manhood ...?"

"How much, loverboy – a tenner?"

"Don't be bloody daft ... yes, a bloody tenner. But it was only a loan ... no it wasn't, I *gave* her a tenner ..." He looked up at me sharply. "What made you say a tenner?"

I burst out laughing. "Because I gave June a tenner."

He gaped.

"Same story, buddy, verbatim, from start to finish. And I reckon whoever wrote the script also shot that holiday film. We've been had, lad, had. That little doodle cost us twenty quid."

"Plus a bottle of vodka."

"I hadn't forgotten. I'll chip in a quid."

"Well, sod me."

"I personally think it worth every penny."

"Oh, don't get me wrong," he protested. "I don't wish to sound a piker after the event, but I do happen to know at least six birds who would do it for nothing *and* make me coffee afterwards. What gets me is the risk these two took – asking for the money afterwards. We might have told them to get knotted and walked out."

"Maybe they're good psychologists and pegged us for honest gents."

"I don't know," he said, shaking his head. "I reckon there's more to it than that. Eileen did it like she really enjoyed it – not just for the money."

"So did June. She was wild."

"Well, we will probably never know. Not a word of this in the *Wellington*, eh? We'll be the laughing stock of Soho."

"Not a word. Hm, fancy paying for it."

He looked at his watch and groaned. "Aw, look at the time – it's nearly three. I've gotta get some sleep."

"Me, too," I said, yawning. I got up and stretched. "I've got to give Croxleys my decision at ten and I don't know what the hell I'm going to tell them."

"You haven't decided?"

"I'm going to have a last word with Mike Spiring before I go to Croxleys. I *think* I'm going to do it."

"What about the rest of the year? What will you do?"

"God knows. But at least I'll have three and a half thousand quid to do it with."

He pursed his lips thoughtfully. "You know what I'd be inclined to do, mate? I'd stick the money in some nice safe place and work abroad for a year. I wouldn't touch that money."

"Work abroad doing what?"

"I don't know ... but I'd get a job in the sun somewhere – building boats in the Bahamas or maybe work in the Snowey Mountains in Australia for a year and come back with another three thousand pounds. I wouldn't blow that money if I were you."

I thought about it. It made good sense. Three thousand pounds took an awful lot of getting. This was a chance in a lifetime to consolidate some worthwhile capital. It really would be daft just to squander the proceeds from White Marvel and have to start from scratch again a year hence.

"Think you've got something," I said. "I'll sleep on it." I opened the door and turned to him. "Well, goodnight, Slimfit."

"That's not what Eileen called me," he grinned.

"Then you got your tenner's worth, didn't you?"

"You're telling me," he said.

CHAPTER TWO

Friday. Less than seven hours after leaving Tony I parked the Lotus in the multi-storey garage in Poland Street and walked zombie-like through naughty Soho towards my agent's office in Shaftesbury Avenue. It was not only lack of sleep that had brought on my stupor but also the amalgam of early morning and the bitter wind that gusted around each corner and cut through my five layers of clothing like cheese wire. It was a terrible day – sleet one minute, snow the next, then a flurry of hailstones that pinged off my raw ears and clonked on top of my head.

I hauled the collar of my overcoat around my ears and trudged on through the slush, wishing like hell it was summer. I hate the winter, the cold. I go rigid, useless. I want to die or hibernate on days like this. The more I thought about Tony's suggestion of working in the sun the more it appealed to me. That was my environment: sun ... warmth ... walking around in shirt-sleeves and shorts, not in four tons of wool and leather.

I reached Berwick Street and crossed over it. On the far corner a ragged hippy, a long-haired kid of about twenty, coloured frozen blue, was tanging out Good King Wenceslas Goes Soul on a battered guitar and blowing on a mouthorgan as though he was trying to keep it warm.

An old brown trilby lying in the slush at his feet bore witness to the dynamic impact of his performance on the early morning Christmas shoppers. In it lay two lonely pennies. I felt sorry for him, fellow victim of the cold. I dropped in sixpence, expecting him, I suppose, to fall to his knees in flooding gratitude – or at least to stop blowing long enough to mutter thanks; but he didn't flutter an eyelid. He was gone, sent, travelling on some private Christmas trip, staring at the gutter with the intense concentration of Ruggerio Ricci negotiating a particularly tricky bit in Tchaikovsky's Concerto in D Major, Opus 35. Up you, I thought. I had a good mind to take back me tanner. Happy Christmas, soul mate, hope it keeps fine for you.

I pushed on, chin down, glancing absently into the shop windows, each one bedecked for Christmas, each window-dressing a monument to hilarious bad taste.

I stopped outside a tool-and-Do-it-Yourself shop, arrested by an electric drill displayed on a revolving, spot-lit stand. It was the same drill I was using in the T.V. commercial to scale the rust off the guttering. EXCITING CHRISTMAS GIFT! a purple silk banner proclaimed.

The window was crammed with similar proclamations and exhortations. Unbelievably a one-inch chisel bore a ticket "IDEAL STOCKING GIFT!" I chortled, visualising somebody's old man ramming his foot into the stocking, desperate to get to the loo on Christmas morning. Yyyaaaarrrrrooooo! Quick – the Evostick!

A brace-and-bit was labelled "FROM THE WIFE WHO *REALLY* CARES!" Oh, darling, just what I wanted! There he goes, boring holes like a thing possessed. Happy ... hole ... CHRISTMAS ... hole ... hole ... EVERYBODY! ... hole .. hole ... hole.... Everywhere – in the piano ... in the sink ... in the goldfish. Now, don't overdo it, Frank, save some for Boxing Day.

"MAKE HIS A *PLUMB-BOB* CHRISTMAS!" exhorted another card. Go on, I dare you, missus. Wrap that two-bob plumb-bob in a bloody great parcel and just watch the excitement, the anticipation in his face as he peels away layer after layer of wrapping paper. Happy Christmas, darl ... Jim? What's the matter, Jim? Why are you looking at me like thaaacccchhhhh!!! Gnarled D-i-Y hands tighten remorselessly on the plumb-bob string. Wife's eye-bulging, tongue-swollen body slithers to the floor amidst mountain of gay wrapping paper. Serves you right, you silly old fart, you should've bought him the three-foot ruler...!

I moved on again, hearing in the next block the Silent Night, Holy Night Cha-cha-chà emanating raucously from the doorway of a cut-price record shop. Suddenly I found myself strangely put out by this commercial destruction of Christmas. God knows, I'm not religious, but this year it seems to be getting to me. I experienced a sudden yearning to hear children singing carols, to recapture my childhood innocence of believing in Father Christmas. I detested this rude commercialism.

Ha! Now that is rich coming from you, a voice reminds me. You with three great fat commercials going out on the box right through the festive season. You, Tobin, flogging Glamour soap, Klippit Construction Kits and Gusto drills for crude monetary reward.

41

Yes, you're right. Shut up and get on with it and let the others get on with theirs.

Mike Spiring, my agent, rents three dingy offices four floors above a chemist shop in Shaftesbury Avenue. I hate going to see him; not for any personal reason because I like the man very much, but because he has no elevator. I went through the street door, took a deep breath, and started to climb. Minutes later I emerged at the top floor knowing how Hillary felt as he staggered up the last few feet of Everest.

Mike called out, "Come in, Russ!"

I staggered into his office and flopped into the lumpy arm-chair in front of his desk, puffing and blowing.

"How . . . did you know . . . it was me?"

"I know every one of my artistes by the extent of their rup-tured breathing."

"How . . . do I compare?"

"Awful. You should give up smoking."

He threw me a packet of cigarettes, having taken one him-self, but I declined.

"Good," he said. "You've started."

"Nuts. Give me two minutes."

"So," he said, lighting up, "you've given White Marvel some thought?"

Mike is a grey man in his fifties. Everything about him is grey – his complexion, his abundant wavy hair, his gentle eyes – even his suit today, though it was relieved by a blue polka-dot tie. He is a kindly man, well respected in the business, as far removed as could be from the tough, cold, grasping image generally held of agents. Not that he's soft. He can bargain with the best of them; but he manages to do it without raising his voice.

"Yes," I said. "I think I'd like to do it."

He nodded sagely. "O.K., but what about the possibility of not working for a year? Given that some thought?"

"As much as I could in the short time allowed. I'd like to work abroad – in a warmer climate."

"Doing what?"

"I haven't a clue. It only came to me last night – from Tony Dane as a matter of fact. He thought I'd be a mug to spend the three thousand pounds from White Marvel and come back broke. And he's right."

Mike was nodding thoughtfully. "Of course he's right. It's a marvellous opportunity for you to see a bit of the world and

– with a bit of luck – there's every chance you can start all over again a year from now, if you want to. It'll be a lot easier than starting completely unknown. The producers you've worked for will still be around next year. Fine ... well, you'd better get around to Croxleys and tell them the good news. I'll start negotiating your contract and finance."

I descended the stairs in a state of elation. I'd done it! Now I was committed. Two weeks shooting on White Marvel in January and then – what? Three and a half thousand pounds in the bank and a ticket to anywhere I liked in the world. It all had a dream-like quality ... and how many times had I dreamed of being in just this sort of situation? Dozens. Now it was reality I couldn't believe it. I paused foolishly on the stairs and pinched my left hand. It was there and it hurt. I was really on my way to Croxleys to tell them I'd accept their six thousand pounds. Whistling the Silent Night, Holy Night Cha-cha-cha I went down the stairs and out of the street door.

At five minutes to ten I pushed through the steel- and glass-doors of Croxleys, welcoming the super-heat of their lush reception hall.

As with most major advertising agencies the reception was designed to impress on impact: green-marble floor, white marble walls, myriad plant life in tropical garden settings, the air subtly perfumed, the tastefulness and expense of its fixtures and fittings immediately obvious.

And in one other way also did Croxleys conform – in the selection of its receptionist for beauty, breeding and bosom. This one was gorgeous, a natural blonde in her early thirties, a dream of elegant sensuality in a superbly-cut grey suit and pink sweater, with, no doubt, a superbly cut South Kensington accent to match. It smiled at me charmingly as I approached, revealing excellent white teeth set in two impeccable rows behind perfect lips. I was attacked by a furious desire to leap over the desk and belt it.

"Good morning. Kern Ai help yar?" she asked.

Yes, love, get your lips round this.

"I have an appointment with Allan Lang."

"End your nerm?"

"Tobin. Russ Tobin."

"Thenk yar."

My name seemed to please her She smiled and crossed her

43

slim legs, entwining them like a couple of copulating boa constrictors, reached for a red telephone and with long, elegant fingers dialled a number.

She smiled at me again while she waited. "Frightful morning."

"Frightful."

"Helleur? Mister Rossell Terbin for Mister Lerng. I see. Thernk yar."

She replaced the phern, the phone. "Please terk a seat, Mister Terbin, Mister Lerng's secretary will be right darn."

"Thernk yar," I said, returning her smile. I positioned myself so I could see up her skirt and pretended to read Punch.

By the time Allan Lang's secretary, Sarah (whom I'd met before) arrived, the bird on reception had shown me the lot twice, though she'd probably have it she was retrieving her ballpoint off the floor. Not much joy, however, she was wearing tights.

Sarah is another little cracker, a dark-haired piece, all tits and talcum, this morning dressed in a green twin-set and light grey mini skirt that barely covered it. They really do know how to pick them in these agencies. It would never do for me to work in one; I'd be on constant heat.

"Morning," she said gaily. "Will you come this way, Mr. Tobin?"

Any way, love.

I watched her neat bottom all the way to the elevators where she turned abruptly and caught me.

"Rotten weather," I said, blinking with something in my eye.

"Frightful. Sorry to bring you out in it."

"My pleasure."

Six men crowded into the car with us and I was forced much against my desire to rub shoulders with Sarah. She smelled divine. She smiled at me once in extreme close-up and brushed an imaginary sliver of lint off her bosom to cover her confusion.

We left the car on the fifth floor and marched along a corridor between walls of offices. Without exception I caught sight of at least one dolly through the large windows of each office who could've qualified for Miss Great Britain. They really are the greatest, all mini-skirted and good-looking. I wonder who the lucky stiff is who interviews them for the job?

Sarah ushered me into Allan Lang's office. I'd met him before several times and liked him very much. He's a mild-mannered, quietly-spoken Canadian, medium tall, medium thin, medium bald, in his medium forties. He got up to greet me and shook hands with a smile.

"Russ, nice to see you, sit down. Sarah, a thumping great cup of steaming hot, freshly-ground Brazilian coffee for Mr. Tobin."

Sarah slid away. This was Allan's little joke. We both knew Sarah was heading for the automatic vending machine in the corridor and would return with a plastic beaker of luke-warm liquid that would look like clouded varnish and taste like cat's pee. He held out a packet of French cigarettes to me which I refused because I think they smell like cat's pee. I lit one of my own.

"I've just had your agent on the phone," he said, "and I'm delighted you're going to do White Marvel."

"How could I refuse when you're offering Fort Knox?"

"We had to, didn't we? We all know detergent is synonymous with death to you fellows. But I'm mighty glad you're doing it, Russ. The Crunchum film was a minor triumph for us and if you can pull something remotely similar for White Marvel I say you're not being overpaid."

"I don't think I am anyway," I said half-jokingly. "You realise I'll be out of work for a year?"

He nodded. "Yes, it was one of the major considerations in determining the size of the money. What will you do? Any plans?"

"Nothing concrete. I'm thinking strongly about working abroad, though what at I haven't a clue."

"How about Canada? I have lots of friends over there."

"What's the weather like? I need sun."

He smiled. "I'm from Victoria – or Little England as it's otherwise known. The climate's much the same as here."

I shook my head fervently. "Thanks for the thought."

Sarah returned, laid down two plastic cups of travesty, and departed. I attempted to pick my squashy thing up and drink. I managed a dribble down my chin.

"The man I'd most like to meet," I said, "is the maniac who invented these. I would hack his nockers off with a blunt and rusty saw, stuff them in one of his own cups, add scalding water and ram the lot up his armpit."

"I'll drink to that," he said, wiping coffee off his knee.

We got down to business, just generally discussing the format for the White Marvel commercials.

In the second week of January, I, with a small mobile camera unit, would conduct spontaneous street interviews outside supermarkets in various locations around London, talking to men and women who had just purchased White Marvel.

During the third week of January we would shoot follow-up sequences in their homes, filming washing results, getting quaint, favourable, humorous, interesting or whatever remarks from their husbands, grandmothers, children and pets to supplement the outdoor sequences. No expense was to be spared. Miles of film stock was to be available and we would shoot anything that looked at all promising. Then from this abundance (they hoped) of material the director and editor would build twelve devastatingly beautiful commercials for transmission beginning March and continuing through August.

"Fine," I said, "but hasn't this all been done before?"

"Sure it has," he said, lighting another of his foul fags. "And it works. There is nothing like the personal testimonial from the woman in the street to convince the other woman in the street. They distrust actresses. They like to hear it from their own kind. The difficulty is in getting their own kind to talk freely and without inhibition. But they talk to you, Russ, we saw that in the Crunchum's interviews. You've got the right face, personality, approach . . ."

"Than . . . kyou."

"I mean it. Sex without superiority, that's your strength. That's why White Marvel can't wait to pay you six Gs."

"I'll do my best."

"I'm sure you will. That's another of your strengths."

I left him and trod air all the way back to the car. I felt great. What a future! A nice idle time between now and the second week in January (everything dies a natural death over Christmas in commercials), two weeks hard but likeable, work and then . . .

I drove slowly out towards Barnes near Hammersmith where Tony was shooting Slimfit. I thought I'd surprise the slob and have lunch with him while telling him I'd said yes to White Marvel. And all the way there my mind was preoccupied with the 'and then . . .' How was I going to spend the whole next year of my life?

46

CHAPTER THREE

The answer came from the most unexpected source, a fact that in no way surprised me. It has always been a cause for wonder how, when a certain problem arises and you begin talking about it, the solution pops up so readily – from the milkman, a neighbour, a friend, a casual contact. If you spread yourself around enough it's bound to happen.

Christmas is, of course, customer relations time in all businesses. Cases of booze travel across the city; turkeys by the thousand wander into clients' offices. It's an accepted way of saying thanks for putting the work my way this past year.

Recording studios and production companies, of which there are many in London, are no exception. And in addition to whatever personal and private arrangements of appreciation are made, the largest of these companies usually throw a Christmas shindig on their premises to which they invite advertising agency producers, film editors, casting directors, theatrical agents et cetera. And these people usually bring along their secretaries or girl friends or secretary/girl friends as the case may be.

It is, though, unusual for us 'artistes' to be invited, since we have no direct influence over the amount of business a, say, recording studio, receives. This year, however, Mike Spiring had felt it profitable to invite me as his guest (this of course being decided before White Marvel had appeared on the scene) in order that I should rub shoulders with agency producers and casting directors. And despite the advent of White Marvel he let the invitation stand.

L.R.S. – London Recording Studios – have their premises in a basement in Soho. Mike and I could hear the racket down below as we entered the street door at nine o'clock on Wednesday night, two days before Christmas.

We descended the stairs and turned into a corridor. Mike groaned. Judging by the number of people who were over-spilled into the corridor it was obvious the studio was choc-a-block.

"Oh, hell," he muttered. "It's going to be a scrimmage. I refuse to fight tooth and nail just to get a free drink."

We reached the end of this corridor and turned the corner.

Mike groaned again, more heartily this time. The big studio was bulging. Obviously a lot of the people were free-loaders. I couldn't imagine L.R.S. inviting this crowd.

Mike touched my elbow. "Look, I'm for one drink just to say I've been here, then bed. You make your own way around, hm?"

Pop music blasted the room from two gigantic loudspeakers high up on the wall. (This in itself was probably a P.R. touch, demonstrating L.R.S.'s reproduction power)

Mike and I threw ourselves into the melee and shoved and pushed across the room to a long, cloth-covered trestle table against the far wall whereat four frenzied waiters were slopping booze into thick tumblers as fast as they could slop. After a mere five minutes I got one of them to acknowledge my existence and at the request "vodka and ..." he pushed into my hand a glass three quarters full (about ten pub tots) of neat vodka and left me to find my own tonic. I eventually did find one, squeezed in a tablespoonful, grabbed a sausage and a cucumber and sardine sandwich and backed away to a tiny space in one corner.

I felt suddenly lost, deserted. Mike had disappeared, swallowed by the crowd, probably trodden underfoot and now lying a mangled bloody mess the cleaners would find next morning. I chewed my sausage and gazed around, completely hemmed in in the corner by grey-suited, bespectacled, bearded intelligentsia and their women, and listened absently to their conversation which reached me as shouted snippets above the roar of the speakers.

"... will undoubtedly see the new I.P.C. commercial as a quite revolutionary socio-politico comment in the guise of the most fatuous mundanity, don't you agree ...?"

"... to be perfectly honest, I hate the bastard's guts ..."

"... perfectly miraculous. Bog paper is so tremendously tricky, isn't it? I mean, fine if the I.T.C.A. would allow us to show someone wiping his ..."

"... new secretary. Like a rabbit, old son. Any time, any place apparently. Over the desk, on the floor .."

I sighed and took a sip of vodka and winced.

"That looked painful."

The voice was low, warm, friendly and very close in my ear. I turned to it. She was out of this world – a petite, green-eyed, golden-haired angel in a white Courtelle dress, low cut at the front, high on the thigh. She smiled sympathetically, showing teeth like Polo mints. The bloom of her unusual sun-tan showed exotically against the snow whiteness of her dress. She was gorgeous, a soft, fragrant memory of hot, forgotten summers, spectacularly out of place in a roomful of pale win-try ghosts. I was instantly smitten.

"It was," I laughed, feeling suddenly nervous and foolish. "It's practically neat vodka. They don't have much time for subtleties tonight."

"I noticed," she said, grimacing at the noise, the crowd.

"Not quite your bag, hm?"

"Let's say I prefer fewer to the square foot and the noise down to mere deafening level."

"I'm Russ Tobin."

"I'm Vicki Hurst."

"Short for Victoria?"

"No. Vicki Hurst."

"I love it. Would you like me to get you a drink?"

"I'd never find you again."

"I'd find you."

She smiled. "Thanks all the same."

"Like a sip of this? I warn you, it takes nerve."

"All right," she said, surprising me.

She wet her lovely lips, no more, and made a face. "Ugh."

"I'm going to sneak it out under my coat," I said. "It'll be great for paint removing, bath stains, polishing brass . . ."

"What do you do? Are you in advertising?"

"Sort of. I'm a visual artiste."

"Visible in what?"

"Telly commercials. Ain't that somethin'?"

She stepped back half a pace and squinted at me, recogni-tion dawning dutifully. "Yes, of course, I've seen you in . . . er . . ."

"Glamour Soap?"

"Yes, of course."

"Nice of you to remember."

"I'm afraid I don't watch much television."

"Good for you. What do you do?"

I expected secretary . . . wife of managing director . . . agent.

"I'm a courier."

"Beg pardon?"

"A courier. A representative of a holiday tour operator."

"Did you gate-crash?"

"No," she laughed. "I came here with an advertising producer who passed out in the corridor about three minutes ago. I'm looking for my coat. I left it on a table over here somewhere."

"Vicki . . ."

"Mm?"

"How would you like me to take you away from all this and feed you? Italian? . . . Chinese? . . . French? Or perhaps a double hamburger at a Wimpey?"

"With chips?"

"With chips . . . and a paper napkin . . . and two cups of coffee. To hell with the expense."

"Help me find my coat."

I took her to a very good Wimpey House I know on the edge of town. Surprisingly hamburgers do vary throughout the Wimpey chain, despite standardisation of raw materials and equipment.

I guided her towards a side-table rather than to a stool at one of the horseshoe bars because I didn't want the fellas in the place ogling her, which they assuredly would have because she was very ogle-worthy with her tan and her golden hair mingling with the fluffy fawn fur of her coat collar. She looked very soft, very feminine and criminally healthy.

We ordered burgers and coffee and I gave her a cigarette.

"Tell me about couriering," I said.
She exhaled the smoke in a thoughtful stream. "I work for a company called Ardmont Holidays . . ."

"Mm, I've heard of them."

"They're quite big. They specialise in package holidays to Spain, Italy, Portugal – anywhere in the Mediterranean. And I represent them abroad during the summer."

"Doing what exactly?"

"Have you never been on a package holiday?"

I gave a cynical laugh. "Vicki, I'll let you into a grave secret. I've only been abroad once in my life – and that was to shoot commercials in Portugal."

She tutted sympathetically. "So you've never had a courier slaving night and day to satisfy your every whim?"

"Ashamed to say, not one. I don't even know what a courier does. I always thought he was a cloak-and-dagger bloke who carried messages in a leather bag or a cleft-stick or something."

"That's one kind. Our kind of couriers take clients on tours,

50

they're the mobile reps. The stationary ones are just called representatives – although most people call them couriers too. A rep – well, let's call them all couriers – a courier lives at the holiday resort and looks after the clients arriving on holiday. He, or she, meets them at the airport, makes sure they and their baggage get on the right bus, books them into the right hotel, arranges for tours, listens to complaints, advises on local entertainment, bails them out of jail, dries their eyes ...'

"Tucks them into bed?"

Her jade-green eyes crinkled. "Against house rules ... and generally holds their hands from the moment they get off the plane until the time they get back on. By which time the next batch have just arrived and away he, or she, goes again."

"Sounds pretty hectic."

"It's very interesting. I love it."

"And where do you courier – personally?"

"I don't – as such – anymore. I've been with Ardmont since they started five years ago. I'm head rep now. That means I'm in charge of an area abroad and I supervise all the reps in that area."

"Keeping an eye on their efficiency, you mean?"

The waitress arrived with the hamburgers. Vicki waited until she'd left before going on. "Yes, I help train new reps, deal with particularly difficult problems – generally keep an eye on things."

"Which area are you in charge of?"

She took a bite of her hamburger. "Mm, this is good. This year it'll be southern Italy."

"The whole summer in Italy? Fantastic."

"Well, more than the whole summer. I have to be out there before the season starts to get things ready. I'm actually going out in two weeks time – then I'll be there right through until the first week in November."

The inspiration and the coffees arrived simultaneously. It must have shown in my face because Vicki stopped eating in mid-bite and said with concern, "What's the matter? Are you all right?"

"Yes," I laughed, "fine. I've just been jolted by a thought." I shook my head. "Crazy."

"Who is?"

"The idea is." I drank some coffee. Vicki waited patiently for me to go on. "Do you believe in fate, Vicki?"

51

"Sometimes. Why?"

"I'm wondering if it was preordained that I should meet you tonight. Seems incredible."

"Why?" she laughed.

"Because you have just described the kind of job that I, without knowing it, have possibly been looking for to see me through to the end of next year."

"Oh, are you out of work?"

"Well, not exactly . . ."

For the next twenty minutes I told her all about White Marvel. And not only about White Marvel. I told her about my selling activities in the North and the other kinds of work I'd done. As our second cup of coffee arrived, I finished . . . "and the way you described the job of courier made me think it could be just the job for me. You said Ardmont employed men?"

"Oh, yes. Not as many as girls but we have a few."

"Vicki, quite seriously, what d'you think my chances would be? What does Ardmont look for in a courier?"

"Well, intelligence . . . personality . . . diplomacy . . ." she shrugged. "That's about it, really."

"What about languages?"

"They help, of course, but they're not always *absolutely* essential. It depends where the courier works. In a place like Majorca, for instance, a tremendous number of local people speak English. Well, to give you an idea – out of the sixteen reps Ardmont has in Majorca only six speak Spanish fluently. The others vary from fairly good to 'The pen of my aunt' standard."

I offered her a cigarette and while I was lighting it for her I said with a grin, "D'you think I'd make a good courier, Vicki?"

She exhaled the smoke and sat back, inspecting me, her head cocked humorously on one side. "When would you like to start – tomorrow morning?"

"No, seriously."

"I'm *being* serious. Philip Ardmont would give you a job, I'm sure."

"Really?"

"Absolutely. I'll, er, let you into a trade secret. D'you know the one qualification *essential* in couriers . . .?"

"Tell me."

Her eyes crinkled mischievously. "Sex appeal. It's as important as good food and clean beds."

"That so?"

"Of course. Sex plays an enormous part in a successful holiday. Holiday is fantasy time – two wonderful weeks of liberty after fifty weeks of dreary work. Think of the hundreds of thousands of secretaries ... factory workers ... typists ... shop assistants who spend those fifty weeks looking forward more than anything else to their summer holidays. They crave escape. They want sun ... and sand ... and sea ... and they want sex. Whether it's a pinch on the bottom from a handsome Italian lay-about or a full-blooded affair with a good-looking stranger." She smiled enchantingly. "Well, you know better than I do how a man feels about it ... but I can tell you from a woman's point of view that if those typists and shop assistants go back to work without so much as an indecent proposition or an offer to 'come outside', they've had a terrible time. Love, in some form, is a must. And what better way to start their holiday than to be greeted at the airport by a tanned, handsome courier oozing sex appeal?"

"Sounds one heck of a job," I said wistfully. "And you honestly think that I ..."

"Oh, come off it. You know you've got sex appeal."

I laughed at her, very chuffed at the compliment. "Tell me about the pay," I said, changing the subject.

"You'd start at ten pounds a week and all found. You'd probably get a room in one of the hotels Ardmont uses – or they might find you a flat, though you'd probably have to share it with another courier ..." she saw the smile in my eyes and said quickly, "... in your case, another *male* courier, Mr. Tobin."

"Shame."

"If you wanted a flat to yourself, Ardmont would probably pay half the rent and you'd pay the rest."

"That sounds reasonable."

"Besides the pay there are certain bonuses that go with the job – some official, some not so official. A good courier can earn quite a bit of commission from car hire, tours – those are the official sources – and from night clubs, shops, cafes on excursion routes if he can persuade his clients to use them – those are the unofficial sources. To give you an idea of how lucrative this commission can be, for the past four years –

while I was ordinary rep – I hardly touched my salary. I just lived on the commission."

"I can imagine. You could persuade me to do anything."

"*And* ..." she laughed, "some of the hotels and nightclubs extend free drinks – even cigarettes – to the couriers who support them. It really can be a lucrative job."

"The more I hear the more I like."

"Mm, well, I haven't told you about the drawbacks yet. Any job dealing with the public's welfare can be difficult. We get some impossible clients to deal with. They start complaining the moment they step off the plane and don't let up for two solid weeks. Everything is wrong – the hotel ... the food ... the service ... the beach ... the heat ... the wind .. the excursions ..."

I nodded. "I know. I've met a few while I was selling sewing machines."

"Fortunately we don't get many of that sort. They're generally very nice people just anxious to have a good holiday – and very cooperative if anything goes wrong." She looked at me steadily. "You're really serious about this, are you?"

"Yes, I think I am. It's all happened a bit suddenly, of course, but it sounds just what I'm looking for. Let's put it this way – the idea appeals to me enormously."

"Well, think about it – and if you decide to go ahead I'll introduce you to Philip Ardmont. But don't take too much time. The season starts early in some places, as early as the third week in March, and Ardmont like to have their couriers all sorted out long before that." She looked at her tiny gold wristwatch. I looked at my watch. It was after eleven.

"I'd better get home, Russ. I'm working at a travel agency in North London tomorrow. When I'm in England I do odd days at different agencies – helping out on the counter – obviously directing as much business as possible to Ardmont."

"Sure, I'll take you home. Where d'you live?"

She hesitated. "Well ... Richmond. I don't want to take you out of your way."

"No trouble at all. I always go home through Richmond."

"Oh? Where d'you live?"

"Maida Vale."

She laughed, knowing Richmond was something like ten miles out of my way.

"No argument," I said.

"All right, thank you."

When we left the Wimpey it was sleeting hard again. We ducked into our collars, sprinted to the car and fell into it, Vicki laughing, me cursing as usual.

"It's all right for you," I said. "You'll be out of this in a couple of weeks. Boy, I envy you."

I started the engine, got the wipers slurping the rotten stuff off the windshield and the heater going, and edged out into traffic.

"Well, you never know," she said, "you might be out of it soon, too."

"I'd give my right arm."

"Oh, not that – you'll almost certainly need it."

I grinned at her. "You reckon?"

"I reckon."

I shook my head. "Ah, it seems too good to be true. There are times I think I'll never feel the hot sun on my face again."

"You really are a sun worshipper, aren't you?"

"I love it – not necessarily to be *in* it, but I like the stuff around me, to feel warm."

"Then I'd say couriering is for you."

"You really feel I'd be good at it, hm?"

"I'm sure you would. I mean, it's only what you're doing now and what you've been doing in the past, isn't it? It's all human relations. Selling sewing machines, collecting debts, doing street interviews for T.V. – it's all contact with people. And if you're successful at those things you'll be successful as a courier. It's only the detail of the work that's different."

"Yes, I suppose so. You know, I still can't get over meeting you at L.R.S. tonight. How did you come to be there?"

"Ardmont is doing a lot of advertising for this summer – and the producer I mentioned ... the chap who passed out in the corridor ..."

"What was his name, by the way?"

"Lee Roper. He works for Whitley, Carr and Banks."

"No, I don't know him. Sorry ... go on."

"Well, Whitley, Carr and Banks are handling our advertising and Lee has been up to the office several times to confer with Philip Ardmont. I met him there and he asked me to go to this party with him tonight."

"Then passed out on you. Charming."

She laughed. "He was pretty sloshed when he picked me up at seven. We had a ghastly dinner. I almost walked out on him in the restaurant. He was telling me a flying story – with ges-

55

tures – and swept his dinner off the table and all over the floor. I nearly died of embarrassment."

"You've had a rough night."

"Not entirely. It . . . quite improved later on."

"Oh, what happened?"

"Met this ugly-looking fella who bought me a hamburger. He was quite nice, really."

"Oh, good."

"Sort of saved the evening."

"Maybe you saved his, too."

"Maybe."

The drive to Richmond took half an hour. I could have done it in twenty minutes, despite the sleet, but I wanted to prolong it. I could have driven all night listening to her talk. She was so easy to talk to, and to be with. Although we hadn't known each other more than two hours she exhuded such a warmth of nature, such instant rapport I felt I'd known her all my life.

During the drive she told me something of herself. She was born in Leicester and after leaving school she took a secretarial course and began work in an insurance office. After a year of that she graduated to something more exotic – a local travel agency, then came down to London to work for Ardmont which had just opened its first office. She became a courier a year later. I put her age at twenty three or four.

I enjoyed hearing her talk. Her voice was soft and gentle. It had a profoundly soothing effect on me and now and again caused little shivers up my neck. It was a curious, hypnotic titillation that made me feel quite dizzy, floaty. An adorable girl.

We entered Richmond and she directed me through foreign territory to a huge block of flats. I ran the car into a civilised carport and out of the sleet, realising instantly that the flats were a big cut above the slum line.

Locking the car, we entered through a revolving glass door into the foyer, a foyer that vied with Croxleys' reception for luxury. Plant life abounded in pots and small garden displays. The walls were pink-mirrored; the lighting concealed, subdued, restful. The deep grey carpet hushed our footsteps to absolute silence as we crossed to the elevators.

Vicki pressed the button. I looked around the foyer and said, "Now, this is what I call suffering," and thinking that the couriering business must be a darned sight better paid than she'd made out.

She must have read my mind because she replied, "Yes, it's lovely. I couldn't afford to live here on a courier's pay . . .'

The elevator doors rolled silently back. We entered the mirror-panelled car and Vicki stabbed the second button. We shot up two floors in the time it takes to breathe. She led the way along a short stretch of hall, carpeted and decorated luxuriously, and opened the door of 206 with a key.

There was no question for me of "what do I do now?". She walked straight in, clicked on a light switch, obviously expecting me to follow. I closed the door behind me.

The small hall was sumptuously decorated — deeply piled pale-green carpet, white and silver wallpaper embossed with an abstract floral pattern in bottle-green velvet, delicate crystal-pendant wall lights. . . . It was warm and silent and rich.

Vicki went to a gilt-and rosewood half-table set beneath a fine gilt-framed mirror and took up several letters from a silver tray. She leafed through them, dropped them back onto the tray, and crossed to a cupboard and handed me a coat-hanger.

She hung up the coats and went down the hall towards a far door, passing several closed doors on the way.

"Loo," she said, pointing at one of them.

We entered a lounge, sitting room, whatever they called it. Vicki pressed a wall switch and said, "Come in," and crossed the room to a silver tray containing bottles and glasses.

The room was beautiful; rich and splendid. Full of warm velvet and gilt and marble and antique splendour.

"Like a drink?" she asked.

"Yes, please — vodka if you've got it. Lord, Vicki, this is some room."

"Sit down. Try the sofa — it's heaven."

I sank into the cushioning of brown ribbed-velvet wondering when I'd stop falling.

"Wow."

"Told you." She brought my drink in a cut-crystal glass and put it on a small marble-topped table in front of me, then kicked off her shoes and sank onto the cushion, curling her legs beneath her.

"Cheers."

"Cheers."

I gave her a cigarette and lit it, then lit mine and looked around the room. "It must be difficult – leaving all this even for the sun."

She smiled and shook her head. "Oh, this isn't mine. I wish it was. It belongs to a girl friend who's father is just a *leetle* bit inclined to indulge his only daughter – his only child, for that matter. Sue is an air hostess with B.O.A.C. As you might imagine, she doesn't have to work for a living but she loves flying. I met her three years ago when she was with B.U.A. on the Spain run. We became very good friends. I stay here during my off season."

"I should have such friends already."

"Sue's a love. Pots of money but she never spends it. She devotes all her spare time to mentally retarded children."

"Quite a gal."

"Yes, she is."

"Where is she now?" I hoped it didn't sound like a leading question. I didn't mean it that way.

She sipped her drink and put the glass on the table. "Australia. She gets to Sydney tonight and has a week lay over."

A week lay over.

"It's a good time to be there, isn't it?" I asked. "Christmas?"

"Fabulous. Really hot."

The mention of Christmas reminded me that since it was now just after midnight it was officially Christmas Eve, and this realisation in turn reminded me I still hadn't made any plans for the Christmas week-end.

"Do you know it's Christmas Eve?" I said.

"No, tomorrow's . . ." she looked at her watch. "Ah, you're being technical. It is, yes."

"How are you spending Christmas?"

"We . . . e . . . ll," she said thoughtfully. "I've got three open invitations. I don't have to let anybody know I'm coming, I can just turn up. What are you doing?"

I shrugged. "No plans at all."

She looked aghast. "You're not spending Christmas alone . . .?"

"No, I don't *have* to. I've got a good friend – a fellow artiste – who's not doing much that I know of. We can find plenty of mischief to get into."

"I don't doubt it," she smiled. "You can't spend Christmas on your own . . ."

She got up and crossed the room to what looked like an

58

antique sideboard. When she opened the front I saw it was a radiogram. She sifted through several L.P.s and put one on. As she came back the music began – dreamy strings and a rippling solo piano.

"Like some coffee?"

"Yes, love some, but I don't want to keep you up – you've got to work tomorrow."

"Haven't you?"

"No," I laughed. "I probably won't do another stroke until the middle of January."

"It's all right for some. Come into the kitchen and talk to me. Bring the drinks."

I followed her down the hallway to one of the closed doors and into a large ultra-modern kitchen tiled in yellow and bronze. Surrounding the centre-floor cooking unit was a breakfast bar with four stools. I sat on one while she plugged in an electric kettle and set out two colourful mugs.

"Do you mind instant?" she asked.

"Not at all. Are you sure you don't want to throw me out?"

She turned and wrinkled her nose at me. "No."

"It's a pity you have to work tomorrow – I mean today."

"Oh . . . why?"

"Well, I thought we might . . . do something."

"Did you now? What sort of something?"

I shrugged. "Oh, I don't know. We've got the car . . . we could drive out somewhere."

"Very tempting, but I'm afraid . . ."

"Will the travel agency be busy – on Christmas Eve?"

"Probably not, but I did say I'd go in."

"Couldn't you . . . call or something?"

She laughed and began spooning coffee into the mugs. "You'll get me fired."

"Oh, I wouldn't do that . . ."

"But?"

"Well, it seems such a waste of Christmas Eve, working in an office."

She stirred in the water and brought the mugs over and sat on a stool opposite me. "I'm sure it would be much more enjoyable driving somewhere, but I really must go in."

"Shame."

"About . . . Christmas Day, though." She toyed with her coffee, turning it in circles. "Would you like to meet Philip Ardmont?"

59

"Uh? Yes, certainly."

"Philip is one of my open invitations. He's got a big house in Wimbledon – and a wife and two children. Christmas with Philip is open-house. People just wander in – friends, neighbours, *his* relatives, his *wife's* relatives ... it's absolute bedlam. If you'd like to ..."

"I'd love to. But wouldn't he mind me, you know, just happening?"

"I'm sure he wouldn't. We don't have to stay long."

"Well, yes, fine."

"Good, that's settled."

"What time d'you plan going?"

"Mid-morning – about eleven. The chaos should be in full swing by then."

"I really appreciate you helping me, Vicki."

"I'm helping Ardmont, too, aren't I? Think of the tremendous increase in business when it gets around the nation's typing pools that Russ Tobin is waiting out there in the sun to pander to their every whim."

"I'm not a lad like that."

"No?" she smiled. "No, of course you're not."

"Scout's honour." I made a face of pensive doubt. "Hm, that's a thought. Do you suppose it would spoil my chances of becoming a courier – being a virgin?"

She spluttered into her coffee.

"Does a lot of it go on?" I asked. "Amongst the *male* couriers, I mean, of course."

"What do you think?"

"I think a lot of it probably goes on."

"You have an evil mind, Mr. Tobin."

"Yeh, I know."

"There's hardly likely to be anything in rules and regulations about a courier's extra-curricula activities, now, is there? And how else would I know?"

"Oh, quite. I just thought you ... might have heard something."

"Not a thing. But I'm quite sure you're wrong. I believe all our couriers are hard-working, dedicated, disciplined, strictly moral men across whose noble minds thoughts of hanky panky never venture – and I'm quite surprised at you thinking otherwise ..."

"Very sorry, I'm sure."

"Our couriers live the life of monastic dedication shared

60

by allied servants of the public – ski-instructors, air hostesses, tennis coaches ... and I'm sure you'd never dream of levelling suspicion of immoral goings on at them, would you ..."

"Certainly not. I'm an idiot. Forgive me."

"As I told you in the Wimpey bar, the *possibility* of sex with the courier must be there, but to suggest it ever actually takes place was the furthest thing from my mind ..."

"I quite understand. I do apologise."

While all this horseplay was going on, we were of course sizing each other up – as we'd been doing since we first met. I'd been analysing the situation since she'd opened the door and invited me in – or at least trying to analyse it. It was difficult. With a certain type of girl the invitation into her flat automatically meant an invitation into her bed. You knew instinctively where you stood. But with Vicki it was different.

Here was a girl who did not conform to the norm. She was experienced, self-assured. For five years she had worked abroad and had undoubtedly had to cope with dozens of tricky situations involving the uninvited attentions of men. And she would undoubtedly know how to handle both situations and men – a cutting remark, a swift kick in the gearbox. She'd match the punishment with the crime and you'd be out on your tail-end before you could say but.

The invitation into the flat meant nothing at all in itself. It could well be that she was so accustomed to lone, civilised, platonic liaison with men and had judged me intelligent enough to realise it that she had invited me in trusting I wouldn't make a stupid play for her.

But, on the other hand, it was also possible that this was her own cool, unfussy way of saying 'I like you. I fancy you. Come in and stay the night' and had judged me intelligent enough to realise that!

I'd have to leave it to her. She knew damned well I fancied her. *Any* man with blood in his veins who was neither mad, sick or kinky would fancy her. And I wasn't that much in love with my own flat that I was yearning to return to it.

So far she'd given me plenty of mild encouragement – if I chose to interpret it that way. The smile in her eyes when she talked about the night-time activities of couriers indicated that at least the subject amused her. I decided to keep on that tack and see which way the wind blew.

"Seriously," I said unseriously. "What *is* the form? I think I ought to know. If a courier's extra-curricular activities *are* hectic, I think I owe it to Ardmont clients to be in top form when they arrive."

"Meaning you're not always in top form?"

"Meaning that perhaps future demands upon one's time and energies might be so appreciably in excess of more normal commitments as to require extra training ... a new diet ... even a week or two at a health farm."

She laughed gaily, a new, sparkly light livening her eyes. I was sure I was on the right track.

"I really wouldn't know," she said, "... though we had one poor chap sent home last year."

"Yes? What for?"

" 'Heat exhaustion' was the official reason. Unofficially he screwed himself into a coma."

My pulse tripped. I laughed with her. The message was coming through.

"What sort of man was he?"

"Good looking – of course – half French, half English. Very tanned. Dark curly hair. The matrons drooled over him. They actually had rows over who should sit next to him in the excursion bus."

"Only the matrons?"

"No, all the girls fancied him – married and single. I saw him get one or two very nasty looks from husbands."

"Did he go looking for it – or didn't he have to?"

She shook her head. "He didn't have to. As a matter of fact he put in a request for transfer out of the hotel and into a flat because the pressure was getting so great. A young girl actually climbed over his balcony one night and crawled into bed with him. Said she was going to throw herself off the pier unless he made love to her."

"Did she – throw herself off?"

She gave me a look. "Would you like another drink? Let's find a more comfortable seat."

As we went down the hall I said, "Don't you want to get to bed?"

"Not yet. We'll have one more drink."

"I can sleep all morning. I'm thinking of you."

"I'll be all right. I'm trained to do without sleep."

We entered the lounge. "Can you handle the music?" she asked.

"Sure."

"Same again – vodka?"

"Yes, thanks."

"Do you always drink vodka?"

"Yes, ever since I discovered its gentle affinity with my head in the mornings. Whiskey had endowed it with some real thumpers. Gin is pernicious and gives me indigestion. Rum stinks. There's not much left."

"Sounds as though you've made a close study of it."

I turned the record over and worked the mechanism.

"Investigation and understanding of every facet of our daily environment," I said, "is a vital necessity for the achievement of a whole and happy life."

"Who said that?" she laughed.

"I did – just now."

"Clever old you."

We met in the centre of the room. I took my glass from her and raised it. "To you, Vicki, lovely facet of today's environment."

She drank and said, "Implying what – that you intend investigating me? Is *it* necessary for your whole and happy life?"

I took her drink from her and put them both on the table, then held my arms out to her. She came into them readily, allowing me to hold her close. The perfume of her hair tickled my nose, strayed into my mind, filled my senses with fragrance.

"Yes, I would say it was."

"How nice to feel wanted," she sighed, jokingly facetious. "Or even merely desired."

"I can't imagine a time of your life when you weren't wanted – and desired."

"Than -kyou."

"You must have to fight a constant battle when you're abroad – against lecherous clients."

"Mm," she demurred. "But one learns to repel without insulting."

"I'll bet. But you've had one or two nasty moments?"

"Mmm," she went again. "When I first started with Ardmont. Now I become terribly brisk and efficient in the face of the enemy. Demoralise him with a smile, a pat on the head and tell him, 'Down, there's a good boy'. It works wonders."

"Rather like a sharp rap from a nurse's ballpoint pen?"

"Is that from experience?"

"Good God, no. I'm far too shy to get randy in a hospital bed."

"Mm," she said doubtfully.

"It's the truth. I really am shy altogether."

"I honestly hadn't noticed."

"Ah, that's because you bring out the . . . the . . ."

"The beast in you?"

". . . the *confident* side of my nature, I was going to say. Why, am I behaving like a beast?"

She hugged me and laughed. "Horribly. I'm scared stiff."

"I can see that."

We were hardly moving, just swaying to the music, using it as an excuse to hold each other. Whoever wrote 'but what is dancing but making love set to music playing?' certainly knew his onions. That purely is what we were up to. She felt good; small and compact in my hands, soft against my front. I wanted very much to kiss her. I could imagine what her male clients must have suffered over the past five years, seeing her flitting about the beach, super-tanned, fair hair bleached by the sun, practically naked but for a bikini. I didn't doubt she'd had one or two nasty moments.

"What are you thinking?" she asked suddenly.

"I was picturing you . . . on the beach in summer . . . in a bikini."

"Were you now? What brought that on?"

"Holding you like this."

"Perhaps you oughtn't to if it gives you those kind of thoughts," she said, making no attempt to break away.

"They were really quite wholesome thoughts. Just appreciative – not lecherous. Is that the right thing to say?"

She gave me another hug. "You're very thoughtful, aren't you?"

"Not always. That's another of my sides you bring out."

"Do I? Well, now, that's your confident side and your thoughtful side. Any others?"

I chuckled. "You'd be surprised. But I'm not anxious for a pat on the head and a 'down, there's a good boy' so I'm keeping them in check."

"You think I'd do that to you, do you?"

I shrugged. "I don't know. I just didn't want to risk it. This is too good to spoil."

She raised her cheek from my shoulder and looked at me. A smile crinkled her eyes as they lowered to my mouth and came up again. She said softly, "Try me."

My heart jumped. I kissed her, very gently, finding her lips

64

warm and yielding. I kissed her like that for a long time. Suddenly she broke away and held me close, uttering a woeful, "Oh ..."

I kissed her hair, her forehead. Her fingers tightened on my back. "I knew ... the moment I saw you I knew you were trouble."

"Oh?"

"I *swore* there would be no one before I left for Italy. Absolutely no one ..."

"I'm sorry."

"And you had to be standing there ... looking all lost and ridiculous ... a sardine sandwich and half a sausage in one hand and a glass of neat vodka in the other ... the only human-looking man in the room ... damn you."

Her mouth came up, anxious for mine. This time it was no gentle exploratory kiss. Her mouth exploded against mine and her body thrust hard. The unexpectedness of her erupting passion took my breath away. You just never can tell.

She broke away from the kiss but clung hard to me with a mournful, "Oh, go home ... now. Please go."

"Sure."

She didn't mean a word of it.

Then she was there again, tongue flying. "Oh, Russ ..." she murmured.

"Can I stay?"

"Oh, yes ... yes."

A moment later we were down the hall and standing in a palatial pink bedroom with a huge pink bed, canopied by a draped white silk awning. We undressed by the light from the hall and hit the cool satin counterpane as one, locked together. Her need was feverish, urgent. She covered my face with kisses and whispered impatiently, "Make love to me, darling ..." and urged me in with repeated gasps, each gasp a voluble expression of her frantic rhythm which ceased as the arrowhead of orgasm pierced her and a husky cry of joyful release escaped from her.

I curled behind her, my arms around her body heat accentuated by the coolness of the sheets, and before long, without another word, she was asleep.

CHAPTER FOUR

I awoke two or three times during the night, aware of her warmth hard against me. Once she moved and made a little satisfied sound and wriggled her bottom to tell me she knew I was there and that she liked the idea and returned again to sleep. But when I finally awoke she was gone.

I propped myself up on an elbow and blinked at the room, wincing at the stream of strong sunlight that slashed through a gap in the curtains with the ferocity of a laser beam.

I panicked a little then, at the silence of the apartment, believing she'd deserted me for the travel agency. But in the next moment, with relief, I heard the chink of a spoon against a saucer from the kitchen and as my other senses awoke I smelled the coffee.

I relaxed against the pillows and waited.

She came in within five minutes carrying a tray. She looked wonderful, enchanting in a pale blue negligee, her pale gold hair free about her face, gleaming in the sunlight. She smiled when she saw I was awake. "Good morning. It's eleven o'clock. I was desperate for coffee."

"I've just had a mild heart attack," I said, making room for the tray. She sat on the bed and handed me a cup.

"I thought you'd gone to work."

She sipped her coffee. "I telephoned."

"What did you tell them – that you had a hangover?"

"No, I told the manageress the truth – that I had a virile all-man man in my bed and I asked her what she'd do in the same circumstances."

"What did she say?"

"She asked me why I was wasting time talking on the telephone."

"You look adorable. I think I'd like to kiss you."

She leaned towards me and accepted one.

"Come back to bed," I said.

"I intend to – as soon as I've finished this."

"You really don't have to go to work?"

"Uh uh." She looked at me over the rim of her cup. "You're a very bad influence, you know that? My desire for work has vanished. The thought of spending today in an office instead of with you was quite painful. Me! Dedicated Doris. I can't believe it."

"What would you like to do today?"

She laughed. "Are you serious?"

"I mean ... when we eventually get up. It looks a lovely day."

"It is. Cold and sunny. Let's see how the mood takes us."

"All right."

She removed the tray from the bed, dropped the negligee and leapt in beside me, cuddling up, making sounds of sensuous pleasure.

"You're lovely," she said, rubbing my chest.

"And pitifully pink."

"I love you pink ..." she kissed my nipple, "... love you ..." kissed my stomach, "... love you ..." the kisses ranged all over my stomach while her fingers tickled the inside of my thigh.

"Hey ...!"

I began to stir immensely and the sight brought her thigh across me. She rolled aboard, laughing at me. "Beautiful," she breathed. "Beautiful." She closed her eyes: her mouth hung open.

"There's nothing quite like it, is there?"

She shook her head. "Nothing. Nothing in life. You can't describe it. It's beyond words. I can feel you in my heart. Right up here in my heart. It makes me tingle ..." She shivered and uttered a quick laugh. I felt her body tighten, tremble. "Russ ... I feel strange ..."

"Are you all right?"

"I feel so *strange* ..."

"Vicki, are you all right?"

"Oh ... yes!" she cried. "Oh, darling, I feel so wonderful ..." the words tumbled out breathlessly. "... it's incredible ... incredible ... oh, RUSS!" Her fingers dug into my arms and she bit her lip savagely as her body jerked ... again ... and again and she fell forward onto me, clutching my shoulders, half laughing, half crying, gasping 'oh' and 'ah' with every breath.

Gradually she became quiet. "I was out of this world ..." she said with a little laugh. "I've never experienced anything like that before. I honestly thought I was going to die of pleasure. It was unbelievable. I feel all weak ..." she sighed deeply and contentedly. "Why did you have to be at that wretched party? ... life was so uncomplicated ... no men ... no trouble ... Italy in two weeks time ... now look what you've gone and done ..."

"I'm sorry."

"So you ought to be ... standing there with a cucumber and sardine sandwich ... upsetting people ... innocent girls ..."

"If I'd known they upset you I'd have taken a Spam."

She gave her helpless little laugh. "I feel so sleepy."

"Then sleep."

"Hold me – as you did last night."

"Certainly not."

She moved from me and curled herself into a ball, took my hand, kissed the palm and placed it on her breast. "Please do something for me?"

"Sure."

"Make me a promise and keep it no matter what ...?"

"What is it?"

"Don't accept any job near me in Italy. Don't dare be anywhere where I can touch you or even see you, because if you are ..."

"What?"

"We've both lost our jobs."

I laughed and hugged her. "All right, I promise."

"I mean it. It's bad enough here ... but with all that sun and sea and warm, moonlit nights ... and soft Italian music ..."

She shook her head and said no more. When we awoke at four the sun had gone and an inch of fresh snow covered the street below.

*

At five o'clock, showered and warmly dressed, we drove to my flat in Maida Vale where Vicki lay on my bed and talked to me while I removed a promising beard and changed my clothes. Then we headed for the city and trudged the slushy pavements, arm in arm, gazing into the wonderously decorated windows of the big stores along Oxford Street, admiring the street illuminations, enjoying the bustle and good humour of the stores and pavements crowded with late Christmas Eve shoppers.

In the warm cathedral vastness of Selfridges we separated by consent to shop for each other's present and we re-met at a prearranged point half an hour later. I'd never known shopping to give me so much pleasure; rarely does it give me *any* pleasure. But I enjoyed shopping for Vicki, visualising her delight when she opened the packages.

I bought her a small bottle of perfume – Arpege – which I knew she used; a ceramic dress-clip that caught my eye; and for fun a quaint gonk-like doll, about six inches high, with a mass of blue hair covering its cheeky face. I had them all gift-wrapped separately in different coloured papers and dressed with appropriate ribbons.

When I rejoined her she eyed the packages suspiciously. "What have you been up to?"

"I didn't buy anything for you. These are all for me. What have you been up to?"

She was doing her best to make little of a carrier bag containing packages. "Same here. Men are impossible to buy for. These are for me."

I put my presents into the bag. "Right – where to now?"

To escape the cold we took two seats in the Paris Pullman and stared at a much vaunted Swedish film for an hour, trying to make out who was doing what to whom and why. After this hour we decided not even the director knew and walked out laughing, childishly high on our sense of independent-mindedness at having rejected a film the world had acclaimed.

We ended up in a little Italian restaurant I'd once been in with Tony Dane. This, at least, was very successful. The head waiter, one of the biggest professional flirts in the business, fell immediately in love with Vicki and we almost suffocated with over-attention when he discovered she spoke fluent Italian. The food was great, the wine nicely mellowing and the softly played background of taped Italian music kept us at the corner table talking, smoking and drinking coffee and brandy until closing time, midnight.

In a rosy euphoria we said a noisy farewell to the head waiter and made for the car. As I started the engine Vicki slid down in her seat to rest her head and touched my knee. "You know, I don't think I've ever spent a nicer day in my entire life. Everything was ... perfect." She took my hand and squeezed it. "Thank you so much."

"And I thank you since you were responsible for it. If I'd gone to the Tratt alone I'd have been given a table just inside the kitchen and a plate of tough, knotted spaghetti. You knocked the poor little headwaiter sideways."

She wrinkled her nose at me.

We reached her flat at half past midnight. As I hung the coats in the cupboard I said, "D'you realise it's Christmas Day?"

She shook her head. "No, it isn't. I refuse to recognise it until I wake up in the morning. It spoils it."

"You're absolutely right. It is not Christmas Day. Would you like a drink?"

"No, thank you."

"Coffee?"

"No, thank you."

"Cigarette?"

"No, thank you."

"What would you like?"

She slipped her arms around me and hugged me. "I'd like an end to a perfect day."

"You got it."

This time there was no fury, no fever ... only gentle, leisurely, skilful, thoughtful love, lasting and rising through an hour to a wondrously fulfilling end.

"A day of days," she sighed, curled once more in my arms. "It's rather sad to think it's over. No other day could be so good."

"I'll try my best. I'll try tomorrow." I kissed her shoulder. "Happy Christmas, love."

She took my hand from her breast and kissed the palm, very gently. "Happy Christmas," she said. "Happy Christmas."

Reluctant to leave her sleeping warmth I slipped out of bed, put on a robe I'd brought from the flat, and went into the kitchen to make the coffee. While it was percolating I dressed the tray with a lace cloth, arranged the cups on it, then placed her presents around them. She was still asleep when I entered the bedroom.

I stood for a moment looking at her, loving the way she lay, one bare arm above the sheet, the other stretched out over the edge of the bed, her little hand relaxed and drooping. Her hair spilled across her pillow; her eyes were lightly closed, lips slightly parted. Her slim form beneath a single sheet, rising and falling in easy sleep, dipped to almost nothing at the waist, rose sharply for the curving mound of hip and thigh. Even in sleep she excited me. For a moment I considered taking the tray back to the kitchen and slipping in beside her for another hour, but it was after ten o'clock and if we were ever to get to Philip Ardmont's ...

I put the tray on the dressing table, knelt beside the bed and began to kiss her ... her fingers ... hand ... arm ... lips ... nose ... eyes. She moved in sleep and turned onto her back, taking the sheet with her, exposing one small, perfect breast. I kissed it gently, tickled it with my tongue. She moved again, opened her eyes, aware instantly of what I was doing.

She smiled and said sleepily. "What a beautiful way to wake up. This surely must be paradise."

"Happy Christmas – properly. I've got something for you."

"Something *more*?"

"Much more – a big, big cup of superbly made coffee ... freshly ground to taste just right."

"You sound like a commercial man."

"I am a commercial man."

"You're adorable."

She propped herself on an elbow, squinted at me through her curtain of hair, still not properly awake, and pouted her lips for a kiss.

"What's that for – coffee?"

"Kiss kiss – then coffee."

I kissed her and brought the tray over. She beamed when she saw the presents. "For me?"

"For you."

"All three?"

"All three."

"I don't deserve them."

"I know it. You're an ugly, unloving, unlovely woman but I'm hoping to change your nature." She took a quick sip of coffee and reached for a package.

"That one first," I said.

She opened the perfume. "Arpege! How did you know?"

"I peeked."

"Oh, thank you, Russ, it's ..."

I kissed her. "Now that one."

She opened the package containing the brooch. "Oh, it's lovely! I adore it. It'll go with at least three of my dresses. Thank you so much."

"Now this one."

"I feel very spoilt. You really shouldn't have ..."

"Hush up and open it."

I watched her expression as she opened the package. I don't think anything would have given her more pleasure than that silly gonk. She took him from his box with a cry of delight and laughed aloud as she parted his hair and saw his cheeky little face.

"Oh, he's an angel! I love him!" She kissed him on the nose and had another look at him, then her eyes came off him and onto me. "And you're an angel," she said softly. "And I love you. Thank you, Russ."

"My pleasure ... and I mean it. You're great to give presents to. You get such a kick out of them."

"What shall we call him?"

"Edward G. Robinson," I said, being ridiculous.

"Yes! Edward G.! Absolutely right." She walked him along the edge of the tray, saying between clenched teeth, "Now, look here, you mugs ... I'm Little Caesar, see ..."

I laughed at her.

"I'll keep him with me always," she said seriously. "He'll stand on the dressing table and come to Italy with me."

At that moment, for the first time, I felt suddenly miserable to hear her talk of leaving. We'd known each other such a short time, hours only, but I'd come to like her very much. It wasn't just sex, though that of course was glorious, but there was so much more. The hours flew in her company. I loved her nature ... the way she talked ... and laughed ... everything about her.

She looked up from the gonk and caught my expression. "Hey, what's the matter?"

"Nothing," I smiled. "Just thinking."

"It must have been serious. You looked quite miserable."

"Heck, no, I'm happy."

She knew though. Her eyes remained on mine for a moment, reflecting her own realisation that we were beginning to mean something to each other. She smiled quickly and lowered her eyes, changed the mood to banter.

"As I, er, told you in Selfridges I couldn't find a thing for you. Sorry and all that ..."

I removed the tray to the dressing table. "That's all right. I don't mind. Just don't expect any more first class lovin', that's all. Just don't expect ..." I rounded on her and she disappeared under the sheet with a scream. "... any more ... beautiful ... doodling ..." I ripped back the sheet and jumped on the bed and began tickling her mercilessly, under the arms, along the ribs. She writhed and kicked, trying to escape, squealing with helpless laughter, begging me to stop. But I kept on, punctuating each fresh attack of tickling with, "...

72

any more ... sumptuous nights ... of indescribable ... pleasure ... just ... don't ... expect ..."

"Oh, sto ... o ... op!" she cried, choking with laughter.

"They're ... in ... the ... ward ... robe ... you ... beast!"

And suddenly I stopped. She gasped and collapsed, flinging wide her arms and legs, shamelessly naked, I stared down at her, breathing heavily from my exertions, stirred by the sight of her body. She saw the look. Her eyes flared with instant sexuality. With a flick I unfastened the cord of my robe and she was reaching for me, hungrily. I fell forward onto her and she took me fiercely, crushing me with thighs of iron, making me cry out as her nails bit into my flesh, bringing me to a state of excitement to match her own, and with a cry she leapt the simple edge of pleasure and flew out into an awesome orbit of ecstasy, taking me with her, all the way, fast as light itself, clean and sharp and clear, all the way to heaven. And this time she was crying, properly crying, crying proper tears. "Oh, Russ ..."

"Yes, love?"

She shook her head.

"What is it?" I whispered, stroking her face, stroking away her tears.

"It was ... just wonderful. Every time I do it with you ... it gets better. It's ... frightening. I really feel I'll die if it gets any better." She heaved a huge sigh and began to settle. "D'you think it's possible ... to die making love?"

"Oh, sure ... if you're eighty-nine and you've got a wonky ticker. But I think you're all right for a couple of years yet."

She laughed and stroked my hair. "It's so peaceful afterwards, isn't it? As though you've sailed through the eye of a hurricane into a quiet lagoon."

"Hm hm, exactly that."

"I feel all floaty ... weightless. I haven't a nerve or a muscle in my body. It's all cloud." She drifted into a small silence, still stroking my hair, then, in the same awed voice she said softly, "Russ ..."

"Mm?"

"Would you mind very much if I said I loved you?"

Funny how that little word stirs fear in a single man's heart. It brings on rushing, primaeval fear, instant horror of responsibilities, disciplines, limitations ... marriage! It's so stupid. It's a lovely word, really, and no greater compliment exists. My instinctive pause for thought, however, misled the dear girl. She said quickly, "I'm sorry, don't answer that, it wasn't fair. Just let me say I do love you ... I don't know how else to describe it. I love your face ... your gentleness ... I love you near me ... inside me. Therefore I must love you. That's all I meant ... and I wanted to say it ... I wanted you to know."

I felt ashamed. Hadn't I thought the same about her while she was asleep? The difference was she'd had the courage to say it.

"Vicki ... men are pretty stupid. *I'm* stupid. Of course I don't mind you saying it. Thank you for saying it."

There was another longish silence and then, so typically, she laughed. "We're getting terribly serious, aren't we? And on Christmas Day too." She kissed my nose. "Happy Christmas, love. What time is it?"

"Oh, about eleven."

"Eleven! Come on, let's get out to Wimbledon. I'm starved."

CHAPTER FIVE

It was well after noon before we began the drive to Wimbledon because we had daudled endlessly in the shower, playing daft games, throwing bubbles at each other, steadfastly refusing to be hurried, not at all anxious to share the day with other people, no matter who. Indeed it was an effort to leave the warmth of the apartment at all for the bleak greyness of the world outside. Still, we finally made it and at half past twelve we were ripping down Park Side, the road that borders Wimbledon Common, me sporting new open-backed driving gloves in black leather – one of Vicki's presents to me (they really were in the wardrobe). When I asked her how she knew the size of my hands she gave me a very quaint look and said, "Are you kidding?"

I was wearing my other present too – a pretty wild-looking shirt with a pale-blue abstract design reminiscent of lace, with a wide tie to match. Very nice.

Near the old windmill we turned off Park Side and meandered through some back streets to a quiet cul-de-sac of very up market houses built in the thirties. The grass-verged road was comfortable, settled and eminently respectable without being dull. The houses, though large and solid, were all freshly painted, jaunty, and had large open front gardens that gave the houses a lightness of spirit. I imagined that in the Spring, with the daffodils and tulips out, and all through the summer with a million multi-coloured roses showing, the road would look a treat.

"That's Philip's – where all the cars are," Vicki said, pointing.

She really looked something, in a leaf-green suede suit and a snow white blouse, ruffed in front to the neck and at the wrists. The green was quite devastating against her blonde hair and sun tan, and the cut of the suit showed off her brown legs and figure beautifully.

Although a circular drive led up to the Ardmont house I had to park the car in the street. The driveway was filled with half a dozen cars and there were already four others at the pavement – Triumphs, Rovers, a couple of new Jaguars, a Mercedes – all good stuff.

We parked the car and crunched up the gravel drive. The heavy oak front door was partly open and before we reached the porch we could hear the noise inside.

We entered a wide hall with an open, L-shaped staircase leading off. Half a dozen kids, ranging in age from about three to ten, were fooling around on the stairs, sliding down the bannisters, shooting each other through them, making a hell of a din.

To our left, through an open door, I could see a big kitchen. There must have been eight or ten women in there, standing around nattering and drinking, preparing plates of snacks. To our right was the door to the lounge. Vicki took my arm and headed me for it, saying, "I told you it would be bedlam."

The lounge was a huge room, running from front to back of the house. It was expensively decorated. A grey-pink curly-twist carpet covered the floor entirely and there was a three-piece suite in green leather that wouldn't have left much change out of a thousand pounds. In one corner a magnificent Christmas tree reached the ceiling; it was abundantly decorated, dripping tinsel, lights and presents. Under it four young lads sat on the carpet building a plastic bridge with a ... yes! a Klippit Construction Kit! Well, at least I'd sold *one*.

There were about thirty people in the room, perhaps more, standing in groups, drinking, laughing, smoking, chatting, nibbling thing on cocktail sticks, all having a lovely time. Vicki peered around the room. "There he is."

She led me through the assembly to four people standing by a long table filled with cold buffet and drinks. A man I supposed was Philip Ardmont looked our way, spotted Vicki and raised his hand. We joined the group.

Ardmont was tall, over six feet, and well built with big shoulders and hands. I put his age at mid-forties. His hair was crinkly and greying; his face ruggedly handsome and intelligent – the sort of face women say improves with age. He met Vicki with a fatherly kiss on the forehead.

"Well done, glad you got here. Happy Christmas."

She said hello to the others in the group, two women and a man, all of whom she apparently knew, and introduced me.

Ardmont welcomed me pleasantly with a handshake like a car-crusher. The other man, a pot-bellied ex-colonel type sporting a military moustache, said predictably, "Hello, old boy," and shook hands heartily. He was introduced as Bill

Cartwright. Mrs. Cartwright was a tall, bony creature with buck teeth and a handshake to match Ardmont's.

The second woman was Liz Ardmont, a titian-haired cracker with big, sexy brown eyes, a lush mouth and a figure to take your breath away, dressed in a white matt-silk trouser suit that had been sprayed on and left no doubt in anyone's mind that she had nothing on under it but tanned skin. She gave me a smile that put my eyes temporarily out of focus and punched me right under the heart.

We were helped to drinks and stood around in the group for a few minutes, chatting about this and that and nothing in particular, and then I found that Vicki, Liz Ardmont and I had formed a splinter group. Liz chatted to Vicki for a while about her coming season in Italy and then turned on me, hitting me again with her smile.

"And what does Russ do? Are you in travel?"

"No, I'm in television. I appear in commercials ..."

Her lovely mouth dropped open; her big eyes got bigger; she stepped back a pace and gasped, "Of course! You're the Glamour Soap man ... ! Oh, how marvellous ..." Then her arm was hooked in mine and she was saying to Vicki, "Darling, I'm going to steal him for a few minutes, d'you mind? There're some girls in the kitchen just *dying* to meet him ..." Then I was being marched away, leaving Vicki laughing.

"Hope you don't mind," she said as we crossed the hall, stepping over children. "But the hens would just adore to meet a celebrity."

"No, not at all ..."

She gave my arm a squeeze, prodding her breast. "That's very nice of you. It'll make their Christmas."

As we entered the kitchen she announced, "Girls! Look what I've got ... the handsome brute in the Glamour Soap commercial!"

Voices ooh-ed and aahed and twittered and giggled. I stuck a Glamour Soap grin on my face and said hello to the ten women, four of whom, at least, were as attractive as Liz Ardmont; then, accepting a drink and a cigarette, I settled down to answering questions. There were dozens of them: Do commercials really take such ages to make? How is this trick and that trick done? How did I get into commercials in the first place? How does one get one's angelic child in commercials? Is the money really so good? Have I met the en-

77

chanting man who rides the white horse along the beach in the chocolate ad? Do I ever get free samples?

It must have been an hour later that I sensed Vicki at my elbow. I was hoarse by this time and my face ached from smiling.

"D'you mind if I pinch him back?" she said to Liz. "Philip would like a word with him."

"All right, if you must . . ." laughed Liz.

Vicki whisked me towards the lounge. There were fewer people in there now. "Thought you needed rescuing, "Vicki said quietly.

"You're a love."

"I've had a word with Philip about you . . ."

"Yes? What did he say?"

"What I said he'd say," she said smugly. "How soon can you start?"

"You're joking."

"I'm not. He had a look at you from the hall while you were holding court with the bevy in the kitchen. He said if you weren't good for a ten percent increase in business he'd eat this year's brochure."

"Go on . . ."

"Honestly."

Philip Ardmont was crouched by the tree, trying to help the four lads with their bridge. As we went in he stood up, sneering at a strip of plastic ballustrade in his hand. "Rubbish," he muttered. He smiled at me. "Well, now, Vicki has told me all about you. Very unusual, I must say. Seems a bit of a come-down financially for you – T.V. star to courier."

"More of a plummet," I said, grinning at the "star" bit.

"You'd really like to try us, eh?"

"From what I've heard about the job I would."

"You don't speak Spanish?"

"No, I took French and Latin at grammar school, but no Spanish."

"You'd be willing to learn it?"

"Oh, sure – what d'you mean – by Linguaphone or something like that?"

"Any way you like. I been thinking . . . the place for you would be Majorca, beginning mid-March. That would give you three months to learn a good smattering of Spanish if you got down to it. You'd be prepared to stay with us right through the summer – until October?"

78

"Yes, I would."

"All right. Come and see me at the office after the new year and we'll go into details. You'll have to fill in an application form and be approved by the board."

I thanked him and he smiled. "You'll earn your money, I can tell you. Now . . ." he turned his attention to the ballustrade. "All you need to build this blasted thing is a degree in engineering and the patience of Job . . ."

I held out my hand. "Let me do it – I've had some experience."

He handed me the part. I knelt down said hello to the lads, and clicked in the ballustrade with a unique twist I'd developed through long practice in the studio.

"I'll be damned," Ardmont said.

We stayed until early evening – until I'd completely built the bridge, done a jig-saw puzzle of the QE2 in mountainous seas; played blow-football until I was dizzy, dressed an Action Man in underwater kit and controlled the radiogram for musical chairs, musical bumps and musical statues. And this is what Christmas is really all about – kids laughing, jumping up and down, excited with their new toys, singing off-key carols. Memories of my own childhood Christmases flooded back at the sight of discarded pillowcases, crumpled wrapping paper, Christmas stockings filled with Hong Kong rubbish, the toys, the sweets. . . . It suddenly struck me I hadn't been a child for close on a million years.

At seven o'clock Philip and Liz Ardmont saw us off at the door with thanks for entertaining the kids.

In the car, as we headed back towards London, Vicki sighed and held her ears. "Wow, the noise! Well, I must say you were a big hit with the Ardmonts – especially Momma Ardmont."

"Jealousy is unbecoming in one so fair. She's quite a dish, hm?"

"Mm . . ." she demured. "A little old, don't you think?"

"Mature, love – mature is the word."

"As in gorgonzola?"

"Don't you like her?"

She laughed. "Yes, of course I do, we're great friends. So – it looks like you've got yourself a job, Tobin."

"I can't realise I could be working in Majorca all summer.

Six months in the sun ... and sea ... and sand ..." I chuckled, "... and s . s . s ..."

"Stop right there," she commanded.

"And s . s . sincerity, I was going to say."

She gave me a playful crack on the thigh.

"It's seven o'clock," I said. "How would you like to spend Christmas night?"

"Abed with you."

"Now, love, you must try to force your mind to other matters *some* of the time ..."

"Do you fancy a party?" she asked.

"There's one party I fancy very much."

"Now who's being filthy?"

"What have you got in mind?"

"It's another of my open invitations – two air hostesses I know. They share a flat in Knightsbridge. It's likely to be just a wee bit noisy and highly alcoholic."

"How d'you feel?"

She shrugged. "Why not? We can always leave if it gets too boisterous."

"O.K. Let's have dinner in town and drop in."

There aren't many restaurants open on Christmas night so we chose the Dorchester to be sure the food was edible. Normally I avoid huge dining rooms because I find myself whispering during the meal instead of relaxing, but with Vicki I found it easy to ignore the room and concentrate on her, as all the other men in the hotel appeared to be doing.

At nine thirty we drove west to Knightsbridge, to a modern block of flats incongruously squeezed between sombre and sooty Victorian terraces.

The door to the flat on the second floor was opened briskly by a character in her late twenties who beamed at the sight of Vicki and exclaimed, "It's come – and it's brought a *man*!"

"Stella – I don't step over the mat until you promise to keep your hands off him," Vicki warned.

"Bitch! Come in."

As we went in, Vicki linked her arm in mine protectively and said, "This is Russ Tobin and don't you dare shake hands with him." To me she said, "This is Stella Ormand and if you value your virginity – keep your distance."

Stella stuck out her hand, took mine and clamped the other hand on top. "Hello, Russ. Vicki, he's lovely."

Stella was one of those women who radiate sunny brashness

and the aura of easy virtue. She was medium tall, slightly dumpy and very full breasted. Her rather attractive face bore the unmistakeable signs of advanced dissipation and in general she appeared untidy, slightly unkempt, as though she'd hastily dressed after a riotous afternoon in bed. I liked her.

From a room down the hall came loud party sounds, female laughter, the boom of male voices and a background of ear-shattering pop music.

"Who's here, Stella?" Vicki asked.

Stella waved her hand. "Oh, God, thousand of them, darling. We invited twenty and forty turned up. Never mind, there's plenty of duty-free booze. Come on in."

She took my other arm and led us down the hall, saying to Vicki, "And where did you find this one, you lucky bag?" squeezing my arm.

"In my stocking. I wrote a letter to Santa."

"All I get in my stocking is holes. I've tried everything – even prayer."

As we entered the lounge Stella bellowed, "Everybody – this is Vicki and Russ! There ..." she said to us, "that's the introductions done. Grab a drink and mingle."

Stella hadn't exaggerated; there were at least forty people in the room, all, I guessed, airport types though dressed in civilian gear. There was just something about them – their appearance, age group, their easy, very easy familiarity with one another. Vicki nodded to several of them as we pushed through the dancers towards a small bar in the corner. Behind the bar, in shirt sleeves, a beefy, red-faced man with a bushy moustache had just finished telling half a dozen men and women a good – and I suspected dirty, story because they all burst into laughter and applauded as we approached.

"That's Ginger Cookson," said Vicki. "Chief Engineer with B.O.A.C. Death and soul of the party."

"How many more d'you know here?"

"Oh, six or seven. That's Pat, over there, the girl who shares the flat with Stella." She pointed to an attractive red head who was dancing with a tall, handsome man in a checkered suit. He had her in a bear-hug and was eating her neck. Pat, eyes closed, mouth open, was obviously not hating it too much. I glanced around the room.

"Are they all flying types?" I asked.

"Yes, I think so – aircrew, ground staff. Stewardesses rarely get a chance to meet anybody else."

"They look a sexy lot."

"Huh, look who's talking. Would you like a drink?"

"Sure – if Ginger will oblige."

Ginger was at it again, holding his rapt audience with another yarn as we moved closer to the bar.

"And so . . . !" he said in a hushed, dramatic voice, spreading his hand for silence, ". . . there it was – the challenge! I thought for a moment – and came up with this:

> What sight more beauteous than a woman's thighs?
> Was fairer texture ever seen?
> A joy that causes man to cry
> Heaven's above! . . . *and* in between.

His audience once again erupted into laughter and applause, punctuated with "Oh, jolly good, Ginger" and "Wonderful!" They sounded well cut to me.

Ginger spotted Vicki over their heads and bellowed, "Vicki, dear heart, wonderful to see you! Happy Christmas, treasure. What can I conceivably do for you?"

"Hello, Ginger – two vodkas and tonics if you've got it."

"For you, my angel, *anything* . . ." he wiggled his moustache lecherously. ". . . and I *do* mean *anything*!" He nodded at me and raised an enquiring brow. "Is he with you, Sugar Lump?'

"Yes, he is."

"Goddam it, woman, now why did you go and do a thing like that? You knew I'd be here . . ."

And so on. A right pain in the cockpit. It was two stories and a small boring eternity before we got our drinks and broke away from the bar.

"If I didn't know better, "Vicki murmured, "I'd think Stella puts Ginger on the bar to keep people away from it."

"He's beautiful."

"You ain't seen nuthin' yet. Wait until he really gets plastered. He'll end up dancing naked."

I laughed.

"I mean it – it's his party piece. I tell you, the party is morbidly respectable at the moment. Wait a couple of hours."

"What about the neighbours – don't they complain?"

"These people *are* the neighbours. The apartment block is known as Runway Six. When somebody sleeps, everybody sleeps. When they kick up a riot, everybody comes. It works well.

82

"I imagine."

The riot developed slowly but inexorably between then and three a.m. on Boxing morning, at which time the scotch bottle crashed through the window into the street below; Ginger Cookson lay three-quarters naked and very unconscious with a busted jaw; one of the intruders was sprawled in the bath, blood flowing freely from a cavity in his head; the police arrived in force to break the festivities up; and Vicki and I went home.

We hadn't intended staying so late. At the beginning I felt a bit out of it. You know how it is when you arrive at a party cold sober and find everyone else has been on the juice for hours; then add to that the fact of the partygoers being a fraternity and me the only stranger in the room and you'll know how I felt.

We began by circling the room, Vicki introducing me to the few people she knew. The talk was exclusively shop – Annabel sends her fondest . . . did you know Phil was marrying Arthur . . . that Ann had had another abortion. I stood around trying to look interested, knowing Vicki was enjoying the gossip. One kind soul brought us a fresh drink, a Ginger Cookson Special – nine tenths vodka with an afterthought of tonic – and within half an hour the dose was repeated, then again, and again . . . and again, so that by one o'clock neither Vicki nor I were feeling any particular pain. The party had taken on a nice rosy hue, floaty, mellow around the edges. At one point I lost Vicki and found myself talking to a dishy brunette about filming. She'd been a model before joining the airline and had done a couple of commercials, so we had a bit in common. I was beginning to enjoy myself when she was whisked away by a rugged brute a good four inches taller and a yard wider than me who gave me a murderous glower.

I wasn't lonely for long. Suddenly I was face to face with one heck of a girl I hadn't noticed before. She must have been a late arrival because I'm sure I would have spotted her when I came in. She was tall, willowy and lightly coloured, Indian perhaps, with lazy brown eyes, snowey teeth and large breasts.

"Hi," she said. "Haven't seen you b'fore. Are you crew?"

She was sloshed. She was talking to my left ear.

"No, I'm . . ."

"Would you like to dance? I haven' danced all night."

"Sure . . ."

She was in there like a homing pigeon, straight in, no messing, arms snaking around my kneck, cheek against mine, everything against mine, as comfy and familiar as an old coat.

"Mm, that's *nice* ..." she whispered in my ear. "Fancy not meeting you before."

She had a pleasant, slightly musky odour, probably an oriental perfume. It rose in waves on the warmth of her body, bending my mind.

"What's your name?" she murmured, kissing my ear.

"Russ Tobin. What's yours?"

"Anita Lesard."

"Sounds a bit French."

"It's a lot French – on my daddy's side."

"What are you on your mummy's side?"

"Celanese."

"Terrific."

"You think so?"

"Your mum must be a very beautiful woman."

"You're nice. Are you here by yourself?"

"No ... I came with Vicki Hurst. D'you know her?"

"No, which one is she?"

I peered around the room but it was so dim by now – somebody had turned off all but one small working light over the bar an hour ago – and so crowded I couldn't see Vicki anywhere.

"I can't see her," I said.

"Good. Perhaps she's gone home."

"No," I laughed. "I don't think so."

"You sound very positive. Is she something special?"

"Very special."

"How long have you known her?"

"Two days." Is that all it was – two days?

"Two days! And already she's something special? You must be a fast worker."

"I ..."

"*Are* you a fast worker?'

Her knee had now crept between my legs and was remorselessly massaging whatever it came in contact with.

"I ... don't really know. It rather depends on the woman's point of view, doesn't it? What's fast for one might be agonisingly slow for another."

"How true." She nestled her cheek into my neck as though preparing to bed down for the night. "You're very wise, aren't you? What do you do? Are you ground staff?"

"No, I'm not with an airline. I'm in television commercials."

She didn't seem to hear. "What a pity you're not a plumber."

"A plumber ...?"

"Mm ... then you could come and fix my pipes. They're knocking."

"Whereabouts are your pipes?" I was afraid to ask.

"Upstairs. At the other end of the block."

"Sorry, I'm not a plumber. What do *you* do?" I had to change the subject.

"Me? I'm in Special Handling."

"Oh ...? What do ... you ... handle – especially?"

"V.I.Ps ..." she giggled, "... amongst other things." Her hand came down from my neck and began massaging my thigh. "I'm *awfully* good at it, "she whispered huskily. "It's a special technique, you know ..." I had a nervous glance about me. "What are you looking for," she asked. "Vicki Whatshername?"

"Well, I ..."

"It's not very flattering, you know, dancing with one girl and looking for another."

"I'm sorry ..."

"Don't you like dancing with me?"

"Yes, love it."

"Don't you find me attractive?"

Oh, blimey. "Yes, of course I do." I didn't like the way this was developing. There was an edge to her tone that could mean trouble if she didn't get her own way. I wouldn't put it past her to shout "Rape!" or threaten to report me to the Race Relations Board if I annoyed her.

"Then re ... lax," she murmured, nibbling my neck, still rubbing my thigh. "And kiss me."

Her lips fell into my mouth. I couldn't concentrate, Vicki was between us. Anita drew away and stared at me, obviously astounded she'd got a man who wouldn't respond to her charms.

"Hey ... you're not with me." Then a slow, drunken smile. "Ah, I see ... you're the 'play it cool' type, aren't you? You like them to come and get you? All ... right ... I'm coming to ... *get* ... you . !"

I half expected something aggressive, but instead she floated back into my arms, pressed herself against me, and the next thing I knew my zip was down and her hand was inside, grabbing me.

"Th . . . ere, now isn't that better? Oops, he's a beauty."

"Look, Anita . . ." My voice was fluttery. I closed my eyes but the room began to spin so I opened them again. I peered into the dark haze surrounding me, feeling suddenly ill, weak, shivery. "Anita . . ." I gasped. "I've got to get out!"

She chuckled triumphantly, taking it the wrong way. "I told you I'd get you. Come on . . ."

I didn't wait to argue. I plunged through the crowd, zipping up, Anita at my heels, and as I made the hall she caught my coat and laughed, "Hey, not so fast, we've got all night . . . !"

I was face to face with Vicki who was chatting to a girl in the hall. I stared at her; she stared back at me . . . at Anita.

"Hi," she said. "That sounded promising. What is it you've got all night for?"

Anita's face was undisguised venom.

"Hi," I said lamely. "Er, Vicki, this is . . ."

Anita was gone in a storm, back into the lounge.

"What was that all about?" Vicki laughed. "Russ, d'you feel all right?"

"Better by the minute. Ginger's Specials got to me back there."

"Who was . . . that?"

"Who – the girl? I dunno. I was just dancing with her when I came over strange."

"What did she mean you've got all night?"

I shrugged. "To dance, I suppose."

"Mm," she went, with an amused look.

A drunken cheer went up and the lights of the lounge came on. We went to the door to see what was happening. Vicki groaned. "It's the bottle game. Ginger's moment has come."

We moved into the room, craning over heads to see what was going on. Ginger was down on the floor, his toes in line with a cigarette packet, and he was "walking" on two beer bottles held in his hands. I'd played the game before. The object is to place one bottle as far forward as possible from the starting line while balancing your weight on the bottle in the other hand. Then, when you've placed the first bottle, you've got to "hop" back on the second, trying not to collapse in the meantime and allowing no part of your body, except your toes, to touch the floor. The strain on arms, wrists and stomach is tremendous; the game is difficult enough when sober; drunk it's impossible.

Ginger was not doing badly for distance but he was now bright purple in the face and his huge hand was dithering badly on the support bottle. Sweat was cascading from his beetroot countenance and down his arm. Out ... out ... out he stretched, teasing the free bottle forward inch by inch. The crowd were urging him on; the noise was terrific. "Come on, Ginger!" "You wanna get some fat off, Cookson!" Ginger was grunting and gasping like a ruptured boiler. Now he'd reached the limit of his stretch, a great distance, and was tipping the forward bottle onto its base. Would it remain upright? Yes ... no ... yes, it was there. A big cheer. Now to get back. He grasped the support bottle with both enormous hands. His breath hissed between his teeth, his eyes were organ stops, sweat just rolled off him onto the carpet. "Come on, Ginger ... nearly there!" Hop ... hop ... hop. The man's strength must have been prodigious to hold up his weight at full stretch lie this. "Come on ... come on, Ginger!"

Then someone yelled, "Hey, Cookson, you've got a hole in your arse!"

Ginger collapsed with a great roaring guffaw, shaking the building, and lay panting like a shot elephant.

"Next one ... next one!" somebody called.

"Who made me laugh!" roared Cookson. "I'll kill him!"

"Come on, who's next?"

A tall, spindly red-haired fellow got down with great determination and looked for a moment or two as though he was going to set a distance impossible to challenge. But before he could set the leading bottle properly his twig-thin arms collapsed and with a yelp he thumped down onto the support bottle, driving it into his stomach. He gagged wretchedly, eyes popping, to the wild delight of the very stoned crowd and someone grabbed his ankles and hauled him off, face down, his nose cutting a furrow in the carpet.

The next contestant was the big, broad-shouldered ape who'd given me the murderous glower earlier on. This big 'ead was going great guns, right from the start. Neck muscles strained magnificently ... shoulders muscles bunched like coiled ropes. The girls cheered him on adoringly. I glared at him, wishing he'd fall off the bottle. Out ... out ... out he went, great muscular thews as rigid as steel girders, effortlessly, not even breathing hard, a superior smirk on his lips.

87

Then ... zing! The support bottle slipped on the carpet. Down he crashed, twisting awkwardly, and let out a bellow of pain as his thumb shot into the neck of the bottle. The last I saw of him he was heading for the kitchen looking for a hammer.

Several other fellas had a go after that and achieved a modicum of success and one split his trousers up the back and was rushed off to the bedroom for repairs. I personally didn't volunteer for the game 'cause I reckoned they wouldn't appreciate a total stranger wiping the floor with them.

Then it was the girls' turn – and half a dozen of them were sloshed enough to try it. It was daft because they're just not built for it. But the men egged them on, mainly because there wasn't a bird there not wearing a mini skirt. One by one, pandemonium mounting, the girls got down. Three of them collapsed with laughter before they'd even started and just knelt on the starting line holding their stomachs. By the time three had had a go the room was in uproar.

Then Anita, the lovely, dusky Anita came into the circle, hands clasped above her head – the champ! She could hardly stand up. She dropped to her knees, grasped both bottles, got her delectable bottom in the air ... and began to walk them. Out she went ... three ... four ... five paces, not doing too badly .. then down she went with a shriek of laughter, rolled over onto her back, legs flung wide, showing everything she'd got through transparent nylon panties. A huge cheer went up from the men. Anita just lay there, helpless with laughter, and nobody moved to pick her up, they were enjoying the view too much. Suddenly Anita wasn't laughing anymore. She was out like a light and probably out for the night. With a wild whoop a young balding chap swooped upon her, picked up the body and waltzed her off to a bedroom. We didn't see them again, either.

The fifth girl, a rather plain-looking bird but a magnificent figure, got down and stretched out on the bottles. Obviously she had no bra on. As her arm went forward to place the lead bottle – plop! – out popped one of her breasts. To tremendous cheers from the men she fought gamely to the finish. She didn't give a damn. Then, when she was safely back home, she popped her breast back in, saying, "So what – you've all seen one before."

The sixth girl was none other than Stella, whose face had disintegrated alcoholically another ten points since she'd opened the door to us. Down she got, weaving beautifully, determined to win or bust. But Ginger Cookson had other ideas. He waited until she was in a helpless position, stretched full length, then crept up behind her and goosed her. With a shriek she toppled, rolled onto her back. Ginger dived on top of her and began pumping up and down. The party was getting rough.

Ginger got unsteadily to his feet and pulled Stella up, then yelled to the crowd, "It's cab . . . ar . . . et time!"

"Ye . . . e . . . e . . . s!" shouted the room.

"Start the music! Dim the lights!"

This was obviously a set party-piece because immediately all but the bar light went off and that great piece of music "The Stripper" with its sensuous bump-and-grind beat belted out. The crowd formed a loose circle around Ginger and Stella. These two circled each other, posing and posturing as strippers do, pretending to peel off long gloves and throw them into the crowd. After a bit of this, Stella stole up behind him and entwined her leg around his thigh, trickled her fingers over his shoulder and unfastened his tie. This she tossed into the crowd. Then she began unfastening the buttons of his shirt, slowly, one by one, and finally jerked the shirt out of his trousers, peeled it off his shoulders and threw that into the crowd.

For a moment she lingered there, rubbing herself against his behind to the beat of the music, tickling his nipples, running her fingers through the hair on his chest. Slowly her fingers descended, found his belt buckle, slipped it open. Down went the zip . . . Ginger kicked off his shoes . . . Stella stole around to the front and with an exaggerated swaying moving began lowering his trousers, going down with them until she was kneeling before him, her nose dead in line with the bulging fly of his boxer shorts.

She stared at it, pretending to be hypnotised by it, to be drawn towards it. The crowd was doubled up with laughter. They cheered her on with bawdy comments. "See it off, Stella!" "Give it a chew, Lolita!" Stella advanced until her nose was within half an inch of the bulge then pecked at it like a striking snake, hissing at it, struck one . . . twice . . . then opened her mouth wide as if to bite it.

Ginger leapt back, kicking off his trousers, looking ridiculous in just his baggy shorts and tiny socks. Stella advanced on him on her hands and knees like a stalking setter, made a grab for his leg, caught it, then ran her hand up until it disappeared up the leg of his shorts. Ginger yelled and jumped away. Stella chased him, hooked her fingers in the band of his shorts and as he leapt away again they shot down to his knees. For a brief moment he was starkers. The crowd collapsed. He escaped her clutches and jerked the shorts up again to cover himself . . .

How far they would have gone is anyone's guess. Probably he would have been prancing around in just his socks within a few minutes. But suddenly there was a row going on in the hall, sounds of angry shouting. The crowd quickly became aware of it and were silent. At the same time the music ended. Ginger and Stella turned towards the door just as a group of people burst in. Two of them were men from the party but the other three were right rough looking punks with wild, dirty hair and filthy clothes, young kids in their twenties, hopped-up yobs from the street. The kid in the forefront was carrying an empty scotch bottle by the neck and looked anxious to use it.

A man from the party shouted at him, "Look, son, get the hell out of here before . . ."

"Piss off!"

Ginger stepped in front of him, towering above him, suddenly sober. "What d'you want, son?"

"The bastards rang the bell and just barged in!" said the fellow from the party. "Now, come on, get the hell . . ."

He made a grab for one of the yobs, a kid in a sheepskin coat. The lad flung him back against the wall.

"We wanna drink!" the kid facing Ginger shouted.

Ginger roared, "What *are* you, bloody hopheads! Get the buggery out of here before you get ki . . ."

Ginger ducked as the scotch bottle came at him. It sailed across the room and disappeared out of the window with a terrific crash. Women screamed. Ginger slung a tremendous punch at the yob and caught him on the cheek. He staggered back. As Ginger advanced on him for a second punch he ran straight into another bottle wielded by the yob behind. It caught him a sickening clout on the jaw. Ginger went down like a felled hippo. Pandemonium burst. Someone from the party grabbed up the bottle and smashed it over the head of the yob who'd thrown it. He went down in a shower of spurting blood. The third yob, right at the back, turned with a scream and tried to make it to the front door. He was booted in the stomach and did a somersault into the wall.

Whoever called the cops probably did it from a phone in one of the bedrooms and five minutes later six husky uniforms came clumping along the corridor and into the flat, by which time Ginger's inert form was fully clothed and respectable and the yob with the spurting head had been dumped in the bath to preserve the furnishings and fittings.

Statements were taken, Ginger was carted off with a broken jaw to the hospital, the yob with the gaping head was similarly disposed of and the other two animals were taken for a swift ride in the squad car.

It was almost an hour before we were able to say goodnight to Stella and get out.

We drove back to Vicki's flat in stunned silence – until we got inside, then we collapsed with laughter, literally fell on each other for support, chokingly recalling fragments of the evening – Big 'ead with his thumb stuck in the bottle ... the tall, skinny bloke being dragged face down across the carpet ... Ginger, naked, with his striped shorts around his knees and his ridiculous little socks ... and Stella being goosed in the bottle game.

"Oh, my stomach aches," Vicki wailed, clinging to me. "What a way to spend Christmas. I'll never, never forget this one."

We were still laughing about it at odd times a week later.

CHAPTER SIX

Vicki left for Italy on the sixth of January and London became suddenly a cold and lonely place.

I saw her off at Heathrow and hated every minute of it. I detest final farewells at airports and stations; but she wanted it so I went. I fidgetted and shuffled and watched the clock crawl round, not really knowing what to say. I couldn't even tell her, "Well, see you in June" or "Keep smiling till next Thursday" because we just didn't know when we'd see each other again – if ever. She'd be stuck in Italy until November and I'd be in Majorca, both of us working seven days a week. Oh, by the way, I'd been to see Philip Ardmont by this time and I'd heard that Majorca was the place for me, but he'd asked me to wait until I'd finished with White Marvel before sending in the application form – just in case something went wrong.

So – there we were, smoking and drinking our last cup of coffee together, trying to make light-hearted conversation about our jobs, about the summer, always about things in the future, never mentioning the past two weeks. Yet I could see the memory of them in her eyes, in a sadness no amount of banter could hide, and when finally the announcement of her flight was made, as she hugged me and kissed me, tears flooded her eyes and her voice broke as she whispered, "Goodbye, Russ ..." and she turned quickly and went through into Passports without looking at me again.

To complete my agony I went up to the waving bay on the flat roof of the terminal and damn near froze to death waiting for her jet, a B.A.C. 111 to take off. When it finally did, some twenty minutes later, I was so stiff with the cold I could barely lift my arm up. The joke was (and I heard this in her first letter which came within forty-eight hours) it wasn't her jet I'd waved off at all. Hers had been delayed over half an hour through some fault or other and all the time I was up aloft losing the use of my limbs, she was down below drinking consoling gins with a fellow courier.

Anyway, I waited until the plane had disappeared through the blanketing cloud then drove back to London. For two days I felt desolate, lost. I began to wonder what I'd done with my days and nights before I'd met Vicki. Then Tony returned from a week in Scotland where he'd been shooting a commercial with a skiing background. He took one look at me, ran a hot bath, changed his clothes, and that evening we resumed our investigation of London.

The Christian spirit is miraculously resilient, isn't it? By the end of that first week I was quite me old perky self again.

And so began my two weeks on White Marvel.

*

We assembled at Croxleys agency at nine o'clock on the morning of the second Monday in January, a bitter, cheerless day though, thank God, windless.

We were a small unit, necessarily; the fewer the better on street interviews. You've got to be nimble, extremely mobile, ready to nip along the pavement after a housewife as she comes tearing out of a supermarket.

The team comprised: a sound recordist, who carried a compact but highly professional tape-recorder slung on his shoulder; a camera operator (who was required to be something between a Roger Bannister and a Charles Atlas. A 35mm. camera, even on a shoulder mounting, is no joke after five minutes); a focus-puller (cum magazine-changer cum clapper boy cum general dogsbody); a continuity girl; and a director. Allan Lang, the Canadian producer, was also in fairly constant attendance during the fortnight.

On camera we had Bert Ford, a middle-aged, lugubrious man with a mournful Buster Keaton face. Bert didn't smile once during the two weeks, though he did reveal an unexpected wit.

In absolute contrast was his focus-pulling assistant, Mickey Maple. Mickey was a muscular, handsome, twenty-year-old sex maniac whose sole preoccupation appeared to be noddy – and how to get enough of it. Mickey, a virile young bull in a state of constant erection, retired on the last day of the shoot and went into the boarding house business. More about that later.

The continuity lady, Alice Naydler, was a quiet, middle-aged woman with years of film experience behind her. Having worked on multi-million pound productions in the past I'm sure White Marvel was a tremendous come-down for her, though she handled this little project with great efficiency.

We had many coffee-break chats about the old days, about the stars she'd worked with and the films she'd worked on.

The sound recordist almost defies description. Apart from "sound running" and "watch that cable, for Crissake!" I don't think he uttered two words during the entire campaign. He was a little bald fellow named Harry Bristow.

The director was beautiful. Paul Ward – medium height, late forties, stooped, quiet, charming – was so agonisingly hung-over every morning every member of the crew physically suffered his headache. Grey of face, huddled deep inside his sheepskin-lined suede coat, he gave the impression that as soon as the project was finished he would wander away and die somewhere. I suppose he was efficient, though I felt time and again that I was directing the action more than he. Perhaps it was his way of doing it. Whatever the case, the films turned out exceptionally well and the White Marvel clients were mighty happy.

At nine forty five on that Monday morning, in a thin veil of freezing fog, we took up our positions outside a gigantic supermarket in Chelsea. Our director looked like death. He staggered out of the minibus, had a quick look around, levelled his pouched, bloodshot eyes at young Mickey Maple and uttered the directive: "Lad, go find coffee!"

Mickey sprang to attention and saluted. "Coffee? Yessir: Right away, sir!"

Ward winced as Mickey bounded away. I'll give Maple this: matching his sexual proclivity was his ability to find hot coffee, no matter how unlikely the neighbourhood as a source. At times, when we were filming in totally residential areas with no shop in sight, he would disappear for ten minutes and return with a box of steaming dixie cups. So efficient was he that I had the feeling he must rap on the first available door around the corner and threaten the housewife with something worse than death if she didn't coff up.

On this occasion he was back in five minutes, due to there being a milkbar right next door to the supermarket. I doubt that Paul Ward had seen the milkbar, however, since it was extremely unlikely he could see the supermarket.

So, fortified by the hot coffee, we began, bright with enthusiasm. I took up my position by the wide glass double doors while Mickey Maple acted as look-out, peering through the huge window at the stand on which White Marvel was displayed.

We waited ... and waited. I walked up and down, stamping my feet to keep the gangrene at bay. The fog was beginning to creep into my bones. Within half an hour I was chilled right through. My ears had died, my nose was froze and I had to keep constantly flexing my microphone hand to prevent permanent paralysis. I thought about Vicki in Italy and longed to be with her. Come on, didn't anybody ever *buy* White Marvel. There were quite a few customers in the supermarket but so far not one had bought a packet.

"No luck, Mickey?"

"Nah, they're all buying Tide and Fairy Snow." He chuckled lasciviously. "There's some lovely Billy Bunt in here, though, mate. There's a young bird in a black plastic mac by the frozen veges – I swear she's got no knicks on. She just crouched down and I saw right up her Blackwall Tunnel ... all dark and 'orrible, it was ..."

"Never mind black pussy, keep your eye on White Marvel."

"It'll be a bloody white marvel if anybody buys any. Christ it's cold." He jumped around for a minute, skipping like a boxer, then suddenly stopped. "Aye, aye – there's an old bird at the stand. She's picked up a packet ... she's put it down again ... she's picked it up again ... come on, you silly old git, stick it in your basket. She has! Tall old crow in a funny green hat. Looks like she's dressed early for Ascot."

"Right – don't lose her, for Pete's sake."

"You couldn't lose this one in a hurry, she's as lovely as mumps."

I paced up and down outside the doors, going over my approach, feeling excited now we were about to start. Now ... good morning, madam. I wonder if you could spare me a moment? ... I see you've bought a packet of White Marvel ... de da, de da, de da ... smile ... pour on the charm ... get them used to the camera, the mike, the crew . . make them laugh to ease the tension ... you've done it all before, boy. It's only Crunchums all over again ..."

"She's going through the cash desk!" Mickey hissed. "You can't mistake her – long streak of misery in a green hat!"

"O.K., thanks."

Then I caught sight of her. Oh, Gawd, he was right. Tall, painfully thin, imperious, with a nasty thin mouth and a long, unfriendly nose. Never mind, it's a challenge, Tobin! Get in there! Overwhelm her with charm. Melt her icy old heart with a smile . . .

Out she came through the swing door, nose in the air, clutching her string-bag of groceries. She gave me and the crew the merest glance and turned away, heading past Mickey, going like the clappers.

"Er, madam! . . . excuse me, madam!"

I was after her. Sound was close behind. Bert Ford with his heavy camera propped on his shoulder was close behind him. Mickey Maple tagged on the back.

"Er . . . excuse me, madam!"

She stopped so abruptly I almost ran into her. Harry Bristow tripped over the mike cable and almost fell into me. Bert Ford, carrying so much weight, teetered on, trying to stop but ran past us. Mickey Maple ran straight into Harry Bristow and exclaimed, "Shit, sorry, Harry!"

The old bird nearly died of apoplexy. She glared at me and at the crew as though we'd just crawled up from the sewers.

"What do you want?" she demanded.

"Er, good morning, madam . . . could you spare me a moment. . . ?"

"No, I cannot, I'm in a frightful hurry."

"Er, I see you've bought a packet of Might Warvel . . . er, White Marvel . . ."

She glanced down at her string-bag, nostrils distended mouth twisted and mean. "What I have purchased is entirely my affair, young man."

"Yes, I'm sorry . . ."

"Now, have the goodness to *remove* yourselves."

She sped away, muttering angrily to herself.

"Sound running," announced Harry Bristow.

We trudged back to the supermarket entrance. I don't think Paul Ward had even noticed we'd gone. He turned to us, hands thrust deep into his pockets, his grey, pinched face peering between the points of his turned-up collar. "I'm going to sit in the bus, I don't feel so good. Carry on, hm? Give me a shout if anything happens."

Not much did happen until nearly noon by which time we were a sorrowful-looking bunch, frozen to the point of agony, dispirited through inaction. Then, just as we were thinking of breaking for a two-hour lunch at the first available pub, Mickey, nose pressed against the window, got suddenly excited.

96

"Hey, hey, hey look at this piece, Russ! A right little belter. Lips like slivers of liver . . ."

Bert Ford yawned. "Mickey, at what age did you first realise you were a psychopathic sex maniac?"

"I was born one. No, no kidding, she's really something and she's just picked up four packets of White Marvel . . ."

"Four! ?" I yelled. "What's she like?"

"I told you – fantastic. Small blonde with a green coat and big tits. About thirty, I'd say. A real cracker."

"Stand by,' I ordered. "This sounds good."

"By golly, she looks good, too," drooled Mickey. "Got a nice sexy barmaidy face ... good figure ... smashing legs. Cor, I wouldn't half like to interview this one meself – in the bedroom. Er, madam, I'd like to see the whiteness of your sheets ... yes, they're lovely. Now, how about the whiteness of your thighs? Smashing. Open wide, this ain' going to hurt a bit ... aye, aye, here she comes ... !"

I paced up and down, working up a smile on my frozen cheeks, glancing through the door for first sight of her. And there she was, just as Mickey had described her. Cheeky little blonde with a corking figure, her green coat tied at the waist, accentuating hips and breasts. She had, indeed, a great pair of legs.

She pushed at the swing door with her bottom and came out, carrying two laden carrier bags. She flashed me a look, came back for a second, glanced at the microphone, the camera, the crew and smiled to herself, as though she knew and welcomed what was coming.

"Good morning, madam ..." I said, approaching her. Lovely – immediate raport. Flirtatious smile in her eyes. Mickey was right again, she could be a barmaid, a nightclub hostess, she had that air of jaunty self-assurance with a touch of bawdy sexiness.

"Could you spare me a moment?"

"Mm, yes, all right." She looked around the crew, taking each man separately, taking her time, very self-possessed, slightly hard. "What are you shooting – a commercial?"

"Er, Mickey, help the lady with the carrier bags."

"Cer ... tain .. ly!" He bounded forward and took the bags from her.

"My name is Russ Tobin. I represent Croxleys advertising agency. Would you mind if I ask you a few questions?"

"I suppose it's O.K."

"Could I have your name please?"

"Jackie Mandell."

"*Mrs*. Mandell?"

"Yes. Are you filming me?"

"No, not yet, but we hope to if you'll answer our questions. We're making a series of commercials for White Marvel. Firstly we do these street interviews, then we hope to do follow-up shots in people's homes – filming washing results, talking to husbands, wives, children and so on. I see you've bought *four* packets of White Marvel. Does this mean you're really sold on White Marvel as a better product than any other washing powder?"

I got the flirty smile again. "Is that what you'd like me to say?"

"Well, obviously . . ."

"And . . . if I appear in your commercial . . . do I get paid?"

The question surprised me. Most members of the public caught by a camera and microphone in the street are so flattered that their views are being sought, so excited at the prospect of appearing on the telly that payment is the last thing they think of. Indeed many of them express surprise at being actually paid for the pleasure.

This bird was different. As I talked to her a thought struck me, engendered by her casual, confident attitude towards the camera, her interest in money, and by her looks, that she was possibly an actress.

I said: "Of course you'll get paid. If you consent to be filmed here and now we give you a token payment of one pound; then, if we consider you suitable for the follow-up filming in your home you get another four pounds. And if you eventually appear in a commercial on TV you get an additional fifteen pounds. By the way, have you ever done any acting?"

She smiled and nodded. "A bit. I was an actress but I retired some time ago. Now I'm a landlady."

"You rent out rooms?"

"Yes, I've got a big house in Blakely Road. I rent six rooms."

"And do all the washing yourself?"

"Certainly. If I sent everything to the laundry there'd be no profit in the business."

She couldn't have been a better subject – a landlady with a mountain of sheets and towels and pillowcases to wash . . . a good photogenic face ... a direct, no-nonsense way of speaking, generating and inspiring confidence. She was perfect.

"How long have you been using White Marvel?" I asked.

"This is my second time.'

My heart sank. "Only the second?"

"Let's face it," she said, raking me with her smile, "soap powders are all the same, aren't they? I just grab the first thing that comes to hand."

I'll just bet you do, love.

"But," I went on, pursuing her," the fact is you *have* used White Marvel – and now you've come back for more. It must mean you were pleased with it the first time."

"Oh, sure – ecstatic."

"And you'd say that on film?"

"Of course. For twenty guineas I'll give the performance of my life."

"Pounds," I corrected. "Mickey – go get Mr. Ward from the bus."

Jackie Mandell was a natural. We shot on her for over half an hour and got some fantastic stuff. We made her go back into the supermarket then filmed her coming out, looking surprised at seeing us. She fluffed and stammered over her words with just the right amount of natural unsureness, searching for her phrases, getting the odd tense wrong, talking in a slightly "off" voice that was neither Cockney nor Chelsea, a voice people of all strata could identify with. She was so good even Paul Ward forgot his hangover and the cold, and she eminated such a wealth of bed-warm, just-possibly-obtainable sexuality she had the crew falling over themselves to please her.

Mickey Maple was beside himself. Every time he caught my eye he'd suck in a breath, raise his eyes to heaven, ball his fist phallically and murmur, "Cor, f..k a duck." He got so carried away I had to tell him, "Steady on, for Crissake," and I'm sure she both saw and heard him but she didn't seem put out. To tell the truth I think it amused her.

It was one o'clock when we finished shooting on her and as the crew broke for lunch and began stowing the equipment in the bus, I told her, "Mrs. Mandell, you were fabulous. We'd very much like to do a follow-up in your home. Would it be possible to interview your husband?"

"No husband." She gave a little smile. "Not now."

"Oh, sorry ..."

99

"Don't apologise, it's my pleasure."

"Well, could you give me a time when it would be convenient to see the house? I'd like to see where you do all the washing and select the best room for the interview."

"Any time you want. How about this afternoon?"

"That'd be fine. Could I come around after we've finished shooting – about four o'clock?"

"Of course. Come for tea."

I laughed. "Lovely. See you at four."

"Will you be coming alone? I'd like to know how many to cater for."

Would you now.

Mickey Maple was hovering close by, loathe to leave her immediate presence. He was fascinated by her, as all the crew had been, but with Mickey it was much more. He was hypnotised constantly attentive. I thought I'd give him a treat.

"I'd like to bring my assistant, Mr. Maple," I said, loud enough for him to hear. His head jerked around. Jackie Mandell looked at him and smiled, really looked at him, as though seeing him for the first time.

"Just the two of you? Right, see you at four."

We watched her cross the road. I stole a glance at Mickey. His mouth was open.

"Fancy it, Mickey"

He released his captive breath. "By the grunge, she really turns me on, mate. What I wouldn't like to do to that."

"What would you do – given the chance?"

Still staring after her, he murmured, "I'd tie it spreadeagled to the bed then leap off the top of the wardrobe yelling 'Geronimo'."

"Nah, she's too much woman for you. She'd turn you into mincemeat."

He nodded, still mesmerised by her receding figure. "Maybe. But what a crazy way to go. I dream about birds like that."

"Like what – older women, you mean?"

"Yeh. These young tarts are all right but you've got to teach them everything, haven't you? You wouldn't have to teach that bird anything. You'd come out of that a much wiser bloke than you went in."

"I think quite possibly you're right. Want to chance your luck, then? She obviously fancies you."

He shot a surprised look at me. "Yeh? Nah, you're kidding."

"No, I'm not. She just had a damned good look at you – all of you."

"Well then . . ."

For the first time that day his cool deserted him. He shuffled his feet. "Naaahhh."

"Go on, get stuck in, man. Think of it as going to nightschool . . . furthering your education."

He grinned at the exciting thought of it.

"Just keep me posted, that's all," I said. "I'm interested in the development. I'll even offer my advice if and when needed."

His grin broadened. "What are you – a sex student or something?'

"Of course. Aren't we all?"

"Yeh, man. O.K. you're on."

"Good lad. It'll be up to you at four o'clock, mind. I'll have a quick squint at the rooms and then you'll be on your own."

"Right." He rubbed his hands together excitedly and shook his head. "Jesus wept . . ."

For most of the afternoon I forgot about Jackie Mandell, immersed as I was in half a dozen interviews, one of which was very worthwhile – a mother of four boys all under eight years old. She was friendly, chatty, absolutely right. I arranged to visit her home, a council house, early that evening to meet her husband who was a lorry driver.

But although my mind wasn't on Jackie Mandell, Mickey's certainly was. I caught him gawping into space several times and Bert Ford on camera twice bollocked him for lack of attention. Mickey apologised sheepishly and grinned when he found me looking at him. Half past three must have seemed an eternity to him.

At last it arrived. The daylight faded fast and a creeping damp brought Paul Ward, our director, out of the bus to urge us: "Wrap it up, lads, and get the hell home."

They needed little urging. Within ten minutes everything was stowed away and within fifteen the bus was disappearing into the evening traffic.

Mickey and I set off at a brisk pace, breathing clouds of frosty air.

"She was an actress, eh?" he mused. "Can't say I ever heard of her."

"The term 'actress', like the term 'Model', covers a multitude of activities, Mickey. I'm not saying she *wasn't* an authentic stage actress, but she might have been a stripper or a chorus girl. They all call themselves actresses."

"Yeh," After a moment he said, "Whatever she was, I bet she's been around, eh."

"I'd venture to say she's no virgin, Mickey."

"That's for sure. Funny, isn't it, how some women just *ooze* sex. I mean, if you really analyse her ... her face, her hair, her body, her legs ... well, you've seen a hundred like her, haven't you? On Kings Road, here, you'd see a dozen dollies a day just as good looking ... but nowhere near as sexy. Funny that. I wonder what it is that gives them that ... that ..."

"Aura?"

"Yeh, aura. It really belts you, doesn't it? You just know a bird like that would be fantastic in bed."

"Fantastic," I said.

We rounded a corner into Blakely Road, a cheerless street of black Victorian terraced houses rising three storeys to their attics. The street lamps were on but they served only to emphasise the January gloom.

We found number forty three and went up a flight of six stone steps to a glass-panelled front door cowering in a shallow vestibule. I banged on the knocker and heard the sound echoing along the hall. How I hate this type of house. I could imagine what this one was like inside by the dozens I'd been in before. Jackie Mandell would occupy the ground floor with its two reception rooms, kitchen and loo. There would be three bedrooms on the first floor and another three on the second floor, then a dismal attic in the roof where accumulated domestic debris was stored. All the rooms would be lofty, never quite warm enough, poorly furnished and indifferently decorated. Soulless *pieds-à-terre* in which six lodgers would sit through the long winter evenings wondering often why they'd ever left home.

A light clicked on in the hall. A wavery figure approached the door and opened it. Jackie Mandell, showing plenty of breast and leg in a blue wool dress, said, "Right on time, come, come in."

She led us along the hall to her living room at the back of the house which, so far, was much as I'd expected. An air of general dilapidation permeated the place, a struggle to make ends meet. I imagined that with very limited funds Jackie had

102

done the rounds of the second-hand shops, preferring good but used to cheap and new.

But from the TV commercial point of view her living room was ideal. It would lend a background of need for economy, thrift – emphasising White Marvel's value for money.

"Well, this is it," she said. "Not exactly Hampton Court but it's home."

"It's fine," I said. "Very nice."

She shrugged. "It's the best a girl can do on her own. Would you like to see the kitchen?"

We went through a door on the far side of the room into a cavernous old kitchen with a quarry-tiled floor and glass-fronted, floor-to-ceiling cupboards. The big Bendix washing machine-cum-trumble-drier in the corner seemed incongruous and anachronistic amongst so much dowdy Victoriana.

"This is the sweat shop," Jackie announced. "Fortunately I don't have to worry about the weather. This machine dries everything ready for ironing."

"And you do all this work yourself?"

"Sure. I've got an automatic ironing machine in here ..." she bent down to a low cupboard and tried to open it, "... the sheets and pillowcases and towels are quite easy with ... oh, damn this thing."

Mickey was there like a shot. "Here, let me do it, you'll break you're nails."

Even muscular Mick had to heave two or three times on the cupboard before it opened.

"It's the damp in here," said Jackie. "It swells the wood."

"You need a bit off this, Mrs. Mandell," said Mickey. "Got any tools?"

She pointed to another cupboard. "There are some things in there my husband used ... but don't bother with it ..."

"No bother," said Mickey.

Good lad, I thought, there's nothing like a few odd jobs around the house for starters.

Mickey pulled out a box of tools and found a small plane. As he attacked the cupboard door Jackie looked on, watching him with the interest women seem to reserve for a deft, practical man fixing something. I in turn watched her, watched her roving eyes paying attention to Mickey's profile, the curl of his hair on his neck, to the width of his shoulders, the strength of his hands. Lost for a moment in concentration an amused smile touched her lips. His activity obviously pleased her.

After a dozen strokes of the plane he tried the door, then removed more wood, tried it again and turned to her, grinning. "There y'are, nothing to it."

"Stupid, isn't it – I've struggled with that door for a year. Thank you so much."

"Nar, it was nothing. Any more odd jobs you want doing?"

She laughed. "Plenty ... but I'm not going to let you do them. You didn't come here to ..."

"No, I mean it! It's my hobby. I've got a workshop in the garage at home. I make all sorts of things. I really love doing it. What else have you got?"

She sighed and laughed. "Oh, all kinds of things. It's a big, old house. One of my lodger's door won't close properly ..."

"Nah, we can't have that, can we ...?"

"But I can't expect *you* to fix it," she protested, though none too vehemently. "I'll get someone in ..."

"And pay some layabout a couple of quid for five minutes work? Show me where it is, I'll do it in a couple of ticks."

"Let him do it," I said. "I won't need him. As a matter of fact I'll have to be going, Mrs. Mandell. I've got another house to see, someone we interviewed this afternoon."

"Won't you stay for tea?"

"No, thanks all the same, I'd better be off. I'm sure your house will be fine, by the way. We'll let you know when we need to shoot in here."

Mickey stayed in the kitchen while I went to the front door with Jackie. As she opened it she said, "I'd really like to do a commercial for you. D'you think there's a good chance?"

"I'd say a very good one. It'll be up to the director and the clients of course – they'll sift through all the material now and make a decision by the end of this week, but between you and me I doubt if we'll get a better interview than yours. It was really excellent."

As I stepped out into the vestibule I said, "Make the most of Mickey while you've got him. It'll keep him off the streets."

"It's very kind of him, but I feel I'm imposing."

"Forget it. Think of it as a small return for a first class interview. Let him do what he likes."

"Well, if you're sure ..."

"He's in his element, believe me. He's never happier than when he's fixing something ..." Or somebody. "Goodnight, Mrs. Mandell, we'll be in touch."

I went down the street chuckling to myself. The lad was in,

boots and all. I was looking forward to his report next morning – if he turned up for work, that is. I had a sudden premonition we might never see Mickey Maple again.

*

He was there, though – late, but there. I was giving my report on the two houses I'd seen to Paul Ward whose face was a study of overhung, bloodshot misery when Mickey sidled sheepishly into the group, trying to appear he'd been there for half an hour. He caught my eye, winked, and got on with taking the camera from its case. He looked terrible – as fragile as Paul Ward.

It was a good thirty minutes before I had a chance to speak to him. Aligned as the day before in front of the supermarket, I wandered over to him as he stood with his forehead pressed against the window, supposedly peering in at the White Marvel stand, but when I got close I saw his eyes were closed. He woke up with a start.

I murmured, "Done any little jobs around the house lately?"

He shook his head. "Godalmighty, I feel awful."

"What caused it?"

"Brandy . . . bloody brandy. I must've drunk a bottle."

"What happened?"

"Tell you lunchtime. It's a long story."

He got progressively more fragile as the morning dragged on, as the cold added to his misery. During the coffee break he disappeared to the pub lavatory down the road and came back looking like death. When we finally broke for lunch he caught my arm with nothing short of desperation. "I've gotta get a hair of the dog, mate, I'm dying. Dying!"

Trying hard not to laugh I said, "There's another pub along there. Come on, we'll get away from the others."

In the pub I bought him a large brandy and ginger and took it to him at the corner table where he looked in grave danger of falling off his chair. He looked up, saw the glass and turned quite green. "Oh, Christ, no . . ."

"Go on, sip it, you'll feel better."

Pulling an agonised face and holding his nose he got a mouthful down. For a moment it looked touch and go whether he kept it down and I backed away just in case. But he mastered it and took another gulp. Colour came back into his cheeks.

"Gotta fag?" he whispered hoarsely.

After a couple of drags and another shot of brandy he breathed a deep sigh and began to relax. "Oh, that's better. Jesus, I thought I'd never see me mother again."

"What in hell happened to you?"

"What *didn't* happen to me! God, Russ, you picked me a right one there. By the crunge . . ."

He got another belt down and began to look quite human, even managed a grin – one of the dirtiest grins I've ever seen. He chuckled and shook his head. "Never had a night like it, mate – never . . ."

I drank some vodka and tonic and waited, knowing he was stringing it out purposely.

"After you left," he said, flicking ash nervously all over the table, "she took me upstairs to the second floor and sure enough the door she was talking about really wouldn't close properly. One of the floorboards wanted shaving a bit. Well, I'd just started on it when she said why didn't I take my coat off and be more comfortable . . ."

"Was there anyone else around?"

"Not a soul. I figured all her lodgers were out at work or something. Anyway, I'd been chopping away at the floorboard for a few minutes when up she comes with a couple of drinks and stands there chatting to me about this an' that and telling me how nice it is of me to do this for her and how she misses having a man around the house to do these little jobs that women are bleeding useless at – you know the old guff. And she tells me her husband buggered off two years ago and left her stranded at a time when she was out of work and also just out of hospital where she'd just had her tubes out and had been told she could never have any kids just to add to her misery."

"Was she morbid about it?"

"Oh, no, she was just chatting and having a drink. Anyway, I finished the floorboard in about twenty minutes and asked her if there was anything else she wanted doing. Well, she said, there was a dripping tap in the bathroom downstairs that was driving her quietly balmy because she could hear it when she was lying in bed at night, so down we went. And there was the dripping tap, the cold one on the bath. I told her if it was the washer that needed renewing I'd have to turn the water supply off at the mains, so she took me into the kitchen and I climbed under the old sink to turn off the cock and that's

106

where I got grease all down the back of my white shirt. Some lunatic had put grease around the washer on the U-bend pipe and I got the lot in the middle of my back. She did her nut. Told me to take my shirt off and she'd wash it right away. Wouldn't take no for an answer. So I peeled off and while she was putting some grease remover on it I got back to the bathroom and had a gander at the tap."

"Want another brandy?"

"Yeh, sure." He drained his glass. "Oh, they're doing me the world of good, mate."

I went to the bar for two more and bought a sandwich for myself. I didn't think Mickey would be interested. I plonked the brandy down in front of him and said, "Go on."

He pulled an agonised face at the sandwich. "Gawd, how you can stomach food, I just don't know . . ."

"I lead a clean, pure life – go on."

"Well, I was fiddling around putting on a new washer – her husband must've been a bit useful because I found a string of washers in the cupboard – when in she comes with another drink and sits on the edge of the bath watching me. She asked me if I mind her watching because she wants to learn to do these little jobs herself. 'Course, I said no I didn't mind because for one thing, sitting on the bath like that she was showing just about everything she'd got and as you well know she's got a pair of thighs like neither of us has ever seen before . . ."

"I wouldn't know, I didn't get that far."

"Well, take my word for it, they're out of this world. Anyway, after a bit I realise she's not so much watching the washer going on the tap as watching my rippling biceps and pecs . . ."

I laughed.

". . . which, I might add, I am now rippling more than is necessary just for her lovely benefit. There I am – heaving and straining to tighten up the old tap with sweat rolling off me brow and me breath coming in short pants. Oh, she says, she didn't mean me to get so hot and dirty on her account and wouldn't I like a bath while I'm practically in it?"

"That's the stuff. What did you say?"

"I looked at my hands – which of course really were filthy by now – and had a glance over my shoulder and asked her if there was any grease on me back. No, she said, it was spotless. What a pity, I said, giving her a grin, because if there had been she'd have had to scrub it off."

"Good . . . good. What did she say to that?"

"She laughed and told me not to be a naughty boy but I could tell from the way she said it that she quite liked the idea. A couple more drinks, I thought, and she'd be in the bath with me. So I said yes, I would have a bath if she didn't mind, and she said go ahead, I'll get a clean towel for you and warm it by the fire and pass it in when you give me a shout."

"Wonderful. Sure you won't have a sandwich?"

"Do me a favour."

"Carry on."

"Well, off she went and I noticed she'd left the door open a bit, just a crack, and I thought there's no point in closing it if she's going to pass the towel in. So I filled the bath and climbed in and there I was scrubbing away with the bathbrush when I heard a floorboard squeak outside the door – just a faint noise but I heard it. By God, she's having a peek, I thought. Well, if she wants a look she can have a bloody *good* look and I started singing and soaping myself and after a minute I stood up with my back to the door. If she *is* having a squint, I thought, I'll make her wait a bit, so I went on soaping myself, showing her me bum and rippling me muscles for about a minute and then slowly I began to turn around. When I'd got almost round and was just about to give her an eyeful, I stopped and turned back again."

"Cruel swine."

"I did this about three times, until I reckoned she was beside herself with frustration, and then I suddenly turned completely around and stuck it right in her eye. I had a quick glance at the door and, boy, she was there! I could just see the white of the towel she was holding. We ... ll, I thought, lady, if you want a thrill here it is and I began soaping me old man then dripping water on him from the bathbrush, giving him a good going over. I was sure I could hear her breathing hard outside the door so I swilled all the soap off, climbed out of the bath and started doing a few bending and stretching exercises right by the door, giving her a real close-up, then I called out 'Ready, Mrs. Mandell!' She's a real actress this one. She flits away down the hall – I could hear her clothes rustling a bit – and calls back from the living room, 'Did you call, Mr. Maple?' I had to laugh. 'Ready for the towel' I shouted and up she trots and passes the towel through all coy, just popping her hand through."

"Superb. What happened then?"

He shrugged. Well, I knew what the score was, didn't I?

She wanted to play games and I was sure she knew that I knew she wanted to play games."

"How very perspicacious of you, Mickey."

"Mm?"

"Go on."

"So I got dressed – still without my shirt – and went into her living room. That's when I noticed."

"What?"

"She'd taken her tights off. Her legs were bare. She was standing by the sideboard pouring another drink. As I went in she said 'Feeling better? Like another drink?' I told her I'd get sloshed if I had any more and she just laughed and handed me one. It tasted like a triple, Russ, solid brandy. Then she went to sit on the couch and told me to sit down with her and tell her all about myself. Well, I was chatting away and she was listening very intently for about ten minutes except her eyes kept flicking to my bare chest and to my flies, when she suddenly went to pick up a packet of fags from the arm of the couch and she knocked it on the floor, over on her side, and before I could get moving towards it she leaned right over the arm to pick it up and guess what . . ."

"She had no knicks on either.'

"She had no knicks on either. Looking at it straight in the eye, I was. I went blind for a minute, straight up, my eyes wouldn't focus."

"I know the feeling. Go on."

" 'Clumsy me', she said. 'Can I help you?' I said, leaning towards her and placing my hand under her to support myself. 'No, I've got it', she said and sat down. 'So have I,' I said. "Ooh!' she went. 'What d'you think you're doing, Mr. Maple?' 'Groping you,' I said, 'as if you didn't know . . .' "

I laughed out loud and all the heads in the bar turned to look at us. "Beautiful, so what happened then?"

"Well, she decides to stop arsing about, pretending she isn't aching for it and falls on me and starts kissing me like the world's coming to an end at six o'clock. And while she's gobbling me, her right hand is undoing my zip and she's moaning and groaning and telling me it's the biggest one she's ever felt which is understandable because by this time he's up over my shoulder somewhere."

"Naturally."

"And she's asking me if I've got to rush away, because if I haven't she's got one or two little jobs for me, one of which

I'm sure is screwing her, provided of course, that we ever make the bedroom because by now she's got it out and is rubbing it against her cheek and showering it with kisses and caressing it like it was a big diamond she'd found while weeding the garden. I tell you, I've heard of female penis worship but this was ridiculous. She just adored it. She even talked to it! Yeh, no kidding. Oh, you're beautiful, she said, stroking its head, kissing it, sticking her tongue down the end of it. I had the feeling she'd forgotten about me. She only wanted me old man. Can you believe she even wanted to photograph it! ?"

"Eh?"

"No, really! This was about ten minutes later. She'd broken off for a minute to fill the glasses up again. I was getting nicely smashed by this time and she wasn't altogether sober. Anyway, she gets the drinks and brings them over and suddenly makes a dive at me and rips my trousers off, then flings her dress off – it was the only thing she had on. She's got a cracking figure, Russ, really stacked . . ."

"I did sort of notice."

"Mm, well, then she's back at it, crawling all over me, still talking to Herbert, telling him what a beautiful boy he is like she was talking to a baby, and she says, 'I think you ought to have your photograph taken' and dives across to the sideboard and brings back one of those polaroid cameras that develops films in ten seconds. Then she crouches down between my knees, takes a photo, counts ten seconds and rips the cover off the film. Gorgeous, she says. Now for a profile shot. Hell, she had me standing, leaning, crouching, lying back across the couch . . . she took shots from ten different angles. Then she asked me did I know it was a remote-control camera, the sort you can take self-portraits with – and what she'd really like to do was take some photos of both of us – together."

"Yes, I've got the picture."

"Brother, so did she. Russ, we were at it for an hour. She must've taken six reels of film. You know these sex books they sell nowadays – forty love positions? Well, I've got news for them. There are at least three thousand six hundred they've never *heard* of! This bird is a real artist. I tell you, we had it off all over the place – on the table, on the floor, up against the wall – even standing on our heads one time."

"Not easy, that."

110

"It's not. We fell over half a dozen times, but we got it in the end."

"Good man."

"Anyway, after all this she reckoned I needed a bit of a rest and asked me if I liked being read to."

"Read to?"

"Yeh, you know, stories. I said I didn't mind though I hadn't been read to since I was a child. I'll read you some short stories by Irwin Shaw, she said, he's one of the finest short story writers of our time. To tell you the truth I'd never heard of the bloke and I expected some real kinky porn, considering the mood she was in. Well, she got the book and came back and said 'I want to sit on him while I'm reading' giving Herbert a stroke. Help yourself, I said, and she climbed on and settled down with a big contented sigh and began reading. Russ, do you know this fella Irwin Shaw?"

"Yes, he wrote 'The Young Lions'."

"Yeh, that's him. There's nothing porny about him at all. He just writes good short stories. I tell you, this bird is fun-ny, sitting there full of Herbert reading stories to me."

"Some people do it watching telly."

He gave me an odd look. "Do *you*?"

"Only Party Political Broadcasts. There's something piquant about having Ted or Harold watching you do it, you know, looking straight at you."

"Mm?"

"Never mind – she was reading to you."

"Got another fag? I must buy some."

"Why change the habit of a lifetime? Here."

"Ta." He lit it, rubbed smoke out of his eye and went on, "Well, she read four stories, then closed the book and suddenly asked me what I'd like to do to her. I asked her what she had in mind and she said, Oh, come on, everybody has sexual fantasies – dreams of doing some secret, awful, funny, kinky things to somebody else and she wanted to know what my fantasies were and she said that within reason I could do them to her. I had to laugh then because I suddenly remembered telling you I wanted to tie her spreadeagled on the bed and leap on her from the top of the wardrobe yelling 'Geronimo'. She asked me what I was laughing at and I told her. Fine, she said, come on you can do it. I'll find some string and you can tie me to the bed just as you want, but as the wardrobe goes right up to the ceiling, can you make do with the dressing

111

table. Certainly, I said, and blow me, she goes into the kitchen and comes back with four lengths of washing line she'd bought but never used because of the tumble drier.

"Then we go into the bedroom and she lies face-up on the bed while I tie her wrists and ankles to the four corners. Then I move the dressing table to the foot of the bed and climb up on it, feeling a bit of a narna by now because fantasy is one thing and reality quite another. But she makes a big joke out of it and I begin laughing so much I fell off the dressing table. I get back on and she says you look lovely up there, all big and masculine, come on, leap on me and sock it to me. So I did. Shouting 'Ger ... on ... i .. mo!' I hurled meself through the air and really socked it to her. Oh, wonderful, she said, jumping up and down. Do it again! And again! Six times I climbed on that dressing table and hurled meself off and the sixth time I caught me toe in the bedclothes and nearly ruined meself on the bedside table.

"Anyway, she'd had enough of this by now so I untied her and asked her what her fantasies were and told her that within reason she could do them to me. You just won't believe what she said."

"Try me, I'm gullible."

"I bet you won't. She only wanted to do it on public transport, didn't she?"

"She did?"

"Sure, Surreptitiously – but in public, know what I mean? Said she'd get a big kick out of having it off surrounded by people who didn't know she was having it off. How are we going to manage that, I asked her. She said, if I wear my long fur coat with nothing on underneath and you wear your overcoat ..."

"Also with nothing on underneath?"

"Nar, with my suit on ... then, she said, I could cuddle up to you and wrap the fur coat around you and nobody would see anything. Well, the idea sort of appealed to me, being a bit unusual. So I said let's have a rehearsal and see if it works. Close your eyes, she said, and open them when I tell you. Then she went to the wardrobe and I could hear her putting clothes on. Open your eyes, she said, and there she was fully dressed. She had shoes and stockings on and a nice black fur coat that came down to her knees and she had a silk scarf around her neck. What d'you think? she asked. I said she looked completely dressed and she laughed and flung the coat

112

open and, blind me, all she had on was the scarf and a black suspender belt to hold her stockings up. Got the picture?"

I cleared my throat. "Yes."

"Come on, she said, get dressed and try it in front of the mirror. I put my suit and overcoat on and she said come and give me a cuddle and by gosh it worked. Looking at ourselves in the wardrobe mirror you'd never guess what we were up to underneath all that fur. Lovely, she said, let's take a ride on a bus first."

"First?"

"Oh, sure ... she wanted to do it on the Underground as well. I tell you, she's wild. So we walk down to Kings Road and catch a bus going to Sloan Square. By now it's nine o'clock and the buses are pretty full. I'm wondering how we're going to manage it but she's got it all worked out. She stands on the platform with her bum against the ticket bin and pulls me against her. Just then the conductor, a little Jamaican bloke, comes rattling down the stairs and tells us we've got to get off the platform. But she gives him one of those smiles that curl your boots up and tells him we're only going one stop and it's hardly worth sitting down as we'd only have to get straight up again. All right, he says, but be careful not to fall off and he disappears upstairs again.

"At the first stop six people get on and have to squeeze past us which gives Jackie one hell of a charge because two of the blokes are vicars. Then the Jamaican comes to the top of the stairs to ring the bell and calls down 'You two getting off?' No, I shout up we made a mistake, it's the next stop. You'll have to go inside, sir, he calls down, you're blocking people's passage, which send Jackie into fits of giggling and all the people on the lower deck stare at us which is just what Jackie wants. Next stop for sure, I call back, and he dings the bell.

"Then came the fun part because the road is under construction just along there and the bus was bouncing up ramps and dropping into potholes, and for about a quarter of a mile Jackie was in ecstasy, and if the road hadn't smoothed out just by the Duke of York's headquarters the game would've finished before we reached the square. We got time for another drink?"

I looked at my watch. "Just about ... but don't go back smashed, for Pete's sake, you'll get it from Ward after being late this morning."

"You want one?"

"No, thanks, I've got interviews to do."

While he was at the bar I pondered on the truthfulness of what he'd told me and found it utterly believable. No doubt there'd been one or two embellishments but in essence it sounded right. I'd pegged Jackie Mandell as a wild woman at first sight and that sort of instinct is rarely misled. I didn't know whether to feel envious of Mickey or sorry for him.

He came back and slid into his seat, unwrapped a packet of cigarettes and offered me one. I was smoking at the time.

"You got off the bus," I prompted.

"And went down the Underground and did it all the way to Victoria. Well, it's only one stop but it's quite a long one."

"And then?'

"We went up into the main line station and bought return tickets to Wimbledon. It's about a ten minute journey."

"I know."

"Tricky bit there. We were standing in the corridor doing it when a ticket collector came along and stood chatting to us for a couple of minutes telling us about a bloke who jumped off the wrong side of the train to avoid paying his fare and got clobbered by an express train going the other way."

"And all the time you were . . ."

"Oh, sure. He thought we'd moved close together to let him pass. Nice old fellow, with a squint. I don't think he could see too well."

"And at Wimbledon?"

"We had a cup of coffee in the buffet and caught the train back."

"Standing in the corridor again?"

"No, this time we tried it in the passage between two carriages. Quite good, there, it swings about nicely, though it got a bit draughty for Jackie."

"I can see it might."

"Then when we got back to Victoria she wanted to try it in a taxi, sitting on my lap."

"O.K.?"

"Smashing."

I checked my watch again. "It's time to go, Mickey."

He swallowed his drink and we left the pub, heading back to the supermarket. "So," I said, "apart from an aeroplane – which might prove a bit expensive – you've just about covered all forms of public transport, haven't you? Is that the end of the project?"

"Hell no, she's got other ideas. She wants to do it in the express lift going up the Post Office tower ... and in Selfridges ... and in the pictures ..."

"How about standing up on a floating lilo?"

"Yeh," he laughed. "Why not? Anything for a challenge."

"I can see you've really caught the spirit of the thing, Mickey."

"Oh, it's a great game."

"What happened after the taxi?"

"It took us home. We were both a bit cold by then so she made us some hot soup and we had a long hot bath together, then went to bed and got down to it properly. We didn't get to sleep until five."

"No wonder you look shattered. When do you see her again?"

"Oh, tonight. I'm going round there after we finish shooting. We're going to try it in the pictures."

"What film are you going to see?"

"Who cares, man," he laughed.

We got back to work and filmed a couple of promising interviews during the afternoon. We also got a crazy old coot with no teeth and hair like a spurting fountain who gave us a great testimonial for White Marvel which lasted half an hour. It included singing, dancing, a couple of very bad jokes and finished up with a bit of conjuring – making a lighted cigarette disappear down his ear. Unfortunately he was either a bit out of practice or his hands were cold and the hot end of the fag dropped off and went down his earhole, poor soul. He went home very subdued with his finger in his ear.

And so we wrapped it up for the second day, not a bad day at all, and Mickey came up and snapped a salute. "Reporting at 0900 hours tomorrow, sir."

"Good luck in the pictures."

"Ta. Let you know."

That evening I thought about going out but after I'd soaked the ice out of my bones for an hour I got interested in a cowboy film on T.V. and decided I was too comfortable to move. So, after the film, I popped a duck a l'orange T.V. dinner into the oven and wrote a letter to Vicki.

I'd had one from her that morning in which she said she was working like a dog, was choked with the weather which

115

was cold and wet, and was missing me like mad, which was nice.

I wrote that I was up to my ears in White Marvel, was choked with the weather which was cold and wet, and was missing her like mad, which was true, particularly since I had a photograph of her propped in front of me as I wrote and felt all the old yearning return as I looked at her.

When I finished the letter I phoned Tony for a giggle and told him about Mickey Maple and Jackie Mandell. True to form he said, when I'd finished, "Well, what's wrong with that?"

"You mean you've done it in a train corridor while talking to a ticket collector?"

"Well, not recently. Keep me posted, hm? She's obviously very inventive. It's refreshing to know there are still some of us around. Maybe we can get together and swop ideas."

I put the phone down, set the table with pleasurable anticipation, and turned my succulent duck a l'orange onto a plate. I poured a glass of wine and took the first mouthful of duck. The remainder I ground to oblivion in my sink Tweeny.

With a Spam sandwich and a glass of milk I sat watching the late night movie, wondering how Mickey Maple was getting on in the pictures.

*

The next morning, Wednesday, he arrived on time but dragging his feet as badly as Tuesday. He sauntered up, gave me a thin, victorious grin and muttered, "Tell you lunchtime. Out of this world, man, outta this world."

I settled down to work, aware that there were only three more days left for street interviews before we moved into the houses. I applied a bit of pressure, made use of every possibility. Just after ten o'clock two young housewives came out of the supermarket, a right cheeky pair, Mrs. Grant and Mrs. Follett.

I approached Mrs. Grant, a small, dumpy bird with dyed blonde hair. She took one look at the mike in my hand – it was about nine inches long and had a bulbous wind-guard made of foam rubber on the end – and said, " 'Ere, watch where you're stickin' your thing, young man. You might do someone a mischief."

" 'Ave you got a licence for it?" asked Mrs. Follett, a tall, thin red-head with a big chin. She looked at it thoughtfully. "You know, Phil, it reminds me of someone I know."

"It reminds me of someone I'd *like* to know," said Mrs. Grant.

"Now, ladies, you've both just bought White Marvel. Can you tell me your experience . . ."

"Cheeky, isn't he?" said Mrs. Grant.

"Dead cheeky, asking respectable married women about their experiences," said Mrs. Follett "Waving that filthy thing in their faces."

"Whose was it, anyway?" asked Mrs. Grant. "Has the poor fella been embalmed or somethin'? Poor soul,' e's going to miss it, isn't he?"

"Yes, someone's lost a very good friend there," said Mrs. Follett. "Whoever it was, he's goin' to be bleeding mad when he finds out what you're using it for. What flavour is it, anyway. Give us a lick . . ."

The crew was falling about and the more they laughed the worse the women got.

"Nah, we're not being fair to the poor lad," said Mrs. Grant. "He's tryin' to do a job of work and we're messing him around."

"Quite right, we must stop messing him around. 'Ere, son, give us another lick it was gorgeous . . ."

Mrs. Grant stroked the end of the mike tenderly. "My old man's goin' to be a terrible disappointment after this. Sorry, Mr. Tobin, you were saying . . ."

They did settle down a bit and talked about their washing, though this serious vein didn't last long.

"Sheets?" said Mrs. Grant. "Oh, yers, White Marvel's marvellous for sheets. Get's all the stains out."

"What stains would they be, then, Phil?" asked Mrs. Follett.

"What stains d'you think, you dirty madam. Tea stains, of course. My old man gets it in bed every morning and every night."

"Mine should be so lucky."

"Tea, you naughty girl, tea. He only gets the other on Father's Day."

Finally I managed to subdue them and we got a very good interview out of them.

Paul Ward was cock-a-hoop at lunch time and broke us

early. I winked at Mickey to hold back from the rest of the crew and we made our way to our own pub.

"The way you look this morning," I told him as we entered the saloon, "you'll never see twenty one."

"That's in two months time."

I shook my head. "You'll never make it. What'll you have?"

"A beer. To hell with brandy."

I got two pints and a couple of sandwiches and we sat down. Mickey took a long draught of beer and gasped, "Oh, that's better."

"Well?"

"We got caught."

"Eh?"

"In the flicks. She wanted it in the Essoldo while watching a film called 'You Can't Stick It Here' – just to prove we could. We took corner seats on the back row right next to the wall and when it was dark she slipped across and sat on my knee."

"She had the fur coat on?"

"Yes, same system."

"And?"

"It was going marvellous until I got cramp, I mean really diabolical cramp in the back of my thigh. Murderous."

"I know how it is."

"I just had to stand up, I was in agony. So I gave Jackie a push and as she stood up two things happened – her coat flew open and the girl cinema attendant shone her torch along the row to show some people in."

"Oh, no."

"Oh, yes. ' 'Ere, what's going on in the corner there!' she shrieks. 'Stop that at once. I'll call the manager!' Of course the place is only full, isn't it. I grab Jackie's hand and haul her out fast. We were followed out into the street by the manager and this bird both shouting the odds. We jumped into the first taxi that came along."

"So that put an end to that caper?"

He grinned at me. "You kidding? We went uptown to the cartoon cinema and had a laugh while we were doing it. It's nice when you're laughing."

"So what's left now?"

"The Post Office tower . . . the Houses of Parliament . . ."

"Eh?"

"Sure . . . she's keen on doing it in the public gallery. She fancies the Old Bailey, too."

"Have you found out anything about her – where she did her acting?"

"Yes, I have. You were right – she was a stripper. She showed me some photos. She went under the name of Glamour Van Belt ..."

I spilled my beer.

"I bet she was really good," he said pensively. "She's going to put on a special performance for me one night – in the house. She asked me if you'd like to come."

"She did?"

"Mm, she said you looked the sort of man who'd appreciate a bit of artistry. She suggested you might like to stay behind on the day we do the interviews at the house. What d'you think?"

"We'll see how it goes."

"I'm sure it'd be worth seeing."

I smiled at him. "You really like her, don't you, Mickey?"

"Course I like her. She's fun."

"And also insatiable. She'll wear you out, man."

"Nar, she's not insatiable. She just loves doing it. So do I, so that's all right, isn't it?"

"O.K." I laughed. "Don't get huffy. It's no business of mine what you do."

"I'm ... not getting huffy, it's just that, well, she's nice to be with. I really like her."

"Apart from sex, what else do you do?"

"We had a meal once ... no, you can't really count that. She sat on my knee half-way through."

"Do you talk sometimes?"

"Oh, all the time. I tell you, she's a lot of fun."

"Sounds like a beautiful relationship."

He nodded, thoughtfully. "It is."

"Good for you."

That was the last time I heard of his escapades with Jackie Mandell. He continued to turn up for work looking terribly haggard but he didn't offer any further information and I didn't press him. I guessed the reason for it but I didn't find out for certain until a week later when we were shooting the interviews in the house. I caught several very tender smiles pass between them indicating an immense fondness had developed in the ten days they had known one another.

At a timely moment I asked him, "Well, how is it, Mickey?"

He winked and said quietly, "It's great, Russ"

"You living here permanently?"

"Sure – over a week now."

"Fine."

"She's lovely."

"She certainly looks very attractive today,' I said.

"I didn't mean just that . . . I mean . . . she's really lovely."

"Done any more jobs around the house?"

"Started papering a lodger's room last night. I'm going to do the whole house for her."

"Great."

"Er, by the way . . . you know what I said about Jackie inviting you to watch her strip . . ."

I shook my head. "Forgotten all about that, Mickey. It never happened."

"Thanks, mate."

At the end of that week he quit the film business and became . . . well, I don't know how exactly he saw himself – house superintendent, perhaps. I know he had at least six months work ahead of him – painting, decorating, plastering, plumbing. Maybe he had more than six months work; it would rather depend on how much free time she allowed him. I've often meant to go back there and have a look at the house. It could well be it's fallen down through neglect.

CHAPTER SEVEN

It was on the Tuesday following the two weeks of White Marvel interviews that Allan Lang, the producer at Croxleys, telephoned my agent to say that Paul Ward and the clients were delighted with the material we'd shot. They would, he said, have no difficulty in cutting twelve good commercials from the miles of film but perhaps would need me some time for one day's filming of reaction shots – smiles, nods, grunts – to be cut into the films at appropriate places.

When Mike Spiring phoned me with the good news I felt, for a few moments, tremendous elation. I'd done it. The money was in the bag. I could now telephone Philip Ardmont and tell him I was free.

But before I did this I phoned Tony to tell him the results.

"Great," he said. "Now you can desert us with a clear conscience."

"What d'you mean?"

"We ... ll, what about our research programme? We haven't done nine tenths of London."

"I'm not leaving tomorrow morning, am I? We've got until the middle of March."

"Right, we start tonight – and you're paying."

I phoned Ardmont then who said, "Fine, Russ, when can I see you?"

"How about ten minutes time?"

"Make it half an hour," he laughed. "You're really keen, aren't you?"

Ardmont's office, near Oxford Circus, exhuded the charged atmosphere of remorseless industry. He was hard at it in shirtsleeves, bent over a big metal desk strewn with papers and brochures. He took a heavy pipe from his mouth, shook hands and waved at a chair.

"How did White Marvel go?"

"Very well indeed. They're pleased."

"So, come March you'll be as well known on telly as the Prime Minister?"

"Oh, easily," I grinned. "Probably better."

"Well, now ... firstly, Russ, I must ask you one question – you're absolutely sure you want to join us as a rep? The reason for asking is that if you were to back out at the last minute it would put us in a hell of a spot. It's happened before."

"Yes, I'm absolutely sure."

"Fine. Well, I've got a position for you in Majorca at a place called Magaluf, eight miles west of Palma. You'll be looking after up to one hundred and fifty clients who'll stay in three big new luxury hotels – the San Vincente, the Hotel Pollensa and the Hotel Palma. We want you to fly out on the thirteenth of March – the season starts a week later, on the twentieth – and you'll stay until October the twentieth, all right?"

"Yes, fine."

All summer in Majorca . . . I still couldn't believe it.

Ardmont reached for a wad of papers. "Here . . . is our staff application form. You'll need a two-by-two photograph for it. Get this into me as soon as you can." He passed me another form. "Here are details of our staff insurance scheme. The company and you share the premium. It'll cost you four pounds for the season. And here . . ." he passed me a sheaf of foolscap papers, typewritten and duplicated, stapled together, ". . . are the instructions to resident reps and couriers – the reps' Bible. This covers everything alphabetically from Airport Taxes to Weekly Returns. I want you to take this with you now and study it very carefully, learn it off by heart. Everything you need to know about the job is contained in there." Now he passed me a bulging manilla envelope. "Here are all the forms relevant to those instructions – Client Reports Forms, Excursion Sales Returns, Expense Account Returns . . . anyway, go through them and call me if there's anything you don't understand. All right?"

"Yes, quite clear."

"Good, now . . ." he looked at his watch. "Sorry to throw you out but I've got a meeting in five minutes. Let me have the application form as soon as you can. By the way, have you decided what you're going to do about learning Spanish?"

"Yes, I've bought a Linguaphone course. There isn't time to take a course in any of the schools."

"Good. Linguaphone is quite O.K. provided you stick at it. Try to do at least an hour every day."

"Yes, I will . . . er, Philip, what about training?"

"Training?" The word seemed to amuse him because he smiled and repeated it. "Training. When you get to Majorca there'll be someone there to meet you. His name is Patrick

Holmes. He's our resident rep in Palma Nova, that's the next bay to Magaluf, about a mile away. Patrick has been with us for three years and he's one of our best reps. He'll show you the ropes."

"Then ... I don't actually get any training in this country before I leave?"

He smiled again and tapped the bulky manual of instructions. "When you've learned that by heart you're ninety per cent trained. Now I must fly ..."

I reached the street a bit confused. It all seemed so simple, so off-hand. Somehow I'd expected to go to school for a couple of weeks, to be tested, to do some rehearsal as we used to do at Ritebuy Sewing Machines before being sent out on real calls. Still, I supposed they knew what they were doing.

I drove back to the flat, made a pot of coffee, settled in the armchair with a packet of cigarettes, and began to study the "Instructions To Resident Representatives And Couriers".

I read:

INTRODUCTION

You have a unique position in the Company as one of our Resident Representatives or Couriers for, in many cases, you are the first personal contact that the client has had with the Company. Only a small percentage of the bookings are made "over the counter" at Head Office; the majority are either made by post or through our accredited local travel agents.

It should, therefore, be your aim to ensure that every client has a really enjoyable holiday, and by doing so enhance the good name of the Company. To do this satisfactorily will require a keen sense of responsibility. You must remember at all times that you have been chosen to render a service to our clients. You will also be required to liase between the Company on the one hand and on the other the managements of the various hotels with which we work in your area; the transfer operator; the excursion operator; the clients. To fulfil this task will require tact and discretion.

You should always bear in mind that to all people whom you meet in the course of your duties, *you* represent the Company. Your personal behaviour and appearance should be beyond reproach.

Aha! Good straight-from-the-shoulder stuff. I re-read it. Remembering my long ago conversation with Vicki about the hopes and expectations of the young girls – the typists, secretaries, factory workers – who take these package holidays, I had a chuckle at the phrases "it should, therefore, be your aim to ensure that every client has a really enjoyable holiday" and "you must remember at all times that you have been chosen to render a service to our clients."

Whatever Lola – or Gladys or Jan or Lucy – wants, Lola etc. gets. The customer is always right. Q.E.D. and P.D.Q.

I opened the twenty-page instructions. On the first page was an index beginning with "Accommodation" and ending with "Your Journey". It took me half an hour to read it all. At the end I was aware of subjects that had never before touched my life – Comfort Stops, Over-booking of hotels, Loans to Clients, Lost Luggage, Memos, Resort Questionaires, Right of Occupancy, Special Transfers, Telex, Thefts, Uplift Permission, V.I.P. Service, Weekly Reports, Weekly Returns ... and many more. Sixty four separate headings in all. I read the whole thing again ... and again, now checking the instructions against the forms in the manilla envelope. After the fourth read-through I was beginning to get the picture.

One fact emerged unmistakeably – discipline was strict. the sixty four chapters were liberally sprinkled with "it is essential that ..."; "under no circumstances will ..."; "it is imperative that ..."; "it is strictly forbidden to ...".

One other fact also emerged, even more unmistakeably – the job was no sinecure. Ardmont said I'd be earning my money and from the formidable list of daily and weekly instructions there was no doubt about it. Even supposing this was just a first impression and supposing the list lost a lot of its terror when I got to know the routine, there was still enough there to indicate a seven-day week and a load of responsibility.

To give you an idea of just how much responsibility, this is what I read: "Clients may also arrive at your resort from Cardiff, Glasgow, Manchester or Newcastle airports, as well as London clients from Gatwick or Heathrow airports".

That meant a continual turnover of around one hundred and fifty people coming into Palma airport on two, three or four flights a week (they called them 'transfers'). These people would have to be met, their baggage checked, baggage and clients put on the bus, taken to the hotel, checked in, settled down, visited everyday, seen back to Palma airport at the end of their holiday, baggage checked again and clients bid farewell – just as the next transfer was arriving.

All this of course was just basic routine!

Added to this there would be excursions and local car hire to be arranged; weekly returns (Reports on Transfers, on hotels, on weather, on clients' problems; Excursion Sales Returns; Expense Account Returns; Return of Rooming Lists; Coded Cables) to be made to either the Area Office in Palma or to Head Office in London (and in some cases to both); and then of course there would be the problems, the totally unforseeable problems that might arise, such as: Delays of Transfers through weather conditions or technical difficulties; Clients wishing to change hotels; Lost luggage; Stolen property; V.I.P. service; Sickness . . .

A very full week's work.

I put down the Instructions and stared thoughtfully at the electric fire. Now was the time to decide – did I want all this responsibility? Life would be a hell of a sight easier in London. I had enough money to last the year without doing a stroke of work. Wouldn't it be madness to take on a job like this when I could afford to live in Majorca all summer as a client!

The welfare, comfort and happiness of hundreds of people were involved. What if I mucked up just *one* holiday? One little bird who'd been looking forward to her two weeks holiday all year? An old woman who was taking her first – and possibly her last! – holiday abroad?

One hundred and fifty people in any two weeks – for eight months. Hundreds and hundreds of them.

Wow.

I lit my eighty fourth cigarette and pondered. Did I really want it?

By two o'clock I was sitting in the photographers' studio. By four o'clock the application form was on its way. I had finally and irrevocably committed myself. In six weeks time I would be in Majorca, courier for Ardmont Holidays . . . courier for Ardmont Holidays. God help us all. And amen to it.

CHAPTER EIGHT

My expectation of having no television work for the next six weeks proved correct, for apart from the one day's shooting of reaction shots not a single job came up. Mike Spiring told me there were quite a few telephone calls but the moment he mentioned White Marvel there was a cough, a meaningful silence and a polite rejection. Russ Tobin was suddenly poison on the London scene; a man of enforced leisure.

But the time certainly didn't drag. I slept a bit later than usual and took all the time I wanted to shower, shave, dress and breakfast and really got stuck into the Spanish course. And it's incredible what you can accomplish with this concentrated study. Within a week I was beginning to get a real feel for the language; within two I was automatically translating in my mind simple phrases in conversation with Tony; and within three weeks I was driving him potty translating aloud and decided I'd better shut up.

This Linguaphone course was a bit of all right. For one thing all the people who spoke on the records were actually Spanish, so the pronunciation was impeccable. Text books are all very well if you want to go deeply into the finer points of grammar, but for my purposes I wanted to hear Spanish spoken and to learn phrases that were going to be of some practical use. I felt there would be scant need for sentences like: "Sir, I think I have just broken your leg" and "Is that your horse on the table?" in the job I was going to do. Possible, sure, but not too likely.

One thing I did manage to do during this time of enforced idleness was to visit some of the places in London that every Londoner should visit and never does – the Tower, the Houses of Parliament (I half expected to find Mickey Maple and the dextrous Jackie Mandell hard at it in the visitors' gallery but I guess it wasn't their day). I stood outside number ten Downing Street with two hundred tourists and pulled tongue at the front door when the policeman wasn't looking. I tore around the British Museum; glanced at the Victoria and Albert and the Science and the Natural museums; popped into St. Paul's Cathedral; had a quick butcher's at Madame Tussaud's, the

National Gallery and Westminster Abbey, then called it a day. Enough is enough. I found it more exhausting than being in the Kum Kum Club. But at least I could now say I'd been and seen. You feel a bit of a twit when an American tourist says to you "Guess ya know St. Paul's like the back of ya hand", and you have to reply "St. Paul's what?".

January dragged itself wearily into February; February blew itself into March. The weather was appalling and made me very impatient for the sun. Yet at least it made it easy for me to stay indoors and practice my Spanish. I kept on and on; one lesson each day. Fifty lessons; fifty days.

During February I heard from Philip Ardmont that the board had accepted my application and two days later I was measured for my Ardmont blazer – a snazzy job in Royal blue with a yellow Ardmont badge on the breast pocket. With a pair of slim-line greys, a white shirt and a mahogany tan it would look pretty devastating.

Ardmont also told me I had a single room in the Palma Hotel. I decided to go along with this until I got out there and had a look at it. If it didn't suit, I was going to get a flat to myself. I was going to get *some* fun out of this job.

The final few days went quickly. There was a lot to do. I let my flat to an American actor who was staying in England for six months on films. I transferred two hundred pounds to a bank in Magaluf. And I sold my car. I had thought about taking it with me but decided against it. It would be easier to hire something in Majorca.

Then, suddenly, it was Friday and my last night in London. Tony and I decided on a farewell tour of Soho in celebration – a revisit to some of our old haunts. At eight o'clock we parked his car in Shaftesbury Avenue and dropped into Len's Den, a dive-bar near Wardour Street. The interesting thing about Len's place is the Graffiti on the wall of the gent's loo. Len, a gargantuan ex-heavyweight wrestler with one ear and a nose like a pock-marked mushroom, personally inspects the wall each morning and removes the offensive and unfunny. Wit is encouraged; filth is not.

Tony and I made straight for the loo for a pee and read. Side by side we scanned the wall to see what was new. Tony started chuckling. "Here's a goodie."

I inclined at an angle and had a look. It was a very good drawing of three faces – two men, with a woman's face in the middle. They all had dour expressions and it was obviously a send-up of the famous anti-body odour product. Underneath one of the men was written: "My name is Pete – it's me feet"; underneath the other man was written: "My name is Jeff – it's me breff"; and under the woman: "My name is Annie...".

There were several others along the lines of: "If you can read this you're peeing on your boots", and somewhat more subtle offering: "My bird is so dumb she thinks a literary bent is a queer author."

"You know," I said, "I have never in my life written anything on a wall."

"You haven't lived," said Tony, shaking it. "G'n, write something as a farewell gesture. Leave something to posterity."

I pulled up my zip, got out my ball-point and wrote, "There's something definitely sick about people who write on walls".

"There," he said, "that didn't hurt, did it."

"You have a go."

He shook his head. "Nah, I'm not feeling very creative tonight. Sort of depressed about you leaving. I won't enjoy this place half as much by myself. A solo slash just isn't the same, somehow."

We went upstairs and got a grunt from Len which is in the nature of an hilarious welcome from him.

"Wotcharavin?" he growled.

We ordered vodkas and he thumped the two glasses down on the bar with all the effeminate delicacy of a shell smashing into a rampart.

"Well, here's to Majorca," said Tony. "And to couriering. Come back a happier and wiser man."

"I'll settle for browner."

"And watch your health. Don't go screwing yourself into a stupor."

"Who – me?'

"You."

"You've got me wrong. Like I told you – quote 'I have been chosen to render a service to my clients. My aim is ensure they have a happy holiday...' "

"That's what I said – don't go screwing yourself into a stupor."

"You have a degenerate one-track mind, Dane. Is that all you think I'm going out for – sun-baked noddy?"

"Yes."

"God forgive you. You can't see dedication when you're face to face with it."

He sighed and shook his head. "Ah, the wonder of it – a constant roll-call of crumpet ... a fresh turn-over every two weeks for eight glorious months." He sighed despairingly. "You'll never last, laddy. I've half a mind to quit London and come out and give you a hand."

"Why don't you?"

He paused in the lighting of a cigarette and looked at me. "Why don't I ..."

"Book now while the best rooms are still going. Come out for a month – June. You can afford it."

He was nodding thoughfully, staring into the distance. Suddenly he looked at me and grinned. "You're on, baby. Write to me next week – as soon as you've scouted the territory. Let me know which is the best hotel."

"Best for what?"

"You tell me, you're the bloody courier."

"Yeh, so I am. It takes some getting used to."

"And you'd better be organised by the time I get there. I'll kick up hell if the service is lousy."

"I'll just bet you would, too."

"Why didn't I think of it before ... a mate with ready access to rooming lists ... names ... marital statuses ... I may even stay for July."

Eleven o'clock found us slightly smashed in a basement Chinese restaurant, dancing with two semi-Lesbians Tony knew. Josie Redman and Clare Cullum, a couple of passable brunettes, who were apparantly more semi than Lesbian this particular night and had quite eagerly agreed to have dinner with us.

We'd just finished dancing and had sat down to await dinner when there was a commotion on the far side of the dimly lit room. A voice bellowed, "Of course you've got a table for us, we've booked the bloody thing."

Tony peered through the gloom and murmured, "Oh, Christ."

"D'you know him?"

"Yes, so do you. It's Pat O'Hea."

"The comedian?"

"The comedian."

Most people knew Pat O'Hea from his occasional appearances on television. He had a reputation, both public and professional, for being brash, crude and almost perpetually drunk.

Tony said, "I worked with him once on a custard commercial. I was the interviewer who had to ask him which brand of custard he preferred – A or B, then I had to hit him in the face with two custard pies. He got so pissed during the lunch break he ruined the set by chucking custard pies at it – and at the camera. We never did finish the commercial . . . oh, no!"

Tony looked suddenly horrified. I saw why. O'Hea and three other people were heading towards us – towards a vacant table next to ours.

As the foursome approached I recognised the other man in the group. It was Ralph Ord, a character actor who specialised in evil parts, mainly because he looked the epitome of evil himself. He was very tall and enormously built and had the most terrifying, piercing black eyes. He also had a reputation, in the business, for being a drunk and a hell-raiser. O'Hea was in good company.

The two birds they had with them were really something, a right couple of tramps in tight dresses that showed big breasts and plenty of bottom.

A nervous little Chinese waiter preceded them and pulled the table away from the wall. Ralph Ord squeezed between our table and his, almost removing our tablecloth completely, and flopped down drunkenly into his seat. His girl, a red-head, sat down with him. O'Hea and his woman sat with their backs to the room.

O'Hea, a balding, beefy individual with a chubby, formless face, struggled to get the waiter into focus. "Sank you, sank you, my little yellow fellow," he smirked, showing his teeth. "That was morst kind, velly kind."

"Would you like some drinks, sir?"

"Would we like some dlinks, sir? Of course we'd like some dlink, sir, we didn't come in her to pick our noses."

The two women sniggered and Ralph Ord simply stared across the room as though hypnotised. He seemed to be in a trance.

The waiter departed. O'Hea looked around, saw the girls at our table and bowed facetiously. "Good evening, ladies, how simply procreatious you look tonight . . ." He glanced at me, passed on to Tony, looked away, came back to Tony,

130

peered hard at him, then recognition dawned. "I don't believe it!" he bellowed. "Tony Dane – the best custard-pie man in the business . . . !"

He lurched to his feet and came at Tony with his hand outstretched. "Howareya, you old cunt . . ." he glanced at the girls, ". . . I do beg your pardon, but I haven't seen this old fart in years."

"Hello, Pat," Tony muttered, wincing.

I was conscious of an uncomfortable stirring at the tables surrounding us. Fortunately the taped music was playing fairly loud and O'Hea couldn't be heard too far away, but he was still reaching tables four or five away from ours.

He weaved over us, blatantly looking down the girls' bosoms.

"As I was saying just the other day," he said in an "I say – I say – I say" voice, "I forget 'oo to, possibly 'Er Majesty the Queen – I said I wonder what ever 'as 'appened to Tony Dane, the best right-arm custard in the business . . ." he wiggled his lips at Clare and threw a kiss at her breasts. ". . . good evenin', my darling, haven't I had you, er, met you before somewhere? If this rude bastard won't introduce me, I'll introduce me for him. My name is Randolph Scott and would you care to dance? No, I don't blame you, my breath smells somethin' 'orrible." He looked at Josie. " 'Ow about you, sweetheart . . . no, you're lookin' at me like poison. Never mind, I've been insulted in better places than this shit shop, did I say shit shop?, I meant chip shop. I do beg your pardon, I've got the wife's teeth in tonight." He gave me a cursory glance. "Don't mind me, sonny, I'll be gone in an hour or two. No offence, I'm sure. You have two very charming old bags with you and I wouldn't dream of insulting them for the world."

He smiled distantly at the girls. "I say, did you know it was Chinese New Year tonight? Hoo Fong Fuck, they call it. A Happy Hoo Fong Fuck to everybody . . ." He shot a glance at the table behind us. "Good evening, madam, a Happy Hoo Fong Fuck to you. It's the Chinese New Year . . ."

"Pat, sit down!" hissed his girlfriend.

He turned slowly and smiled coldly at her. "And a Happy Hoo Fong Fuck to you, too, you old bat. Where's that bloody slant-eyed kid with the drinks. He's a Commie, I tell you. They're all Commies. Well, Hoo Fong Fuck him to Pekin and back . . . hey, kid!"

He bellowed across the floor to a passing waiter who falt-

131

ered, changed course, and approached. "Happy Hoo Fuck to you," said O'Hea.

"Sir?"

"Happy New Year, you c ... c ... Cantonese gentleman. Don't you know it's Chinese New Year?"

The waiter grinned uncertainly and looked at all of us in turn to see whether it was a joke. "It's not Chinese New Year, sir."

"There, you see, they're all Commies. They don't even know it's Hoo Fong Fuck night. Get us some drinks, kid, I'm dying the death, standing here with egg foo yong on my face."

At that moment the first waiter arrived with a tray of drinks. He looked flustered, very angry with O'Hea. Before he could set the tray down O'Hea picked a glass off it and tossed down a good double whiskey. "Bring me another one, sunshine ... no, make it two, I can't hang around for you all night. Where did you go for these – Mother Russia?"

I glanced at the people at O'Hea's table to see how they were taking his behaviour. Ord was still in his trance and his girlfriend was peeling nail varnish off her thumb and flicking it in the ashtray. O'Hea's girlfriend was reading the menu.

The waiter off-loaded the drinks and got away quickly, muttering to himself. "And you," O'Hea called after him. "They're the trouble-makers of this world – the Commies ..."

Clare said quietly to us, "Excuse me," and made to get up.

"Me, too", said Josie, collecting her handbag.

"Oh, allow *me*!" said O'Hea, moving quickly behind their chairs. "Going for a little pee-pee, darlings? Don't forget to wipe them nicely now."

Tony hissed, "Pat, take it easy, for crisssake. Why don't you sit down and leave us alone?"

O'Hea's eyes snapped angrily. I got ready to move. If he went for Tony I was going to hit the crude sod over the head with the food-warmer. But he backed down and said, "Sorry. Don't call us, we'll call you. No offence, only a bit of fun."

He sat down in his own chair and snapped at his girlfriend, "Let's have a butcher's at the menu, you silly cow, you know you can't read Chinese. Now, what shall we have to celebrate Hoo Flung Fuck? How about some Hong Kong Dung with Flied Lice and a side order of Shitty Chow Mein? No response was the stern reply. Right, we'll have the set dinner for four and fuck the lot of you. Where's that heathen waiter ... Hey, Yellow Peril! Get your feet over here, we're starving!

And tell the wine waiter to stop playing with himself and come too!"

The waiters took his orders very quickly and rushed away.

"Come and dance, you fat faggot!" O'Hea said to his girl-friend.

They got onto the crowded floor and began jigging about. Then O'Hea dropped to his knees, threw his arms around the girl's legs and began kissing the junction of her thighs. The place was in uproar. Then his girl stalked off the floor and O'Hea followed her on his hands and knees, calling, "Here, pussy, pussy. Here, kitty, kitty, kitty. I wanna kiss your little pussy . . ."

The management obviously wanted him out of the place fast because their meal came up instantly, and the wine. O'Hea's girlfriend served some of the food onto their plates and then O'Hea raised his glass of red wine. "Here's a Happy Hoo Fong Fuck to everybody . . . !" then drank some wine and dropped the glass into his food. "Oh, shit," he said. "Never mind, I never did like this Commie crap," and with that he picked up the bottle of wine and poured it all over the table – into the food on the warmers, all over the table cloth, into Ralph Ord's plate.

"Look!" O'Hea exclaimed, pointing at a big fried prawn. "The bastard's swimming, Ralph, the bastard's swimming!" Then he flicked the bottle and spattered Ord's white shirt all over.

That did it. Ord came out of his drunken trance, picked up a big fried prawn off his plate and flung it in O'Hea's face. "Make that bastard swim too, O'Hea!"

O'Hea let out an exultant yell as the prawn hit him in the eye. "What d'you do that for, you big cunt!" and scooped up a handful of fried rice and slung it at Ord. Back came the crispy noodles to land in O'Hea's hair. Back went a salvo of sweet and sour pork in thick gravy. And as the chop suey hurtled through the air towards O'Hea the girls swept away from the table and three of the brawniest Chinese gentlemen I've ever seen ran across the floor, literally hauled O'Hea and Ord out of their seats and frog-marched them towards the stairs.

O'Hea left, singing at the top of his voice, "Goodnight, campers! We'll meet again . . . don't know where . . . don't know whe . . . e . . . e . . . n! And a Happy Ding Dong Fuck to the lot of you!"

Their table looked like the battlefield of some terrible Chinese food war. Pacific fried prawns, chicken chow mein, sweet and sour spareribs, shrimp chop suey, crispy noodles and gravy lay scattered all over the place – and everything swimming in Nuits St. George 54. There was even a meatball up on the wall light.

"I don't think I feel very hungry," said Clare.

"Neither do I," said Josie. "Do you mind if we go home."

We put them in a taxi because they insisted on that, and Tony and I laughed all the way home.

As we stopped outside my flat he said, "Buddy, we'll never forget your last night in London, for sure." He held out his hand to me. "Good luck, mate. Drop me a line next week. See you in June, hey?"

"Sure thing. Keep it in shape, now."

I got out of the car, waved to him, and walked towards the front entrance.

"Hey, I forgot!" he called.

I walked all the way back to him. "Forgot what?"

"Happy Hoo Fong Fuck, son," he said and shot down the street and out of sight.

CHAPTER NINE

I flew out to Palma seated between a nutty millionaire named Harry Onions and his leggy mistress, Pamela, an odd arrangement you might think but Pamela insisted on the window seat and Harry wanted to stretch his feet in the aisle.

Harry, a fifty-year-old Cockney, had made his million "graftin' scrap iron twenty hours a day and the way he bought champagne on the flight seemed dedicated to spending it as quickly as possible.

He hardly stopped talking during the two hour flight, and when he wasn't at it his mistress was, digging me in the ribs, telling me to look at this cloud and that field and those little houses, and while I was leaning across to peer through the window, Harry was pulling me back again to tell me yet another joke.

"There was this bloke, y'see," he said within minutes of introducing himself, which was three seconds after we'd sat down, "who was dead set on marrying a virgin. He just *had* to marry a virgin. So 'e goes to the doc and asks him how he can be sure his girlfriend *is* a virgin . . ."

Pamela's elbow caught me a beaut right under the heart. "Russ, just look at that Jumbo jet over there, in'it big?"

"Yes, terrific.'

Harry's scrap iron hand eased me upright again. "Don't interrupt, love, there's a good girl. So this fella is told by the doctor: 'Go to a chemist shop and get a Virgin Detector Kit' – have you 'eard it?"

"No, I haven't."

"It's a good one, you'll like it . . . hang on."

The B.A.C. 111 thundered down the runway and flung itself into the air. Pamela had her nose pressed to the window; Harry had his fingers in his ears. He removed them as soon as we'd levelled out. "Cor, the pressure don't arf hit me."

An air hostess was fluttering close by.

"Hello, Rita," said Harry.

Rita dazzled him with her smile. "Hello, Mr. Onions, nice to see you again."

"Bring us a bottle of bubbly soon as you're able, love."

"Certainly, Mr. Onions. Anything else I can do for you?"

"Not just now, thanks. Who's flying – Bill?"

"No, sir, Captain Anderson today."

"Oh, it's Frank. Give him my best."

"I will, sir."

She tottered off and Harry turned to me. "So, this bloke goes to the chemist and gets one of these kits and takes it home. And when he opens it up he finds it contains a pot of blue paint, a pot of red paint . . ."

"And a cricket bat," interupted Pamela. "Russ, just look at that cloud formation. Fantastic, isn't it?"

"And a cricket bat," said Harry, pulling at my arm, "Pam, I do wish you'd shut up and let me tell 'im. So this bloke is a bit flumoxed, y'see, and he goes back to the doctor and says I got one of them virgin kits but I don't know how to use it. What's the pot of blue paint, the pot of red paint and the cricket bat for? . . . oh, 'ere we go . . ."

The champagne had arrived. I've never seen such service. Harry poured out three glasses and passed two along, then took a gulp and said, "Well, says the doc, paint one of your balls blue and the other one red, and on the first night of your honeymoon, whip back the sheets . . . and if your wife says 'Coo, I've never seen a pair of bollocks that colour before . . .'"

"Smash her over the head with the cricket bat," said Pamela. "Russ, come an' look, is that the sea down there . . . ?"

"Smash 'er over the 'ead with the cricket bat." Harry sighed patiently. "Pam, 'ow many times have I told you not to finish my stories for me." He shook his head at me. "Bloody hopeless, women. Eh, did you hear the one about the three tramps – damn good one this – three tramps sitting by the side of the road, cooking sausages, just chatting away. One says to 'is mate: George, if you had ten thousand pounds, what would you do wiv it? George thinks for a minute, then says: If I 'ad ten thousand pounds I'd build meself a big, white marble hall. And in the middle of this white marble hall there'd be a white marble dais and on this dais there'd be a big, white double bed – and on this bed there'd be the most fabulous, fantastic blonde you ever saw – stark naked . . ."

"Don't forget the elephant, Harry," said Pamela. "He always forgets the elephant and spoils the story."

"Look, love, I was just going to tell you about the elephant, now shut up, for Gawdsake. And I don't always forget the

136

elephant. You always remind me about the elephant before I can mention it."

"You forgot the elephant once, Harry, and you spoilt the story."

"Once, for crissake! I forgot it once! And you remind me every time."

She said to me, "He forgot the elephant when he was telling the story to the President of the Board of Trade."

"It was the Foreign Secretary," said Harry grudgingly, "Anyway, George says, and by the side of the double bed I'd have this enormous white elephant . . ."

"Not white, Harry – the elephant was the only thing that wasn't white."

"Yeh, ordinary elephant – this enormous ordinary elephant by the double bed. And in one corner of the hall, says George, I'd have the Liverpool Philharmonic Orchestra – all dressed in white. And in the second corner – a mighty church organ, all in white. And in the third corner – a really hot jazz band, all in white. And in the fourth corner – the Luton Girls Choir, all dressed in white. Then I'd enter the hall . . . walk across the marble floor . . . up the white marble dais . . . onto the double bed . . . and onto the blonde. Then I'd shout LIVER-POOL PHILHARMONIC ORCHESTRA – START PLAY-ING! . . . MIGHTY CHURCH ORGAN – START PLAYING! . . . HOT JAZZ BAND – START PLAYING! . . . LUTON GIRLS' CHOIR – START SINGING! Then I'd turn to this big elephant and say: put your big foot in the middle of my back and beat time to *that* bleedin' lot!'"

He collapsed with laughter. Pamela was tugging at me again. "It *is* the sea, come an' look." Harry went into a coughing fit and I thought he was going to be sick. "Ooh . . ooh," he went, trying to get his breath. "Oooh, that's a good one. Always makes me laugh."

"I wish you wouldn't tell it," said Pamela. "You're going to have a heart attack one day. Russ, come and look at this little boat . . ."

Harry had me by the arm. "One I've just got to tell you – about the rabbit, the lizard and the turtle . . ."

It was like that all the way to Palma. By the time we got there – at four o'clock in the afternoon – I had a very bad case of Wimbledon neck. Still, it helped pass the time.

"Come and look us up," insisted Harry as we shook hands

on the tarmac. "We're staying at the Belle Vista this trip. We like to try 'em all. If I like it, we might buy the bugger . . ."

They went off towards Customs, Harry laughing uproariously, Pamela looking at cloud formations.

I took a deep breath of warm Majorcan air and gazed around the airfield. Well, I'd made it. I was here. An exuberance seized me. I felt excited. Treading air I headed for the main building to meet Patrick Holmes.

He spotted me – or rather the Ardmont labels on my luggage – as I left Customs with a porter.

"Russell Tobin, is it?"

The soft Irish brogue suited the man perfectly. He was an inch or two shorter than me – about five feet ten, slim, athletically built, wiry. His features were dark and handsome, his hair curly, worn long on the neck. His eyes, I noticed immediately, were an unusual shade of olive green. They were fascinating eyes, even to a man. To a woman they'd be mayhem.

He was probably a bit older than me, in his late twenties.

"Patrick Holmes," he said, holding out his hand. "Welcome. I've got me car out front." He spoke to the porter in rapid Spanish, telling him where the car was parked.

"Did you have a good flight now?" Patrick asked as we followed the porter.

"Great. I've got a stiff neck from playing conversation tennis with a scrap metal millionaire and his girl friend but apart from that . . .'

"Ha, that would be Harry Onions no doubt."

"You know him?"

"All Majorca knows Harry Onions. He makes five – six trips a year here and always lives like a king."

"That explains the treatment he got on board. He had a hostess almost to himself. We drank champagne . . ."

"That's Harry. Never drinks anything else."

"He invited me up to the Belle Vista . . ."

Patrick laughed. "Then go – I'll come with you. He's a good pal of mine. You'll have the night of your life I promise you. The girls will be thicker than flies on a hunk of old horse meat . . ."

We stowed the luggage on top of his little Seat and drove out of the airport towards Palma.

"I take it there's plenty of it here during the season, then," I said.

"What – girls?" He gave me a devilish grin. "Have you

never been to Majorca before? What a treat you've got in store, Russell. The sights you'll see before the summer's gone will keep you in wicked memories for the rest of your natural life. Big German girls with thighs of steel to crush a man to his smiling death ... and the Swedes! ... the Swedes. Sun tanned angels with long white hair and wondrous lips ..." His voice had taken on a hushed reverence. "And of course the little English roses ... and the Irish, Scots and Welsh. They all have their lovely moments. They come here in their thousands — a vast multitude of provocation thirsting for sun and sand and sea and sex. This is four-S country, for sure. It's enough to drive you blind."

I sighed dispiritedly. "Just my luck."

He looked at me, anxiously. "What is?"

"To meet a connoisseur on my first day. I was hoping you'd be a middle-aged, dedicated eunuch who'd keep reminding me of the earnestness of my calling and the dangers of straying from the professional path."

"I see," he said with mock seriousness. "So it's the tendency towards naughtiness you've got, is it." He tutted and shook his head. "That's sinful."

"Worse still, I've got a buddy coming out for the whole of June who is steadily working his way through the world's entire population of good-looking women."

He looked appalled. "Aw, the shame of it. Well, keep him well clear of me. I'll not be contaminated by such a reprobate ... now, just look at those two, would you ..."

Two young, long-haired girls in summer dresses were walking beneath the palm trees on the pavement. They glanced at the car. Patrick waved. They waved back and laughed.

"There, you see," said Patrick dolefully. "Temptation lies at every hand and the season hasn't even started yet. Remind me to get a bigger car, Russell, this dinky toy is no good for anything."

"Do you know those two?"

"Not to my certain knowledge, but alas the human memory is not entirely boundless in its capacity. I try hard, believe me, if only to avoid embarrassing moments, but there is a limit."

"You need a filing system."

"Och, I've got one of those — at least, a small library of little black books, but as the season progresses the sheer numbers defeat yuh."

We were now entering the city of Palma, travelling on a

dual carriageway ring road which followed the harbour, avoiding the city centre. The sight of the ships and boats in the harbour, the horse-drawn open carriages clopping along the wide road, and the broad palm tree-lined pavements gave me a terrific thrill. What a difference from London. The air was clean and fresh and smelled of the sea; the buildings sparkled in the late afternoon sun. I breathed in deeply and sighed, "Ah, this is terrific, Patrick."

"Aye, it's a lovely island. Palma's a nice city, too. "Would you like to learn something about them as we're driving along, now?"

"I want to know everything about them – eventually."

"Right, stand by for a wee travellogue ..." he cleared his throat dramatically. "Majorca, largest of the Spanish Balearic Islands – being 1405 square miles in area – lies one hundred miles off the coast of Spain. The population is 365,000 ..."

"That many, eh?"

"Oh, sure. 160,000 of them live here in Palma, the capital. It's not one of your piddly little places, you know. It's a fair sized city. Anyway, to continue ... Majorca's climate is excellent, it's scenery magnificent. It's history has involved Iberians, Carthaginians, Romans, Vandalls and Moors ..."

"And Irish."

"Begob, you're right, I almost forgot. In 1276 Majorca became a kingdom in its own right but in 1343 Pedron IV of Aragon made a take-over bid for it and Majorca has evermore remained tied to Spain."

"Fascinating."

"Now to Palma, a gay, bustling city of 160,000 souls and more than thirty nightclubs. The shopping is excellent and the stuff to buy – tell your future clients – is leather goods, suede, glassware and artificial pearls."

"They have bull fights here, don't they?"

He pulled a face. "Aye, every Sunday from May to September."

"And they kill the bulls?"

"Often with more enthusiasm than skill. They don't often get the top matadors here. I've been the once but never again. I think you ought to go once so you know what it's about – the clients are bound to ask. But if you're anything like me the sight of the poor thing dying will turn your stomach over. Meself, I'd rather spend a Sunday evening sitting with a pretty girl at a pavement cafe on the Plaza Gomila Terrano than watching some poor beast being slowly hounded to a bloody death. Still, that's up to you of course."

"That Plaza Whatsitsname sounds all right."

"Gomila Terrano. Och, it's lovely ... sitting in the shade on a warm summer afternoon, holding her wee hand, drinking cold beer and watching the world go by. There's nothing like it."

"Yes, I'd like to try that, Patrick. Sounds like my cup of tea."

"So you shall, my boy."

"You really like it out here, don't you?"

"I love it – just love it. Would you believe I used to work in a men's store in Dublin selling socks and ties? Well, I did, until three years ago. I'm twenty seven now and I'd worked in that damned shop – it belonged to my uncle – since leaving school at seventeen. I was supposed to take the place over eventually and he wanted me to learn the trade from the shop floor up. Russell, I died the death. Hated every blessed minute of it. There was the deuce of all rows when I left but I couldn't stand it any longer. From the moment I joined Ardmont and came out here I was a happy man. The job's not easy – the public can be a mite difficult – but once you've got into a nice routine and you've met all the problems at least once then you can have an awful lot of fun here. I swim all summer and water ski and skin dive and run around in a fast little motor boat I bought for meself – and of course there's the girls ... never a shortage of the lovely things just aching for a bit of holiday fun. It's heaven on earth, Russell. What more could a man want? When I think of the poor gumps back home travelling up to the city on the 7.55 every morning and sweating it back home on the 5.55 in the evening ..."

"You could be me talking. That's exactly how I feel."

"Which reminds me – I *am* doing all the talking. How about yourself now? How did you come to be out here ...?"

"There'll be plenty of time for that, Patrick. Just keep on talking. I want to know everything about everything – the island, the job ... the girls."

He laughed. "Sure, he's a man after me own heart. I think we'll get on famously. All right, I'll keep talking, but just tell me to shut up when you've had enough. Now, what d'you want to know first ...?"

"What place is this?"

We had now left the city behind. The road had cut inland a
141

little and we were passing through a small township of very attractive shops and cafes and bars, all new and clean and very smart. Many of them were faced with multi-coloured terrazzo and were decorated with flowers, particularly geraniums, in pots and window boxes.

"This is Cala Mayor," Patrick said. "Lovely little place. The shopping here is almost as good as in Palma."

The road continued to meander towards and away from the sea, sometimes quite far inland, at other times close enough for us to catch a glimpse of the blue water.

"Illetas," said Patrick sometime later, pointing to a forest of pine trees. "Nice quiet little place. You can't see it from here because the land drops down to the cove. Not much doing there except dancing in the hotels but there's a good bar with a nice garden."

"Do you know the whole of the island like this?" I laughed.

He shrugged modestly. "I guarantee you'll know it pretty well by the end of a month.'

We now turned left off this main road onto a secondary road, passing more shops and some villas, gaily painted places with walled gardens.

"We're coming into Palma Nova. This is my territory. I look after two hotels here – the Marbella and Don Pepe."

"Do you live in one of them?"

He laughed. "No, I've got a nice little flat right on the beach. We'll pass it in a minute."

"I've been thinking of doing that myself."

"Well, it suits me fine. Living in the hotel puts you right on top of the clients all the time and if you're seen you're available, no matter what time of the day or night. I like to get away from them some of the time. Besides ..." he grinned, "living in a hotel sort of cramps your style. Most of them are pretty broadminded but there's always the fear that the passkey will grate in the lock and a chamber-maid will burst in and catch an eyeful. The possibility of it dulls your concentration."

"How much d'you pay for your flat, Patrick?"

"Twenty-five pounds a month, fully furnished. Ardmont pay fifteen of it. I've got a good-sized bedroom, a living room with a balcony overlooking the beach, a well-equipped kitchen and a bathroom with bath and shower. I pay extra for hot water. I've got a little Majorcan girl coming in three hours a week to clean for me."

"Sounds good."

"Och, it's nice. If you want something like that for yourself you can get it with no trouble at all. Just let me know and I'll have a word with an estate agent pal of mine in Palma."

"Wonderful."

Now the road ran very close to the sea, bordered on our right by a succession of brand new, multi-storeyed hotels and rows of shops. Almost everywhere I could see construction work in progress. Huge dumper trucks laden with rubble rumbled towards us, spewing white dust. Giant cranes hauled buckets of concrete and prefabricated units into the air.

"The island's gone building balmy," said Patrick. "Five years ago there was hardly a hotel along here. Now look at it. Fifty hotels and apartment blocks must have gone up in this area in the past three years. They seem to grow out of the ground overnight."

"They all look good, though."

"Aye, thank God they've got good architects and lovely natural stone here. They look pretty enough."

The road left the sea briefly as it cut across a small promontory, then rejoined it as we entered yet another small township of hotels and shops.

"And this is your territory – Magaluf. Very nice beach here that sloped gently into the sea. And there are your hotels – the San Vincente, the Palma ... and down the road there the Pollensa. You've got a room in the Palma, haven't you. We'll get you settled in there, then I'll take you to the other two hotels to meet the managers. After that, if you like, you can come over to my place for a drink. I generally eat at one of my hotels, the Marbella, but I always keep something in the flat in case I don't want to go out. We can decide on dinner when the fancy takes us."

"What's the local entertainment like?"

"Not bad. There's flamenco dancing and singing if that's your meat – personally a little of it goes a heck of a long way with me. And there are a couple of good clubs and a disco-theque – the Whiskey Frou Frou. Och, the talent that passes through those portals during the season is beyond belief. Then, for a drop of good draught beer there's the Bar Tabu in Palma Nova ..."

"That sounds enough to be going on with."

"And, of course, it's only twenty minutes drive into Palma. Oh, by the way, what are you going to do about a car?"

143

"I'll rent one."

"Right, leave that to me, too. We'll go to the Garage Rossello where Ardmont does all its car-hire. You'll get a special rate there."

He turned into the grounds of the Hotel Palma, a forecourt beautifully landscaped with flower borders and palm trees. As we pulled up at the impressive entrance a young boy in smart brown uniform came down the steps to take the luggage.

We followed him into the cool marble-floored reception. Facing us was the bar and beyond it I could see the beach and the sea.

On reception was a young, olive-skinned chap of our age. He was dressed very formally in black suit and tie. He looked up from a drawer of cards he was searching through and grinned at Patrick.

"Top of the afternoon to yuh, Tony," said Patrick. "Greet Russell Tobin, our new rep who will grace your lovely hotel with his ebullient presence from now till October."

Tony, obviously used to Patrick's blarney, shook hands with me and said in a strong Spanish accent, "A hundred thousand welcomes, as we Paddy's say."

Patrick laughed. "Sure, you're comin' along fine. We'll make an Irishman of you yet. Is your manager in, then?"

"Yes, he is."

Tony left us, popped his head through a door behind the desk, and came back to us. "Go right in."

We went into the office through a door in the foyer. Senor Almeria, a dark, saturnine man with patent leather hair, laid down his gold fountain pen rather gravely.

Patrick said, "Good afternoon, Senor Almeria. May I introduce Russell Tobin, the Ardmont representative for Magaluf?"

Almeria rose and shook hands with a slight bow. "A pleasure, Mr. Tobin."

We talked for five minutes, pleasantly though formally. I assured him I would do my very best to keep my clients – his customers – happy and he assured me of his fullest cooperation at all times.

Then we left, collected my key from Tony, and shot up in a fast elevator to the tenth floor. As we followed the young porter along the corridor Patrick said, "Don't mind Almeria, he's a nice chap. It's just his manner. You'll find all these

144

managers a little stiff. They live very formally but they're always polite and helpful. They just seem to take life very seriously."

We entered room 1023. It was a fair-sized room with a bathroom and loo leading off, all very clean and modern. A sliding glass door led out onto a small balcony. I pulled back the door and went out with Tony and gazed out over the land at the rear of the hotel – or what we could see of it between the pressing line of hotels and apartment blocks on the far side of the road.

"What a pity," I said. "This would have been superb on the other side of the hotel."

"Aye, that's the trouble, but you'll not find one rep with a sea view. The rooms are too valuable. That's one reason why I got myself a flat. I just couldn't see the sense of letting all that water go to waste."

I nodded, making an instant decision. "Patrick, let's find me a flat, eh? I'm going to be here for eight months and I want a few home comforts."

"Right you are, me boy, consider it done."

He sat on the bed while I unpacked my clothes and hung them in the cupboard. "Some fancy old gear you've got there," he grinned. "I'm thinking you're a man of considerable property on the quiet."

"It's a long story, Patrick. I'll tell you later."

We went downstairs and as we climbed into the car, he said, "Russell, I've got a thirst like two dry camels. Let's leave the other two managers until tomorrow and drink some cold beer, what d'you say to that?"

"I say let's leave the other two managers until tomorrow and drink some cold beer."

"Och, I thought you might."

We drove back along the road to Palma Nova. Now, at six o'clock, the evening was drawing in fast. The crimson sun was falling behind us, setting the tall white buildings on fire, and a cool calm had begun to envelope the land.

We skirted the wide, shallow bay and turned off towards a new apartment block set right on the beach.

Patrick's flat was on the ground floor. He let us into a long hallway, floor-tiled in pale green terrazzo stone. All the rooms – the bedroom, the bathroom and the lounge – led off left from the hall. The kitchen was the exception. It faced us at the far end of the hall.

We went into the lounge, a lovely airy room floor-tiled the same as the hall. The furnishing was modern and comfortable. There was a dining table and four chairs, a long settee and two easy chairs, several ceramic lamps and a few seascape prints on the walls. A cotton rug added a blaze of colour to the stone floor. The facing wall was all glass, divided into four panels. Patrick drew back the centre two and we went out onto the balcony. On it were a metal table and two plastic-weave seats.

The view was magnificent – open sea to the far horizon, with the curving bay of Palma Nova to the right and a spreading arm of land stretching to infinity on the left.

"Fan-tastic," I said.

"Aye, it's a joy to sit here in the evenings, See there ..." he pointed to a mass of twinkling lights way out along the arm of land. "That's Palma, eight miles away. Sit yuh down and sniff away all you like, I'll get the beers."

I took the chair facing Palma Nova bay and breathed in the cool sea breeze. Now the sun was almost gone and stars were winking in their millions in the dark turquoise sky. Evening calm had hit the land and sea alike. The water trickled into the beach in lethargic little waves and licked the sand with a surging swish. Sitting there, fanned by the breeze, all tension slipped suddenly away. My body drooped, my eyes felt heavy, and a pleasurable shiver trickled up my back and roused the hairs on my neck.

Patrick came through with two tall glasses and bottles of iced larger and said, "Now, there's a picture of a man relaxed. What were you smiling at?"

"Patrick, you know what it's like when a girl kisses your ears, tickles your neck ...?"

"Aye, you go a bit soft in the head."

"That's what just happened to me."

He jerked the cap off a bottle and handed it to me with a glass. "This place does it to me, too. Sometimes I just sit here in the evening and marvel that life can be so beautiful. Dublin and London and all the rush and bustle are of another world and I'm very happy to keep it that way." He plonked down in the other chair and raised his glass. "Well, here's to a great summer for both of us – and I've a feeling it's going to be beautiful." We drank some beer and got cigarettes going. "I've been wondering what sort of fella they'd send out to Magaluf. Last couple of years we've had a right cold fish down here, chap named Walter Payne, Mr. Efficiency himself. One of these fellows that blows his nose by the book. Payne by name and pain by nature – doesn't drink, smokes a pipe and thinks a woman is a statistic marked female on a rooming list. You'll be meeting him on Monday. He's our area manager in Palma."

"Oh."

"Oh, don't worry, he won't bother you too much. As long as you get all your returns in on time he leaves you alone. Still, thank God I've got a man here with an affinity for the subtle pleasures in life. Now, tell me about yourself . . ."

We talked for three hours.

I told him about life in Liverpool, working for Turners Removals and Wainwrights, the builders, then Ritebuy Sewing Machines and Karefree Kredit, and finally of moving down to London and starting in commercials.

And he told me about his years of boredom and frustration in menswear in Dublin and of his three years with Ardmont. It was interesting how much we had in common and it wasn't difficult to see why we'd liked each other on sight.

"I'll never go back," he said finally. "At least not permanently. I'll always work in the sun from now on. Oh, I'll take the odd trip just to remind meself what a miserable bunch of buggers they are with their lousy weather and whiskey at three pounds a bottle and their strikes and murders and riots. Sure, there are problems wherever you live, but a quick dip in a warm sea and all this beautiful colour puts you right back on your feet again in no time." He laughed suddenly. "I'm goin' on a bit, aren't I but I think you feel the same way yourself."

"As I said before, you could be me talking."

"Then you'll love it here, Russ. Now, what's the time? God, it's after nine, you must be starving. Let's go over to the Marbella and eat, then we might drive into Palma for a look around, what d'you say?"

The huge and beautiful dining room of the Marbella was practically deserted. White-jacketed waiters hovered around, fidgetting with little jobs to kill time. Six of them served us, no less.

"Another two or three weeks and the joint will be jumping," said Patrick. "There'll be five hundred people eating in here. The hotel's only a tenth full at the moment – mostly English people, old couples, who can't stand the winter and can afford two holidays. I've only got a small handful of clients at the moment – eight in here and four in the San

147

Pedro. They're no trouble at all. Tomorrow I'm taking the old dears over the mountains to Puerto de Soller on the north coast. It's a lovely run. I think you ought to come with us. It'll give you an idea what a day excursion is like."

"Yes, I'd like that."

"The trip starts at ten thirty. We'll go to see your two other managers at nine, O.K.?"

We finished the very good dinner and drove towards Palma at an amble, not wishing to spoil our relaxed mood. As we approached the city, passing the harbour which shimmered with reflected light from the boulevard and from the ships riding at peace on a gentle swell, Patrick asked me, "How's your Spanish?"

I laughed. "Don't honestly know. I've been hammering a Linguaphone course for nearly three months. *I* think it's not too bad but God knows what a Spaniard would think."

"Would you like to try a little for ten minutes?"

"Yes, sure."

"Right, Spanish it is and not a word of English."

By the time we had parked the car and were sitting in a little bar I realised I had an awful lot of Spanish to learn; but I was pleased to be able to carry on some degree of conversation with him.

"Och, not bad at all," he said generously. "A little short on the vocabulary but the pronunciation is very fair. We'll keep on practicing from time to time. As a matter of fact you can practice a bit now and buy the drinks."

We'd been sitting there for twenty minutes, talking, idly listening to the juke-box, watching the people pass by in the square, when Patrick suddenly leapt to his feet and rushed outside. He was back a moment later with two girls. One was a small, light-weight blonde, dressed in well-cut navy blue trousers and a white, well-filled sweater. The other was a tall, aristocratic brunette in a light blue dress under a dark blue coat. Neither was ravishingly beautiful, but they were attractive and nicely tanned. Both were in their mid-twenties.

"Spotted them across the square," said Patrick, giving me a wink behind their backs. "Russell, meet two of Ardmont's finest – Anne Franklin and Jean Ford."

Jean was the little blonde.

"Ladies – Russ Tobin, Ardmont's latest acquisition for Magaluf. Sit you down. What're you drinking."

Anne Franklin, it transpired, was the resident rep at a place

148

called Camp de Mar, and Jean was the rep at Paguera, two resorts very close together and both just along the coast from Magaluf. Anne had been with Ardmont for three seasons; Jean for one.

"You doing the town?" Jean asked me.

"Just settling in. I only arrived this afternoon. Patrick is showing me around. It's all a bit strange yet."

"I know the feeling," she laughed.

She had a nice laugh.

I noticed Patrick appeared to have an affinity with Anne. A couple of times she laughed at something he said and touched his knee with a familiarity that told me she'd done it before.

"Well, now, what could be nicer," he said, turning to Jean and me. "Four of the brotherhood taking a breather before all hell let's loose. I think we ought to make a big night of it, what d'you say, girls?"

Jean looked at her watch. "It's eleven now. What did you have in mind?"

"I had in mind a little dancing for an hour or so just to get the blood circulating for the season. How does that appeal? Russell, here, was Frou Frou champion of Knotty Ash three years running and will give you the thrill of your life. Come on, now, before they all close for the night."

The girls needed no urging. Within ten minutes, in a dimly lit discotheque not unreminiscent of the Kum Kum Club though a trifle quieter and easier on the eyes, I had my arms full of little Jean. She danced passionately, arms entwined around my neck, body pressed against mine, and she danced in silence, eyes closed, fingers playing affectionately with the hair on my neck.

One time we passed close to Patrick who was similarly locked together with Anne. He spotted me and winked meaningfully although I had to wait until we were standing together in the gents before finding out what the wink meant.

"Well, how d'you like them?" he asked.

"Fine, Jean's very nice. I find Anne a bit cool."

"Aw, that's just her way. There's nothing cool about her when she gets going."

"Oh?"

"Not at all. She's as hot as wee Jean and Jean lights a fair old fire, believe me."

I looked at him.

"Sure, I've slept with them both, though not, unfortunately, at the same time."

"Yeh?"

He laughed. "The blood gets a little warm during the long summer and the girls get as agitated as anyone else. The big muscular bucks on the beach get them all worked up and ... well, there I am with the flat ..."

"Patrick ... how soon could I get a flat?"

He laughed out loud. "I daresay you could have one by the end of the week – maybe sooner. Things are quiet at present. I'll phone my estate agent pal in the morning before we go off to Soller. He may even be able to get you one in my block, I know there are several vacant. Though maybe you wouldn't fancy one so close ...?"

"I'd fancy one."

"Right, then, I'll ask him."

"What's going to happen tonight?"

"Tonight?" He thought about it. "Why – d'you fancy sleeping with Jean?"

"I don't know. I think maybe I'm too bushed, I wouldn't do her justice."

He nodded. "All right, let's be good boys tonight. We'll just see them home and get some sleep, eh? I'm feeling a little tired myself."

We left the discotheque at one o'clock and drove home under an immense full moon. It blazed down, lighting the road like day.

Jean was driving me in her car. Patrick had taken Anne. We had arranged to meet on a promontory overlooking the sea at Camp de Mar. There, when we had said our goodnights, I would transfer to Patrick's car and we would drive back to Magaluf.

Jean, sitting on my left, drove the Fiat confidently, zipping through the gears expertly along the winding coast road. She looked very attractive in profile, her tanned skin dark against the whiteness of her sweater.

She talked about her previous season with Ardmont, making me laugh with stories of terrible mix-ups at the airport when, on one occasion, all the luggage for one hotel finished up at another on the far side of the island. On another nightmare occasion a transfer of fifty people were stranded all night at the airport because of last minute engine failure.

150

"I hope you won't get that sort of problem," she said, "though I'm sure you will. I don't think there's a rep on the island who hasn't had something go drastically wrong sometime or other."

"How do the clients usually take it?"

"Oh, they vary, of course. It depends very much on how you handle them. Most of them are sympathetic and helpful but you do get the other sort who rant and rave and threaten to write to Head Office and complain. They rarely do, though, thank heaven. If they're inconvenienced at the beginning of their holiday, they've got two weeks to get over it; and if it happens at the end, they've usually had such a good time they're too relaxed to stay mad for long."

We passed through Magaluf and I pointed out the Hotel Palma where I was staying.

"Not for long though, I hope. The room overlooks this road. I want a sea view."

"Don't blame you. What are you doing about it?"

"I'm going to try to get a flat in Patrick's block. He's speaking to an estate agent tomorrow."

"I spent last season in the hotel in Paguera," she said. "This year I've got a flat. The same thing happened to me – I got a room overlooking a pine tree. I found it maddening to know the sea was so close and I couldn't see it. And besides, clients were knocking on my door at midnight asking about excursions for the following day. There was no privacy. Now if they want me they've got to telephone first and that's a bit too much trouble for them unless it's urgent."

"What about Anne, has she got a flat?"

"Yes, in Camp de Mar. Most of the reps have flats. For one thing, no matter how good the hotel food is you get fed up with it sometimes and it's nice to cook something for yourself – and have a few friends in for a drink. There's a big danger in this job of never being able to get away from it. We all realise it's a seven-day week job but it doesn't have to be twenty four hours a day too. You've got to have a bit of freedom."

"How far is Paguera from here?"

"Only three miles. Camp de Mar is six miles beyond that."

"Patrick tells me Majorca's a beautiful island."

"It is. The mountains are adorable. They're not all that high but some of the views are breathtaking."

"I'm going there tomorrow. He's taking a bus-load of old dears to Soller."

"You'll love it. Puerto de Soller is very picturesque, surrounded by mountains. I love doing that trip."

We were now entering yet another shopping centre. Here as everywhere else I'd seen, the shops were new and very attractively dressed.

"This is the main street of Paguera," Jean said. "The Carratera de Andraitz."

"The Majorcans are awfully good at this mosaic work, aren't they? They really seem to care how their buildings look."

Towards the end of the main street Jean pointed towards the sea, towards an apartment building barely visible through a thin forest of pines.

"That's where I live, down by the beach."

"What's the beach like?"

"Lovely – nice clean sand."

"I'd like to see it."

"What – now?"

"Mm, sure."

"All right," she laughed. "I don't suppose the others will miss us too drastically."

She turned off the main road and drove along an approach road between the pines and stopped the car in the forecourt of the apartment block. Then we walked into the pines and along a narrow wooded path towards the beach.

I slipped my arm around her waist and she hugged me. "Just look at that moon," she said.

We stopped and stared at it. It blazed down brilliantly between the pines from a cloudless sky.

"Just listen," I said.

We stood absolutely still. A gentle breeze murmured through the trees, barely moving the branches. It smelled strongly of pine and of the sea.

"D'you hear it?" I whispered.

"What?"

"Nothing. Absolute silence. No jets screaming ... no cars ... no people ... everybody's gone. We've got the world to ourselves."

She chuckled. "What a lovely thought."

We went on down the path, hearing the swish of the sea as

we neared the beach, then we broke from the trees and stopped, astounded by the sight of the shimmering tail of moonlight on the black water. For quite a while we just stood there, breathing the soft, perfumed air, listening to the steady, soothing sigh of the sea.

"Can you tell me," I said at last, "why I've wasted so much of my life in cities ... in a cold climate? I should've done this years ago. Do you ever get tired of the sun and the sea, Jean?"

"Oh, occasionally, I suppose. I miss my family now and again and feel a sudden yearning to be back home but it's not very often. In any case, I spend four months of the year in London. That's enough."

"Where d'you live in London?"

"Putney – not far from the bridge."

"Slight difference, isn't there – between this and Putney?"

"Yes, slight," she laughed. "Would you like to paddle?"

"Mm? Yes, sure."

"The water's cold yet but I often walk in it at night time, with the beach all to myself."

We stripped off shoes and socks and rolled our trousers up and walked through the cool sand to the water's edge. I dipped a toe in. It was freezing. Jean laughed and pushed me further in. After a minute it seemed warmer. Then, with our arms around each other, we strolled through the shallows for perhaps a mile, gazing at the huge stars, looking at the hotels, watching the play of moonlight on the rippling sea talking about Majorca and the job.

Towards the end of our return walk, close to the apartments, Jean suddenly shivered. "I'm a bit chilly. It's the cold water. I think we'd better go in and dry our feet. Would you like some coffee?"

"Sounds wonderful."

"Come on, I'll race you up the beach ..." And she was off, running like a hare, throwing up sand behind her.

I let her win.

She let us into the apartment. It was so similar in design to Patrick's it could have been built by the same people and probably was. She pointed at the bathroom. "Put some hot water in the bath and wash the sand off while I make the coffee."

As I sat on the side of the bath soaking my feet I wondered what would happen now. Patrick, I supposed, would realise the plan had changed and would leave it to me to get home under my own steam. I now felt fine, no longer tired. The walk in the water had done the trick. I felt anything *but* tired.

As I dried my feet I heard music coming from the lounge. Jean came into the bathroom, sat on the bath and dangled her feet in the water, swishing off the sand.

"Coffee's ready, it's in the lounge."

"Here, let me have a foot."

I dried her feet and tickled them. After this horseplay we went barefoot into the lounge. Tom Jones, in romantic mood, was coming quietly from a portable record player.

"The radio here is terrible," Jean said. "You can only get foreign language stations and you know what that means – ten minutes of gabble to one minute of music, so I brought my record player this time."

"He's too good to be ignored," I said, opening my arms. She came into them, holding me as she'd done in the discotheque, only more so. After a minute she said, "Let's dance in the moonlight."

She broke away, turned off the lights, drew back the curtains covering the balcony door and led me out. Bathed in the brilliant moonlight we clung together. She massaged my neck and I could feel her breasts begin to rise and fall more urgently against me. I let my hand stray towards her left breast. I placed it there, squeezing it gently.

"You're naughty," she murmured, slipping her hands under my jacket to massage my spine.

I dropped my hand to the hem of her sweater and went up underneath. Her skin was warm, soft as silk. She had nothing on. I cupped her breast and suddenly she kissed me, passionately, pulling on my neck. She bit my lip, searched my mouth with her tongue, and her hand came down to rub my thigh. Then she stiffened against me.

"Russ . . ." she gasped.

"Mm?"

"Let's do it here . . . in the moonlight."

She broke away and went quickly indoors, emerging a moment later with three cushions from the settee. She threw them down on the balcony. In one quick movement she had her sweater off and in another she was standing before me naked. I was only a moment behind her. She reached for me, melted into me. Her body was hot and trembling. Taking my hand, she lay down on the cushions and drew me down beside

154

her. We clung together, kissing, for only a moment before she opened her legs and drew me over her.

"Don't move just yet," she gasped. She was shivering beneath me, from the cold air or from excitement, maybe both. I knew she was looking at the full moon over my shoulder. "Oh, this is wonderful," she breathed. "It's so beautiful." She made a sudden jerking movement and gasped, "The moonlight and the sea give it something ... extra. It's so exciting ...!"

Her legs came up quickly to grip me hard. Her hands tightened on my back. I sensed her rushing to a quick finish.

"Russ ..." she gasped. "Come ... come ... !"

She thrust out her legs; her body arched beneath me and a cry, a subdued cry escaped from her. Breath gushed from her as she relaxed, "Oh, that was wonderful ... wonderful ..."

We lay quite still until the chill night breeze caused me to shiver. She rubbed my back to warm me.

"We'd better go in," she said.

I helped her to her feet and she came against me, throwing her arms around me. "Take me to bed. I'll drive you to Magaluf early."

I was in bed when she came into the moonlit room from the bathroom. She scrambled in and snuggled up against me, shivering. "Oh, that's lovely ... you're so warm."

I stroked her gently and held her until she had warmed enough to stretch out her legs and relax, then we lay on our backs and looked at the swathe of moonlight on the ceiling.

"That's the first time I've made love in the moonlight," she said. "Actually looking at the moon. It was wonderful. Funny – how different circumstances can vary the enjoyment."

"Variety is the spice of love."

"I'd like to do it on the beach one night – and in the sea."

"That'd be fun."

"Will you do it with me in the sea sometime?"

"Sure, just say when."

"Later on – when it gets warm."

"It'll have to be warm," I laughed. "I wouldn't be able to find him."

"I'll find him. You couldn't lose *him* easily."

She slid her hand down and stroked him.

"Are you keen on getting any sleep tonight?" I asked.

"Why?"

"Because if you carry on like that I almost guarantee you won't get any."

She giggled and kept stroking. "You're going to have a very hectic season, you know that?"

"Oh, why?"

"Because you're going to be chased by half the girls on your transfers."

"Oh, only half? What about the other half?"

"They'll be married. You'll have your work cut out accommodating the single ones. It'll need some clever planning to fit them all in."

"I'll also need a course in vitamin injections."

"I've got a feeling you'll cope, somehow."

"I suppose I'll have to. Don't forget – it's my duty to 'remember at all times that I have been chosen to . . .'"

"'. . . render a service to our clients,'" she finished for me. "Yes, I've often wondered how far Ardmont expect us to go with that one. I've been half expecting some of the dirty old men to throw that phrase at me when I've been ducking fumbling fingers."

"They try it on, then, hm?"

"Constantly. 'My dear, you've been so frightfully helpful – you must have a little drink with me. Say – my room in ten minutes?'"

"I can't say I blame them. I'd try it on myself."

She laughed and squeezed me. "I'd let *you*."

She threw a leg across me, crawled on top and lay there, looking down at me, tracing my mouth with her finger, then she kissed me once, twice, three times. "I'm not going to bother you. If I don't see you, I don't see you. We'll both be very busy. But don't desert me altogether, will you? Ring me and say hello now and again. I want us to be good friends. And don't forget – when the sun gets to you and you're feeling fruity, don't waste time looking for it. It'll always be here."

"You're very nice."

"I'm very selfish."

She kissed me again and rolled to my side. "I'll set the alarm for seven. You'll be at your hotel by eight, all right?"

"Fine – but won't they be a bit suspicious – me coming in at eight in the morning?"

"No, they're very broadminded. What you do is your business."

"Very civilised."

"Very. Here they regard sex as a natural part of life, not as a dirty adjunct to it."

"*Very* civilised."

She kissed me again and turned around, taking my hand to her breast. "Here endeth your first day. What's your opinion of the job so far?"

"You know, I think I'm going to like it. Yes, I definitely think I'm going to like it."

CHAPTER TEN

The sun went off before the alarm clock. I awoke staring down at the green tiled floor and for a moment thought I was looking at green English fields from an aeroplane. Another few inches and I'd have fallen off the bed.

Pushing myself further on, my behind touched another. Jean woke up as I turned. The covering sheet was down at our feet, but not in the least did she mind being seen completely naked. She smiled, blinking at the strong sunlight, and popped me on the nose.

"Morning."

"Morning."

"You have a golden halo around your head."

"Very fitting," I said, "I *feel* saintly."

She chuckled.

"What time is it?" I asked.

She stretched for the alarm clock and squinted at it. "It's seven. I'm glad it didn't go off. I hate being shattered awake. Much nicer to be touched."

I leaned across and kissed her stomach, tickled it with my tongue. She laughed and brought her knees up. Then I kissed her breast. The large dark nipple rose instantly. "Hey" ... she looked at me in a strange, direct way. My pulse raced. She reached for me, kissing me furiously. In the next moment we were making love, frantically, with all the strength that a good sleep in the fresh air can bring to waking. I felt like a giant, endlessly durable, and it communicated to her, exciting her to volcanic passion. It was over quickly, but duration was not important. It was what we both wanted and the intensity was incredible. We lay bathed in perspiration, panting noisily. "Wow!" she gasped. "Oh! That finished me for the day."

"How about me? I've got to climb mountains!"

She laughed and flopped her hand on the bed. "Oh, that was wonderful. What a way to start the day."

After a while, when she had calmed, she said, looking beyond me to the sea and sky, "It's a very beautiful day. You'll enjoy your drive to Soller. The mountains will be wonderful."

158

"I wish you were coming with us."

"So do I. But we'll do it sometime – before the season ᵥ over."

We showered and had a quick breakfast of fruit juice and corn flakes on the balcony. The sun dazzled us off the sea and the air was cool and incredibly fresh. I breathed huge lungfuls of it. I couldn't get enough of it.

Jean laughed at me. "You'll burst."

"I'm starved for it. In London I take the smallest breaths possible. This stuff is pure ozone. It certainly makes you sleep very well."

"It also appears to make *you* waken very well. Come on, alarm clock, I must get you back to the hotel."

Just after eight o'clock I walked into the foyer of the Hotel Palma. Tony was not on duty. Another young fellow about my age shook hands when I introduced myself and handed me the key, expressing no surprise, either by word or look, that I'd wandered in at that time of the morning needing a shave.

When I had shaved and changed my clothes I walked down to Palma Nova. I strode along the road feeling marvellously well. A sunny morning anywhere puts me in a good mood but this new environment and the sight of the sea filled me with sense of supreme well-being.

Patrick answered his door sipping a cup of coffee.

"Aha! The prodigal returns. Come in. Where did you get to, as if I didn't know. It's written all over your face. Come in and have some coffee."

The table on his balcony was set for breakfast.

"I've had breakfast," I said, "but I'll have some coffee."

"You've had breakfast, have yuh? I'll lay safe money it wasn't served to you in the Hotel Palma." He handed me the coffee with a grin. "Was I not right about the darlin' girl? Is she or is she not something to write home about?"

"Nobody at home would believe it."

He cackled a laugh. "Lovely, lovely. I'm glad your first day on the island was successful. Begin as you intend carrying on, is what I say, and I can see you fully intend carrying on."

"Er, what time did you get home, Patrick?"

He looked at his watch. "Half an hour ago, if that. She's a very demanding lady, is Anne. Bejez, I could do with a couple of hours sleep but it'll have to wait. Maybe I'll squeeze a couple in the bus at Soller when the old dears are having a

nd. Now, as soon as you've had your coffee we'll
ound to the San Vincente and the Pollensa and bid
agers hello. Then we'll call Carlo about the flat and
clients into the mountains. It'll be lovely trip today,
as a bell."

"Yes, so Jean said."

He raised his brow. "Oh, you got around to talking, did you?"

"She's a very nice girl, Patrick."

"So she is. Well, it looks as though you've got your boot nice and firmly in the door there and it couldn't happen to a nicer fella. We'll see about that flat and get you comfortably bedded down. That's one of them up there, by the way ..." he pointed to a balcony on the second floor, two apartments away from ours. "And there are two or three more further along. I'll get Carlo down to show you around."

At nine o'clock we went to the San Vincente, a gigantic fifteen storey hotel with two dining rooms and four bars. Having presented myself to Senor Brunay, a reserved, charming man, we then went along the road to the Pollensa, a smaller hotel though still ten storeyed, and I presented myself to Senor Millor, another reserved, charming man.

"Well, that's that," said Patrick as we descended the steps into the sunlight. "Duty done – now let's call Carlo."

He used a public telephone in a bar across the road, speaking such rapid Spanish I had difficulty in following him. He finished with a flurry of "Si ... si"s and glanced at his watch. "Si, Carlo, muchas gracias."

He put down the phone, shaking his head and grinning. "He's a keen boy, is Carlo. He's jumping in his car this minute. He'll be here in twenty minutes. He says he's got three flats vacant – the one I pointed out to you and two others on the third floor. You can have any one you like."

"Marvellous."

"It's half past nine now. He'll be here before ten – so that'll give us half an hour to look over the flats."

"I can't believe things are working out so well. Something's got to go wrong in a minute."

He laughed. "That's British training making you talk like that. You're subconsciously expecting this to take at least ten days – if it ever gets done at all because of strikes or forms to fill in or Government permission being required, isn't it so?"

I grinned. "Something like that."

160

"I know the feeling well. It takes some getting over. Och, I know some things are slow here but not where money is involved. Look around you – at the building going on. Can you imagine anything happening this fast in the old country? It takes them a year to widen a hundred yards of road because they've got no incentive to go faster. I tell you, you'll probably be sleeping in your own flat tonight if I know Carlo."

"Tonight!"

"Sure and why not? You give Ardmont as a reference and pay your first month's rent and Bob's your uncle, you're in. They've done it for us reps before many a time."

We drove back to Patrick's flat to wait for Carlo. He appeared precisely at ten to ten, a small, very dapper Majorcan with a pencil moustache and polished black hair.

He talked incessantly in machine-gun Spanish, pointing out the features of his three ultra-fine apartments which were identical apart from their positions in the building. There was little to choose between them. It was all over in twenty minutes. I chose the one on the second floor.

"A wise choice," Carlo said to me, in slower Spanish, realising I was a novice. "It saves the legs and does not leave the girls breathless." He beamed at me, displaying a mouthful of huge teeth.

"When can I move in?" I asked him.

He shrugged, mystified. "! Ahora esta bien! Right now!"

Patrick grinned at me. "What did I tell you? He's a man of the moment, is Carlo."

Carlo whipped a contract out of his briefcase, hastily filled in my details, and presented it to me for signature.

"It's all right," Patrick said to me in English. "It's the same as mine. You're bound to a month's notice, that's all. You pay a month's rent in advance plus a tenner deposit against breakages."

I signed the contract, wrote out a cheque on the Spanish bank in Magaluf for the equivalent of thirty five pounds, took the key from Carlo, shook his hand and it was done.

"You wish the telephone, of course," he said. "I will arrange that you may use it from tonight."

When Carlo had left, Patrick and I went around the flat once again. Apart from the colour scheme it was the same as his. It smelled a bit musty but that would go when the windows were opened.

"Well, there you are – quick and painless," said Patrick.

"A home of your own. God Bless all who enter – or perhaps God *help* all who enter might be more appropriate.

"Thanks very much, Patrick."

"Aw, t'was nothing at all. You'll have to let our area office in Palma know about this immediately and send a memo with eighty five copies to Head Office and they'll probably have a dozen fits and tell you you should've notified them first of your intentions and waited for their confirmation, but just plead the ignorance you're entitled to on your first day, don't mention Patrick Holmes, and they'll forgive you. Now, come on, let's take the old things to Soller.

*

It was a fabulous day, as Jean had predicted. I sat up front with Patrick in the thirty-seater sight-seeing coach, listening to his commentary on the excursion. He had a way with him, this Irishman, and charmed the twelve elderly English people – six married couples – with his wit and humour, getting them laughing before we left Palma Nova. By the time we got back at five in the evening all the old girls were in love with him.

We drove from Palma Nova to Palma at eleven o'clock, then turned onto the inland road to Vaildemosa, an ancient mountain village where Chopin and George Sand spent a winter in a monastry, stopped there briefly to let the clients stretch their legs, then on through the rugged, purple-hazed mountains, down the twisting mountain road, and through the lush Soller valley. Here we sat at a pavement restaurant overlooking the placid harbour and lazed for a couple of hours in the sun over lunch.

I said to Patrick, whose eyes were constantly closing, "Is this a typical tour? Are the clients always this easy?"

"The wee kids get a bit irritable on some of the trips but they usually go pretty smoothly. It all depends on yourself."

"You've got this bunch nicely hypnotised. They're loving it."

He grinned. "There's nothing more boring than a straight commentary of facts. You'd have the clients yawning in no time. A few little jokes and a bit of a flirt does the world of good. Get the facts over, by all means, but give 'em a bit of a giggle and they think they're having a wonderful time."

"Who writes your scripts for you?"

"Sure, it's a good thing the clients don't take more than one trip to the same place or they'd hear the same corny old jokes over and over again. I've been rehearsing for three years so they ought to be good."

"Why don't you put your head down in the bus for an hour before you fall off that chair and into the harbour?"

"If you can keep an eye on things I think I will. I must have an early night tonight, I must . . . I must . . ."

He wandered off, yawning.

But of course he didn't have an early night. It was after five o'clock when we disembarked the clients (who all insisted on shaking his hand and thanking him for a wonderful day), and then he came with me to the Hotel Palma to tell Tony I'd be moving out immediately and into the flat.

We loaded my cases into the car and drove to the flat. By seven o'clock I was all packed away and we were sitting on my balcony drinking a beer that Patrick had gone out to buy, together with a few groceries, while I was hanging up my clothes.

"Well, here y'are," he said, "all settled in and raring to go."

"It's the quickest move I've made in my life."

"And I hope it's one of the best. With a comfortable H.Q. you can put up with all sorts of problems during the day. Nothing seems so bad if you can put your feet up on the rail here, drink a beer and look at the sea." He took another swig and said, "You know, I think a little celebration is called for, what d'you say? You just can't move into a new place without wetting the furnishings and fittings."

"What about your early night?" I laughed.

"Aw, I feel fine. That hour in the bus did the trick. Let's call the girls and have a little party, what d'you say?"

"I say let's call the girls and have a little party."

"I thought you might."

He leapt from his seat and went to the phone in the lounge. "It's on!" he called. "Aw, that Carlo . . ." He dialled a number. "Is it the lovely Jean, then" he laughed. "The boy's moved into his new pad, number 26, and wants yourself and Anne to see it. What are you doing this minute? Och, the thought of it . . . well, love, dry everything thoroughly but quickly and get the gorgeous lot over here quick as you like. And could you bring your records? We'll cook you something later on. Where's Anne? Right, I'll call her right now. G'bye."

He rang off and called through, while he was dialling the

163

second number, "She was just out of the shower ... standing there stark naked and dripping water all over the floor. The mind boggles. She'll be here in half an hour ... hello, Anne, darlin', it's me. What are you doing right now? Well, save it for tomorrow and get over here for a wee celebration. Russ has got himself a new home, number 26, and is just dyin' to cook you dinner. Right, angel, soon as you can."

He put down the phone and came through, rubbing his hands with glee. "Aw, that's lovely ..."

"Patrick, I can't cook ... !"

"Never mind that. I'll make you all a paella like you've never tasted before. Come on, we'll nip down to the supermarket and get some shrimps and chicken and peppers ..."

What began as a small intimate celebration for four, finished as a full-blooded party for twenty. It was all Patrick's doing. He seemed to know everybody in Magaluf and Palma Nova. Before we'd left the supermarket we'd invited, through Patrick, the local taxi proprietor and his wife, the supermarket owner and his, a retired English real estate agent who lived in Magaluf and a widow who owned a local gift shop.

"Hope you don't mind, Russ," he said as we left the shop. "But they're all lovely people and it'll do you good to know them."

"I don't mind at all," I laughed. "But what about food? You can't cook for all that crowd."

"Aw, sure I can. I just make twice as much. Paella's dead easy."

On the way back to the car we met – and Patrick invited – a nice-looking girl who worked in the local car-hire office and her girl friend who ran a hair-dressing salon in one of the hotels. We then went back to the supermarket for more shrimps and chicken.

The other eight people at the party were Patrick's neighbours in the block who happened to be walking on the beach and were invited in or had come down to see what the noise was all about.

Anyway, it was a great party. Nobody got drunk and they went home reasonably early, and Patrick was right when he said it would do me some good. For one thing I spoke mostly Spanish and by the end of the evening I was chatting away and looking for a chance to speak it.

Apart from that I began to feel I now belonged to the community. I'd received eight invitations from the people who lived in the block to drop in one evening for a drink and the supermarket owner promised me ten per cent reduction on everything I bought there. The widow told me she'd be delighted to see me in her gift shop, implying – without actually saying – that if I had thirty clients with me she'd be thirty times as delighted and my patronage would not go entirely unnoticed.

The young birds from the car-hire and the hairdressing salon politely and guardedly implied the same thing, though what sort of reward they had in mind I couldn't think. I made a mental note to ask Patrick about that.

He, of course, was in his element, dressed in a chef's apron, serving steaming paella from the kitchen, drinking beer and talking the whole time. He didn't kiss the Blarney Stone, he'd swallowed huge chunks of it.

At last he closed the door on the last guest and came back to us with a grin, peeling off his apron. "Well, how was that for a small housewarming? By tomorrow Russell Tobin will be known the length and breadth of the island."

"I don't know why you're taking your apron off," said Anne. "There's the washing up to do."

"I was thinkin' how much prettier it would look on you, sweetness and light."

Anne and Patrick left us about one o'clock on Monday morning. At the door I thanked Patrick for organising the party.

"Aw, nothing at all. I enjoyed meself. Come down to my place at eight tomorrow morning and we'll go to area office in Palma. There'll be rooming lists to check with hotels and a hundred bits an' pieces. Goodnight, now."

Jean and I sat close together on the balcony drinking a final cup of coffee and looking down on the moonlit sea. Now, after the noise of the party, the peace was indescribable; only the gentle soughing of the sea against the sand disturbed the silence.

"Tired?" she asked.

"A bit. I feel marvellous, though, so relaxed. I haven't had so much sun and fresh air since last summer. My whole body is tingling."

"I know, it's a wonderful feeling. And wait until you're swimming every day – it's almost payment enough for doing the job, without the money."

"I'm very glad I came."

165

"So am I – very glad you came."

She was looking at me, wanting very much to be kissed. I got up and she came up with me, wrapping her arms around me, offering her mouth. I could feel her heart thudding beneath her thin dress. She broke away from the kiss, saying softly, "How's the bed? Is it comfortable?"

"Don't know . . . haven't tried it yet."

"Shall we risk it?"

After that night I didn't see Jean for a month. The next evening, at ten o'clock, her first clients arrived at Palma airport and for her the season had begun.

I telephoned her during those weeks and made several dates but each time she had to cancel because of some emergency or other. And Patrick fared little better with Anne. On one occasion, three days after the party, he put down the phone and shrugged. "Nope, she's got a sick woman on her hands. Sounds serious. She's waiting for the doctor now. Ah, well – that's the courier business. We don't get paid for sleeping around."

But to return to the morning after the party – Monday morning. Patrick drove me into Palma and we got to the area office at nine. It was an attractive place with an abundance of terrazzo stone-work and tropical plants I had now seen so many times.

Three young female Majorcan typists were already hard at work, clattering away. They looked up as we went in and fluttered their eyes at Patrick who blew them all a kiss and called, sotto voce, "Mornin', me darlin's!"

A thin-faced young man, also a Majorcan, was at work on the counter. Patrick said to him, "Good morning, Alberto. Is he in?", nodding towards a door with "Manager" painted on it.

"Yes. You'd like to see him?"

"Not by choice but by necessity," Patrick whispered.

Alberto smiled conspiratorily and went to knock on the door. He came back nodding. "Go on in."

Walter Payne, the area manager, was small, stocky, and English, the prissy, overgrown schoolboy type of fellow who, back home, plays field-hockey furiously on Saturday afternoons, swills pinters with the chaps in the clubhouse afterwards, and never gets the front of his hair cut. It hangs down in a great clumpy wave to one side of his face and he irritates you beyond endurance by pushing it back every five seconds. I hated him on sight.

He shook hands unsmilingly and limply and drawled, "Glad you got here, Tobin." He waved his pipe at a couple of chairs, sat down, stuck the pipe in his mouth, and sorted through a hundredweight of papers. "Right," he said eventually, "got your bearings down there in Magaluf? Hotel accommodation all right?"

"I, er, I'm not staying at the hotel. I've moved into a flat."

There was a short, shocked silence before he looked up at me. "Mm?"

"I didn't like the hotel room. I've moved into a flat in Patrick's block."

"When?" he snapped.

"Last night."

"On whose authority?"

Right, I thought, this is where we sort each other out for all time. Give this type of man half an inch and your life is just not worth living. I didn't need this job; I didn't have to take any guff from Mr. Walter Payne. I could belt him on the jaw and fly home on the next plane. It was a wonderful feeling.

"With no one's permission, Mr. Payne. I didn't like the room so I moved, it's as simple as that. Philip Ardmont told me in London I had a choice – the hotel or a flat – and I've chosen a flat."

"Yes, but you do realise that Ardmont will be contributing to the rent and therefore need to be notified. And that we also need to officially notify the Hotel Palma that you will no longer be staying with them."

"All of which would take ten days," I said, touching Patrick's foot.

"Quite possibly. The notification would have to go to London, processed, and then returned here. But that's not important . . ."

"It is to me. The flat I wanted might well have been let by then."

"And that would have been too darned bad, Tobin, but there is a procedure to follow, in this as in everything else. We can't have sixteen representatives just taking the law into their own hands . . ."

"Look, Mr. Payne, let's not exaggerate. I'm not about to embark on a programme of anarchy designed to demolish the Ardmont procedure system. All I've done is move my room.

Pretend I'm still at the hotel and that I've just now notified you of wanting a flat. If Ardmont is out of pocket between now and when the confirmation comes through, then I'll pay."

He glared at me. His hands were shaking. "I don't like your attitude," he said with ominous quiet. "You've made a bad start."

Patrick cleared his throat. "Walter, it was all my fault . . ."

"It was not Patrick's fault," I interrupted. "He told me Ardmont would need to confirm the flat, I took it on impulse."

Payne looked at both of us, tight-lipped. "I'm . . ." He swallowed what he was going to say. "Send me the details of the flat, Tobin, and I'll submit the application." He slung some papers at me. "Here are your rooming lists for your first transfer this Saturday. Check them with two hotels involved and return them to Head Office on Monday next with your weekly returns. All right, that's all."

Out on the street Patrick whistled and laughed, "Boy, you gave it to him. I thought he was going to choke."

"Officious prick. I've run up against men like him all my life, Patrick, but fortunately I don't have to take it any more."

"Good for you. I think he'll treat you with more respect in the future – though I also think he'll be waiting for the chance to pounce on you."

"That's just fine with me. I'll do the job to the best of my ability and if it's not good enough for Ardmont I'll pack it in. One thing I'm not going to do is lose any sleep over that pipe-sucking ponce."

"That's the stuff. The eejet never got over his promotion to manager. He was, as I told you, a dry son of a bitch before, but now he's quite beyond hope. There's not a rep on the island that likes him. And while I'm thinking of it – thanks for taking the blame in there. I didn't mind taking it but it was nice of you all the same. Come on, we'll go and see the Garage Rossello while we're here and fix you up with a car."

I hired a Mercedes, though not a very pretentious model. It was five years old. But the interior was clean and the engine sounded good. After we had completed the transaction Patrick, standing on the pavement while I warmed the engine up, looked around the interior and said, "Aw, you've got yourself a nice car – bags of leg room and a good back seat. I'd have the divil's own job executing anything subtle in mine. Now, don't forget to drive on the right-hand side of the road, for God's sake. You go and check your rooming lists and I'll have a peep at me dear clients and I'll see you back at my flat for a beer before lunch, O.K.?"

I got back to Magaluf without mishap – I'd already done a bit of right-hand driving in Portugal when I spent that disasterous three weeks making commercials there – and I checked the lists with the hotels.

There were sixteen people on my first transfer, a nice little bunch to cut my teeth on. Ten were to be accommodated at the San Vincente; six at the Pollensa. The flight was due in at five past ten Saturday night. I studied the names on the lists, looking for the single girls. There was a Mr. and Mrs. *and* Miss McLeish staying at the San Vincente, and a Miss Thompson and a Miss Lowndes at the Pollensa. No ages given but all over twenty one.

I joined Patrick on his balcony, opened a beer and watched the sea kiss the beach.

"Another month, me boy," he said, "and that beach will begin to fill. Another two months and you'll not see too much sand at all. And from July on ..." he sighed longingly, "... it'll be one great heaving mass of gorgeous brown pulchritude, one vast, undulating mirage of noddy. Every conceivable size, shape and inclination will be lying there, basting itself with suntan oil, or running through the warm water, tits flying in the breeze, little bums wobbling like jellies. Aw, the thought of it. I must get me binoculars fixed. I dropped them in the sand last year and broke a lens, me hands were shaking so much."

"I reckon, Patrick, that if we had a good stout pole with a noose on the end we could lassoo them and whip them over the balcony here before their mothers missed them."

"Sure, there's no need to spend your strength doing that. All you've got to do is whistle."

"Looks like it's going to be a long, hot summer, Patrick."

"It'll be hot all right – there hasn't been a cool one yet. But keep away from the married ones if you can possibly help it. They're trouble you don't need to bring upon yourself." He smiled, reminiscing. "There was one down here two years ago, an English girl, nice little thing with three young kids, though you'd never believe she was old enough to have them. She was here with an au pair; her husband was going to join her after her first week.

"I met her with some friends in the bar along the road one evening and we took to each other straight away, though

169

knowing about the kids and the husband, I didn't push it. Well, we said goodnight in the bar and I came on home here, and within a few minutes she was knocking on the door, inviting herself in for a coffee. Russell, within ten minutes we were going at it like a couple of alley cats and when she hit her climax I thought I was going to have a corpse on my hands. She went berserk – crying and gasping for breath and staring up at the ceiling as though she was about to die of apoplexy. Then, after a while, she told me – it was her very first climax. She'd never had one in her life! Three kids, mind you, and never come before. I've heard of such things happening but I'd never met a case personally.

"She told me her husband was a one-minute merchant, no patience, no thought for her. Wham, bam and thank you, mam. Terrible shame. Do those fellas not know the true beauty of the thing is making the woman climb up the wall and across the ceiling?"

"Apparently not," I said.

"Well, the point of the story is I couldn't get rid of her. The au pair was looking after kids all day and everywhere I went I kept bumping into this woman – accidentally on purpose. And every night she was knocking on the door and demanding the same again. It got very difficult – especially when one night she told me she'd never be able to sleep with her husband again."

"Uh uh."

"Yes, quite – very tricky."

"How did you get out from under?"

"I told her I was going away for a week – to the far side of the island. It wasn't nice having to creep about the place, constantly on the look-out for her. But I think she finally saw reason and kept away. I saw her once, during the second week, on the beach with her husband. Big, strapping fellow he was. Should have been giving her all the satisfaction she wanted. I felt like taking him aside and giving him a tip or two."

"Have you had any other narrow squeaks?"

"Oh, yes," he laughed. He shook his head. "There was a big German girl last year – staying at the Palma Hotel. Gob, she just loved it – anyway you liked – backwards, forwards, upside down and hanging from the curtain rail. Anytime of the day or night. Well, she was booked in as *Miss* Gerta Holstein so I was quite happy to oblige the dear lady. Wonderful figure she had ... big breasts and long, terrible long legs. She'd wrap them around you and damn-near break your back.

"Then, after a couple of days, a fella arrives on the scene, old enough to be her father – or even her grandfather. He must've been seventy, very distinguished-looking German, arrived in a chauffeur-driven Rolls Royce and booked into the Palma also. That night she's around here for her usual nightcap and not a blind word does she say about knowing this old chap. Next day she's sporting the most terrible black eye you ever saw – livid purple and as big as your fist. And I get a quick visit from the chauffeur who's as big as Henry Cooper and eight times as mean. He tells me to leave this bird alone and not allow her into the flat again – or else. Frightened the living daylights out of me."

"You don't know who the old fellow was?"

"Name of Gunter. Big industrialist, I heard. Rich as Croesus. Looked to me as though she'd run away from him and he'd come tumbling after, trying to persuade her to go back to him, though he'd need to be a lot fitter than he looked to satisfy that galloping big sexpot."

"Point taken. I'll stay clear of husbands and sugar granddaddies."

"Watch out for jealous boy-friends, too" he laughed.

"Oh, no – more trouble?"

"I was sitting at a pavement cafe, just down the road, one warm summer night last year, minding me own business, in fact I was reading the paper, when two people come and sit at the next table. The girl was gorgeous, blonde, tanned as brown as your hat, really built. The boyfriend was a drip of the first water, a regular Walter Payne, English, prissy and white. She rounded on him and told him in Swedish English to piss off and stop annoying her. He, being the twit he was, started whining for another chance, but she was adamant and told him he wasn't going to spoil the last night of her holiday like he'd spoilt quite a few of the others. Anyway, after a while he slunk away with his tail between his legs.

"What a terrible thing, I said to her, to end your holiday with a flaming row. Would she take a drink to console her sweet self. Yes, she said, she would. And she took another and another and another – the last one being here in the flat – and she finished her holiday on a high note of glorious abandon, shaking the pictures on the wall and zinging the bedsprings as lyrically as a zither solo in a Russian jam session. Well, I drove her out to the airport next day and was saying a fond farewell to her in the foyer when who should pop up but the boyfriend. He started screaming and shouting at us louder than if he'd caught his balls on barbed wire. Up storm the airport police and the airport management and before you know it half of Majorca knew I'd screwed his girlfriend on the last night of her holiday. Fortunately I was able to tip the wink to the airport manager, who I know like my own brother, and he tipped the wink to the chief of airport police, who *is* his brother, and the girl disappeared through the barrier as though by magic. I disappeared into the manager's office and Sonny Jim is left there all by himself in the deserted concourse wondering where everybody's gone. Nasty moment, though."

"I'll look out for jealous boyfriends, too," I promised.

"It'll not be easy. It's them divilish women that are the trouble. Once upon a time – long ago, mind – I used to think it was only the fellas who were randy, that did all the chasing. Perhaps it was some maternal influence that had me believing the poor, put-upon females were merely the victims of their carnal oppressors and never had an original dirty desire in their angelic minds. Gob, I know better now. There's not one ha'puth of difference between the sexes. The girls love it as much as we do and the tricks they get up to in order to get it would put ours in the shade. So be warned ... och, I'm teaching my father to suck eggs, you're a man of no mean experience yourself. But perhaps you don't know the female on holiday as I do. They're a different breed altogether. The sun and sea do something to them. Maybe it's being closer to nature that makes them romantic, I don't know, but whatever it is, give the driest, the most juiceless old spinster a couple of days out here and she begins to look at the lads like she's never looked at them before. I've seen it happen dozens of times and lovely it is to see.

"Well, now, how about a spot of lunch ... and while we're having it I'll throw a few questions at you to see how you'd handle certain difficult situations."

"What sort of situations?"

We got up and made our way into the kitchen to make a sandwich.

"For instance – what action would you take if you arrived at Palma airport with a returning transfer of fifty clients and found all flights to London had been cancelled due to weather

172

conditions. It is one o'clock in the morning and all the hotel rooms the clients have just vacated have already been occupied by an incoming transfer?"

"Jean told me about that one."

He laughed. "The poor girl still wakes up screaming about it. You butter the bread and think about it."

CHAPTER ELEVEN

The first week flew by and I've never enjoyed a week more in my life.

I was with Patrick constantly. Every day we went out on an excursion. We visited Cala d'Or on the south east coast – beautiful, unspoiled sandy cove; Cala Millor, a resort on the east coast, set in pine woods sloping down to the sea; Cala Ratjada, a superb little fishing port overlooked by towering mountains; Playa Esperanza, on the Bay of Pollensa in the north of the island. And we saw Manacor, the centre of the artificial pearl industry; the Caves of Drach, where an orchestra plays on a huge floating barge; the leather factory at Inca; the liqueur factory at Santa Maria; and by Saturday evening I was shagged. I could hardly keep my eyes open. Patrick and I sat on my balcony, drinking vodka, carefully, because for me it was going to be a long night, and I found myself drifting off to sleep now and again.

"This is no good," I said, rousing myself. "The clients will be waiting at the airport and I'll be right here, snoring me nose off."

"It's been a busy week for you," he said, looking irritatingly fresh and wide awake. "The fresh air and the change of air does it, too. You've done very well to keep up. You've seen an awful lot of the island in the past six days."

I looked at my watch. It was eight o'clock. I'd be leaving for the airport in an hour. The thought brought a flutter of anxiety. My first transfer. Well, hell, there was nothing to worry about. Sixteen people to say hello to, sixteen lots of baggage to check and load onto the bus, a cheery word over the microphone, book them into the hotels – and that was that. Nothing to it. I'd be fast asleep in bed by midnight.

"We're in for rain," said Patrick, peering into the night sky.

Since sunset, cloud had rolled in from the sea; thick stuff, bringing with it a cool wind that made it necessary to wear a sweater on the balcony. I prayed it wouldn't rain. The clients wouldn't be very happy. The cool wind they wouldn't have to mind; it was the penalty for taking an early holiday. But rain would be taken very much amiss.

174

"D'you feel confident about meeting the transfer?" Patrick asked. "I'll gladly come with you . . ."

"Thanks, Patrick, but I want to do this on my own. Hell, we've been through the instructions a hundred times this week. If I don't know what to do by now, I'll never know."

"Och, of course you know what to do. But you know where I am if you get into any difficulties."

"Thanks very much – you've been a tremendous help."

"Not at all – you've been a good pupil. Get this first transfer over and you'll be away."

"Have you ever had anything go wrong?"

"Oh, sure. Lots of little things, but nothing we didn't eventually put right. We even lost a child once, a little boy of six. We disembarked thirty clients and their children at the hotel after an excursion and the little tyke crept back on the bus without our knowing. The driver took the bus to the garage and we found the wee fella fast asleep on the back seat three hours later. It wasn't altogether the most congenial three hours I've ever spent."

At a quarter to nine I went back to my flat, put on my Ardmont blazer as per regulations, and drove over to the Hotel Pollensa where I'd arranged to meet the bus. It was already there when I arrived. I boarded it, said hello to the driver.

He said, "Va all over, Russ." It's going to rain.

He wasn't kidding. We'd hardly cleared Palma Nova when it hit us. It bucketted down, lashed the windshield in fury. Zipping rips of lightning split the sky and thunder claps exploded with terrific crashes every few minutes. I cursed all the way to Palma.

At the airport I went straight to the airline office to check on the aircraft's arrival time. Yes, there was a small delay. Head winds were adding fifteen minutes to the e.t.a. I rang the two hotels and told them we'd be a bit late, then went into the bar and drank three cups of coffee.

At ten o'clock I went back again to the airline office. A further small delay. The storm that had hit us – and was still hitting us – was throwing the jet around a bit. Latest e.t.a. – ten thirty.

I paced up and down and chain-smoked, tried to read a magazine. The minutes crawled by . . . ten twenty . . . twenty five . . . thirty.

The announcement came at last over the public address system. "B.U.A. announce the arrival of their flight . . ."

175

I checked that our bus was parked directly outside Customs and went back into the building. People began emerging slowly from Passport Inspection. God, they looked terrible ... pale, shaken. Could these possibly be my clients?

Within minutes a hundred people thronged the Customs hall. Not one of them looked very well. It had obviously been one hell of a flight. Many of them were elderly. The men guided the women immediately to the bench seats and fussed over them, comforting them. I saw two stewardesses amongst the crowd, attending elderly women.

I made my way over, identifying myself by my blazer. An elderly man, tired, washed out, approached me.

"Are you the Ardmont courier?"

"Yes, sir ..."

"My name is Leach. We've just arrived from Gatwick ... had the most awful flight. The aircraft was hit by lightning and ... well, my wife is over there with the stewardess. She's not at all well. Can we get to the hotel as soon as possible?"

"Yes, of course, sir. We'll hurry it up as fast as we can. The baggage should be up very soon."

Next moment I was surrounded by clients all appealing for the utmost speed – Mr. and Mrs. McLeish, Mr. and Mrs. Anderson, the Carstairs ... the Edwards ...

I promised them all the same thing and prayed the luggage would come up the belt. It seemed to be taking ages.

I wandered over to one of the airhostesses who was attending a client. She came to meet me, smiling grimly. "We've had a rough one," she murmured. "We must have dropped five hundred feet in one of the falls. Food all over the place – we'd just finished the meal. Nobody's hurt but most of them are sick."

"My commiserations."

"Was a bit nasty. How many have you got?"

"Sixteen."

"Best of luck."

"Thanks."

The first luggage began emerging on the belt. Eager hands pulled them off and lugged them to the Customs table. The Customs men, thank God, were appreciative of the situation and waved the passengers away before they could place their luggage on the table.

I watched for Ardmont labels and got the porters over to

them fast, then hustled them off to the waiting bus while I guided the clients out and onto the bus.

Well, so much for "instructions". There wasn't a word about aircraft dropping five hundred feet and clients arriving sick as dogs and just wanting to lie down and die. "Check the luggage *before* it is put onto the coach" instructions said, "and assure yourself beyond all doubt that *all* the luggage is being loaded. You should follow this procedure: on arrival of a group, count the luggage and initial the reverse side of the labels ..." ha! I could just see myself telling this sorry bunch "now hang about a bit while I stick my name on sixty seven labels".

It took me a good fifteen minutes to load all the luggage and the poor old dears onto the bus and at last I was slamming the door and telling the driver, "Vaya – rapido!"

I walked down the centre aisle and had a look at Mrs. McLeish. She looked like death, pale green, and was lying with her head on her husband's shoulder. As I approached he whispered, "Have you a paper bag my any chance?"

Oh, Gawd.

We did have a few on board for such emergencies, especially for children on excursions. I went forward and came back with some and on the way both Mr. Anderson and Mrs. Edwards asked me for one. I handed McLeish the bag and turned around to see if anyone else wanted one. No sooner had I turned my back when the dreaded sound was heard. Poor Mrs. McLeish; she'd missed the bag. All over her husband and some over me. What in God's name did instructions say about this? I was searching for a solution when someone threw me a box of tissues. I took a handful out and gave the rest to McLeish who looked completely stunned by this latest development.

"I'm so sorry," his wife was whimpering.

He patted her hand and began scrubbing himself. "Never mind, dear, it couldn't be helped. We'll soon have you in bed."

Whether it was the sound or the ensuing odour or both, I don't know, but suddenly it was happening all around me, fortunately into the bags. Eight people were sick between then and arriving at the San Vincente. I've never spent such a ghastly half hour in all my born.

I plunged off the bus, ran up the hotel steps, gabbled a warning to the night receptionist, "Forget the guest book – just get 'em upstairs fast. And get all the porters you can muster. I want these people in bed in five minutes."

In a great flurry of activity my ten clients were off the bus and heading upstairs in the elevators in seconds. McLeish smiled wanly as he passed me. "You've been very kind. So sorry about the mess."

"Don't think about it, it was nothing. Get to bed. I'll see you in the morning. If you want a doctor – or me – just tell the night porter, he has my number."

I told the others the same thing. It was good to see the relief on their faces that they didn't have to hang around.

I fled back to the bus through the deluging rain and shot over to the Pollensa. Same routine there. As the last piece of luggage came into the foyer and the last client disappeared into the elevator, I breathed a huge sigh of relief and went out to the driver. He was soaked to the skin, poor fella. I slipped him a good tip and he took it with thanks.

"Le estoy muy agradecido," I said. I'm very grateful.

He shrugged and grinned. "De nada, Russ, de nada."

When I got in my car I realised I stank to high heaven.

As I entered the apartment block, Patrick's door opened. I'd had a feeling he'd be keeping a friendly eye on me. He popped his head out. "Well, and how did ..." His eyes popped. "Holy Mother of God, just look at you. You're soaked! Come in ... come in."

"I stink."

"Stink?" He wrinkled his nose as I got close. "Well, I do detect somethin' that's not your usual after-shave."

In the lounge I took my coat off and flopped down on the settee. Patrick handed me a huge slug of vodka and a cigarette then sat silently while I told him what had happened. When I'd finished he nodded solemnly then burst into laughter. "Welcome to the club, me boy. You've been initiated – and so soon in your career. Until you've been sicked on you're no courier." His laughter died. "But seriously, well done, you did the right thing getting them to bed fast. To hell with signing in. The comfort of the clients is the prime consideration and to hell with the bloody instructions. I'll pop over with you tomorrow, if you like, and see that nobody's seriously ill."

"I think they'll be all right. They just wanted bed."

"Sure ... sure. And now ..." the twinkle returned to his eye. "I've got a nice little surprise for you – somethin' that

178

will drive all thoughts of nastiness from your mind and restore your former good humour ..."

He got up, went to the table and brought back what looked like a coloured holiday brochure.

"Just clap your eyes on that lot and tell me what you think."

I took the folder. It *was* a brochure, but not a holiday one. It was for Gaytime swimsuits. Ladies swimsuits. I opened it out ... and out ... and out. There were four pages, printed on both sides. Each page contained four photographs. Two girls – one a smokey blonde, the other a deeply tanned brunette – modelled one-piece suits, sun-suits and tiny bikinis in a variety of highly provocative poses, legs wide apart, hands on hips, draped over rocks, sprawled in the sand ...

"Wow," I murmured.

"I thought that might be your reaction. You're a highly predictable fellow in some ways."

"I don't think any of these are quite you, though, Patrick ... oh, I don't know – this see-through net job might look pretty devastating ..."

"Russell, they're here."

"Mm?"

"The darlin's are here – in Palma Nova. I met them tonight in the Don Pedro. They drove in from Palma this morning. They're here for a week with their photographer, as queer a coot as you'll meet in many a ponsy mile. But the girls are gorgeous!"

"What nationality are they?"

"English! That ... is this year's catalogue. They're here to shoot another batch of photographs for magazines. And I ... that is *we* ... have volunteered to show them around the island to look for locations."

"No!"

"Oh, yes! None of them has been here before. That catalogue was shot in Jamaica. Now what d'you think about that?"

"I think ..." I sighed, "... I think you are the most intelligent, thoughtful, considerate and sophisticated man I have ever met."

"There you go again being predictable. I *knew* you were going to say that."

"When do they want to start?"

"Tomorrow morning, weather permitting. About ten o'clock."

"Couldn't be better. We'll nip over and see how the clients are, first ... I doubt if any of them will want to go touring tomorrow ... and then ..."

"Lovely."

"Which one's mine?"

He grinned lasciviously. "Well, to tell you the truth I did rather fancy the brunette. She's a pixie-faced angel with the name of Ruth Dell, slim as your finger and a pair of Bristols Venus herself would've given her right arm for."

I tapped the catalogue. "So I see. And the blonde?"

"Francine Dupres – Franky for short. And I doubt very much her ancestors got closer to France than Southend, but nevertheless she's a lot of bundle and one can't be over-critical in these difficult beginning-of-season times."

"She'll do very nicely. No competition?"

"Och, the wee fella taking the photies is as bent as all get out. Peter Telfer is his lovely name. He was making a play for the barman in the Don Pedro for two hours last night, wigglin' his lips and flutterin' his eyes. Still, he's pleasant enough company if you can overlook his slight aberrations."

I finished my drink and got up. "Patrick, you're a genius."

"Well, I wouldn't go so far as to say that."

"Wouldn't you?"

"Well ... if you insist."

"See you here at nine?"

"Nine it is. Goodnight, me boy, and leave it alone tonight, there's a good chap, you may need all your strength for tomorrow."

"You reckon?"

"Have I ever let you down?"

"Never."

"Well, then, have faith in this instance. If they're a couple of virgins, I'm Des O'Connor's uncle."

"I know the feeling. A week is a long time in Majorca as well as in politics."

*

I awoke at eight to the sun streaming through the window, all sign of the previous night's storm gone. The sea looked fat with rain water. A wallowing swell oozed in in lolloping undulation and rippled up the beach to dissipate itself in harmless little waves. There was not a cloud in the sky.

I flung the balcony door wide, breathed the freshness of the

180

morning and felt marvellous. What a way to start the day. For a moment my memory flew to Liverpool, to the view I had had from my little back room at Ravenscourt ... Aunty Barne's back yard ... old man Mathews' house on the other side of the cobbled alley ... the grey slate roofs of that line of grimy terraced houses ... what a difference.

I showered and dressed quickly, swallowed a cup of coffee and went to collect Patrick. He opened his door with a mouthful of toothpaste. "Hun in," he said. "Won' me a mimit," and ran back to the bathroom.

I heard him swill and spit. "Wonderful day, eh?"

"Terrific."

"Should be an interesting one, too, bejez." He came into the lounge, combing down the back of his hair. "Right, me boy, let's have a look at your clients."

We went first to the San Vincente. Yes, they had all slept fairly well and most of them had ordered their breakfast in their rooms. From the foyer I telephoned each in turn. They sounded very cheerful. It was probably the sun. No, they hadn't planned anything more ambitious than a stroll along the beach and to the local shops and they wouldn't be needing me during the day.

Then we nipped over to the Pollensa and did the same there. One woman, Mrs. Kennedy, was still feeling poorly but her husband thought another day would put her on her feet.

As we came down the steps Patrick checked his watch. "Five to ten – just right. Russell, let's be after it."

We drove to the San Pedro in the mercedes, having decided all five of us would be more comfortable in it than in his two-seater."

"I'll do my share of the driving, of course," he said generously, "and I'll give you a turn in the back with the girls."

"How very kind. And Tooty Fruity stays up front with the driver?"

"Och, he's harmless. If he tries anything funny – slap his wrist with your handbag."

We parked the car and went into the luxurious foyer of the San Pedro. Patrick said, "I'll give them a tinkle and hurry them up."

We were sitting in the foyer when the girls appeared from the elevator.

"There," murmured Patrick. "What did I tell you?"

Both were tall and very slim, extremely chic in pastel cotton

trousers and loose silk blouses, their hair held by silk band-
anas. Ruth, as Patrick had mentioned and I had witnessed in
the catalogue, was well endowed up top. Franky, the blonde,
was less so, though they were still very adequate. Their features were nicely-boned, very photogenic, and well tanned,
presumably from Jamaica. They wore very little make-up,
just eye shadow, false eyelashes and a touch of lipstick.

They came across the foyer all legs and stealth, graceful as
cats, smiling at Patrick, inspecting me.

"Good morning, ladies," said Patrick, leaping up. "You
both look nothin' short of absolutely radiant this morning.
Meet a fellow guide and mentor, Russell Tobin."

Laughing, they shook hands.

"Is he always this complimentary," Franky asked me.

"His father was keeper of Blarney Castle. He used to
sprinkle ground Blarney Stone on Patrick's porridge as a
child."

"How did you know that?" said Patrick. "I never told a
soul." He said to the girls. "Where is Mr. Peter Telfer?"

"Probably taking his curlers out," Ruth said.

"You're jokin' . . . of course?" said Patrick.

The girls gave bitchy smiles.

Peter Telfer came out of the elevator as though on cue,
spotted us and came over with small, quick steps. He was on
the short side, about five seven, a little chubby and his head,
a mass of tight brown curls, seemed much too big for his
body. He had a small nose, small blue eyes and a full mouth.
His walk and his hands were the immediate give-away. He
moved them in loose, flowing gestures, as a woman does –
with a floppy wrist. He was dressed in tight grey hipster pants,
a light-blue woollen sweater, buttoned to the neck, white
leather sneakers and sky-blue socks. He looked devastatingly
clean and gave the impression he'd never in his life been otherwise. I put his age at around thirty.

Over one shoulder were slung two cameras and over the
other a leather equipment case.

As he approached us his eyes swivelled to me. Having already met Patrick and dismissed him as a possible conquest,
he was having a good gander at Tobin. I met his gaze with
pleasant disinterest and shook his hand.

"Right," said Patrick, "where would you like to try first?
Any particular background you fancy, Peter?"

"No, leave it to you, love, we've got all week. How about a

182

general ride round today – and if I see anything that takes me fancy, we'll have a bash."

"In that case, let's tour the coastline. We'll start west from here and look at Santa Ponsa, Camp de Mar, Paguera, then along the north west coast to Puerto de Soller and the mountains."

"Absolutely super."

We went out to the car, stowed the girls' small wardrobe cases in the boot and got in, Patrick and the girls in the back, Telfer in the front with me, at a decent distance.

"What's the name of this first place?" Telfer asked Patrick. "Santa what?"

"Ponsa."

"Mm, sounds homey," he laughed.

At least he could take a joke against himself.

Patrick said, "Santa Ponsa is one of the least built-on beaches and one of the best. If you want a long stretch of empty sand, this is the place."

"Oh, good. Drive on, Russell and let's have a butcher's at it."

As we approached Santa Ponsa, only a few minutes drive from Magaluf, Patrick said, "If anyone is interested, this is the place where James I of Catalonia landed with his sweaty knights in 1228 to mix it with the Saracens for possession of the island."

"How frightfully interesting," drawled Telfer. "Who won?"

"Jimmy, of course. And close by there's a splendid 13th century castle called Ben Dinat, which is Catalan for "I have dined well", because these were the very words that Jimmy said, interspersed with burps, when asked how he'd enjoyed his dinner of scampi, chips and tinned peas."

"There, now, girls," said Telfer, with a yawn. "We learn a little something every day. Keep your lovely ears open and who knows what you'll grow up to be."

They sneered at him.

I drove close to the beach and we all got out and had a butcher's. Telfer went into a mild paroxysm. "Wonderful ... wonderful! Girls, we'll take a few here. Get your white stuff on. Virgin white against a virgin beach. Quickly, now, chop, chop ..."

I don't know where I'd expected them to change – behind a tree, in the car perhaps. I really hadn't given it any thought. Idly Patrick and I watched them return to the car and take out

183

white bikinis and towels from their cases in the boot while Telfer was tearing up and down with a viewfinder and a light meter.

The girls talked quietly between themselves, looked up and down the deserted beach, over towards the nearest hotel which was five hundred yards away, then came to some decision and laughed conspiratorially.

Franky called, "Boys . . . would you do something for us?"

We were over there in a flash.

Franky said to me, "Would you hold my towel up while I change, please, Russ?"

Ruth offered hers to Patrick. "Would you do me, please?"

"But of course, darlin', where are you going to stand?"

"Around here," she said, heading for the far side of the car.

"I'll do it here," said Franky, already standing close to the side. "D'you mind?"

"Violently."

She cocked a brow which said "You kidding?" and threw me the towel. I opened it out, fully, stretching my arms. It was deep enough to cover her from shoulders to knees.

"No peeking," she said.

"Who – me?"

With four deft flicks she'd undone all the buttons on her blouse; with a shrug it was off – and she was standing there naked to the waist. My pulse exploded. I raised the towel quickly, but not that quickly – not before I'd got a good eyeful of small, uptilted breasts as tanned as the rest of her. Then she threw the blouse over the towel, draping it there bringing the towel below my eye level again.

She kicked off her sandals, unzipped her trousers, dropped them and stood on one leg to take them off. They came over the towel too. All she had on was a pair of white transparent knicks – her full tan and everything else showing through. Down came the knicks. She turned and placed these on the bonnet of the car and picked up the pants of the bikini that she'd placed there. For a full fifteen seconds she stood with her back to me, completely naked, while she sorted out the front from the back of the bikini pants. I couldn't believe it was happening. I glanced over the car to Patrick. His mouth was open. Ruth was also starkers. She had magnificent breasts, larger than Franky's as I'd seen from the catalogue.

I looked back at Franky. Her body was superb; her skin

184

flawless. Her waist curved down to a perfect bottom and long, slender legs.

Suddenly she turned, faced me, and stood on one leg again to put on the bikini pants. "Does this embarrass you?" she asked. I could detect the laughter in her voice. "We're used to undressing in front of men. When you've got twenty five quick changes in a show there's no time for prudery."

"I'm glad. You have a wonderful figure, Franky."

She stood up and eased the pants up her hips. "Thanks. I'd like a bit more up here, though . . ." she pushed up her breasts, making them fuller. "Especially for swimsuit work. But the rest is all right."

"I think they're very beautiful."

"Have you seen Ruth's?"

"Er, yes, I did have a quick peek."

"Now, hers are ideal – especially for bikini tops. I'd like mine that full."

"Don't change a thing," I said.

She threaded her arms through the bikini top, took her trousers and blouse off the towel, took the towel and threw them all in the car, then turned to me. "Will you do me, please?"

I fumbled with her strap hook, touching her skin.

"Thanks," she said, adjusting the cups, easing the strap. She turned and posed for me, one knee inclined in front of the other. "Will I do?"

"I'll take six."

Telfer was striding towards us through the loose sand. "Come on, cherubs, hurry it up. Put the boys down, you can play with them later."

Patrick and Ruth came from around the car. She looked stunning in a tiny white bikini with a gold chain at the waist.

"Over there by that tree," said Telfer, charging off. The girls followed him, skipping like golden fawns, hair flying in the breeze.

Patrick sidled up to me, gasping. "Holy Mither, did you ever see anything like it? I couldn't believe my eyes when she whipped it all off and stood there mother naked, those wonderful Bristols starin' me in the eye, pubics rustlin' in the breeze . . ."

"They just don't give a damn, do they?"

"Not a tinker's – and a lovely, healthy attitude it is, too. I just wish more young and beautiful women would follow their example, there'd be so much less wanton, lustful lechery and who the hell am I kidding? She got me so knotted up there with carnal desire I'll have lovers' nuts for a fortnight."

"Think of what it's going to be like by the end of the week, Patrick. Seven whole days of this lie stretched before us . . ."

"Aye, and seven whole nights, too. And if I don't lay that lovely thing this very evening my name's not Patrick Gilhoolie O'Connell Holmes – and if you breathe a word of that to anyone I'll break every bone in your body."

We watched Telfer for fifteen minutes, ripping off shot after shot, leaping about like a leprechaun, while the girls posed and postured against the trees, against the sea, against the backdrop of endless virgin sand. Then he ordered them back to change. We heard him call, "Try the wet-look stuff and hurry it up, loves."

Back they trotted. Patrick was already in position on the far side of the car. I got the towel out and held it up as Franky reached me. She laughed and said "Keen, aren't we?"

Up went the towel . . . off came the bra and pants . . . and once again it was all displayed before me. Unbelievable.

In the next hour they had two further changes, the final one being into one-piece swimsuits. Then it was back in the car and on to Paguera.

"Got some beautiful stuff there," panted Telfer, re-loading his cameras. "I must say you chaps are being wonderfully helpful. Sure you don't mind holding the towels for the girls?" He flashed his eyes at me in a coy smile.

"Well," I sighed, "we did promise to help. It's not exactly the sort of job we would have volunteered for, but under the duress of a promise . . ."

Patrick guffawed and I got Franky's hand on the back of my head.

"Couldn't agree more," Telfer drawled. "I mean, what *is* pleasant about a naked woman. . . ?"

Poor soul.

We stopped only five minutes at Paguera. It was just more beach to Telfer. But at Camp de Mar he became quite ecstatic about the pine trees and once again it was all out . . . towels up . . . trousers down . . . band . . . bang.

As Patrick passed me when the session was over he murmured, "I'll never last a week, so help me."

He took over the driving for the fast run along the north coast to Puerto de Soller where he had a very good lunch on

Telfer, then we began the homeward journey back through the mountains to Palma and on the Palma Nova. We got back to the San Pedro at five o'clock.

"Wonderful day," said Telfer, "just wonderful. Where d'you recommend tomorrow?"

"Let's do the east coast – get a combination of harbours, coves and mountains."

"Too splendid ... too splendid ..." He wandered off towards the elevators, yawning.

"What plans have you girls got?" I asked Franky.

She shrugged and looked at Ruth who also shrugged.

Franky said, "First – a long hot bath. Second – I haven't a clue."

"Then we suggest ..." said Patrick, "... a couple of drinks at my place, a drive into Palma, a superb dinner at a little place I know and whatever takes your fancy afterwards ..." he looked at me, "don't we?"

"Indubidably."

"We'll pick you up at seven, O.K.?"

"I don't know," Ruth said hesitantly. "I mean, we don't know you very well. Girls can't be too careful. How do we know we can trust you?"

"I'll put your minds at rest," said Patrick. "You absolutely can't."

"Then we'll see you at seven," said Franky.

*

Well, that was one week ago tonight. Franky and Ruth leave tomorrow, back to England, and we'll miss them. It's been a fabulous week. The weather has been good and we've been all over the island. And every night we've been dancing and dining and ... and what else? Oh, yes, I had my second transfer in – thirty six of them – and this time without mishap. They're mostly older couples because it's still a bit early in the season, though there are three younger birds amongst them, three secretaries from the same company who missed their holidays last year and have been given two this year. They're not all that terrific but it does seem to indicate that the trend has started ... harbingers of things to come.

Anyway, I'm more settled in the job, now. I met this transfer with a lot more confidence and it's going to get easier all the time. By the way – Walter Payne, our area manager, actually phoned me and congratulated me on the way I'd handled that first transfer! Apparently Mr. McLeish had taken the trouble to tell Payne how grateful he was for the attention his wife had received and Payne passed it on to me. He still was not exactly overflowing with friendly cheer but I did detect a slight easing of snide, so maybe we'll get on better in the future. Even if we don't, you know how much it's going to worry me.

Oh, had a letter from Tony Dane to say he'd booked into the Pollensa for the whole of June and told me that if I didn't have something really good lined up for him on arrival he'd make complaints about me until I did. He also said my White Marvel campaign was going out on T.V. and how bloody horrible I looked and he said there had been letters in the Times complaining that the series was racially slanted and demanding that the commercials be withdrawn until a series called Black Marvel was made, lying swine.

He'd been down to Len's Den again since I'd left and some-one had written on the wall: "Russ 'White Marvel' Tobin is a screaming great poof" and told me he'd searched his heart assiduously for an honest opinion of the comment before adding "Hear hear!".

God help us all when he gets out.

Well, there you are, everything up to date. It's now eleven o'clock and I must have an early night, it's been a hectic week. If – and I *mean* if – I get a bit of spare time later on in the season I'll let you know how I'm getting on and how things went with Tony out here. And ... excuse me just a moment. "Er, Franky, love ..."

"Mm?"

"Look, I don't want to nag, but if you're going out on the balcony don't you think you ought to put *some* clothes on ... ?"

Honestly, the way this bird walks around ...

Tarra.

THE GOD OF THE LABYRINTH 40p

Colin Wilson

What has the most prolific of England's younger authors got into this time? Book-buyers have been waiting keenly for a new direction from Colin Wilson, and now they have it: *"The score up to page 50 is two sex experiences for the narrator, plus a whipping with a cat-o'-nine-tails which he gives on request to an eccentric colonel, plus several other sex fragments from the forged or genuine papers of Esmond Donelly, eighteenth century rake. This is roughly par for the 300-page course, with passages of Johnsonian pastiche and nutty mystical musing"* breathed the *Sunday Times*, while Janice Elliot of the *Sunday Telegraph* claimed *"the plentiful sex is never prurient: there are some mind-boggling performances (but) he talks a lot of sense"*; meanwhile the Sunday *Sun* raved on about *"a well-written book with lashings of sex – entertaining and informative."*

Make up your own mind on this new line for Wilson (in fact an extension of his enquiry into existentialism and murder) by reading *The God of The Labyrinth* yourself. As the narrator says, "I have always been obsessed by the way that sexual experience seems to slip through the fingers like fairy gold."

General Fiction

The incredible sex sagas of
STANLEY MORGAN

Have you read the amazing amorous
adventures of Russ Tobin – Stanley
Morgan's hilarious romeo-rapist? Thousands
of book-buyers have, and we bet they're still
reeling from the blows of bawdiness and
beauty inflicted upon them by the wit and
action of Mr. Morgan's rapier pen. Few
books in their genre are as popular as these:
they are constantly being reprinted.

THE SEWING MACHINE MAN   30p
THE DEBT COLLECTOR   30p
THE COURIER   30p
COME AGAIN COURIER   35p

BEST SELLING MAYFLOWER TITLES

☐	583 11692 2	THE MOVIE MAKER	Herbert Kastle	4(
☐	583 11574 8	THE "F" CERTIFICATE	David Gurney	3:
☐	583 11717 1	LAST SUMMER	Evan Hunter	2:
☐	583 11683 3	FANNY HILL (unexpurgated)	John Cleland	3.
☐	583 11186 6	WANDERERS EASTWARD, WANDERERS WEST	Kathleen Winsor	4(
☐	583 11650 7	GOAT SONG	Frank Yerby	4(
☐	583 11710 4	THE DEAL	William Marshall	4(
☐	583 11715 5	THE MADONNA COMPLEX	Norman Bogner	3:
☐	583 11734 1	WORLD ATHLETICS & TRACK EVENTS HANDBOOK/70	Compiled by Bruce Tulloh	2:
☐	583 11703 1	WORLD MOTOR RACING & RALLYING HANDBOOK/70	Complied by Mark Kahn	2:
☐	583 11711 2	OCTOPUS HILL	Stanley Morgan	2:
☐	583 11377 X	THE SEWING MACHINE MAN	Stanley Morgan	2:
☐	583 11336 2	STILETTO	Harold Robbins	2:
☐	583 10339 1	ETERNAL FIRE	Calder Willingham	3:
☐	583 10429 0	LUCY CROWN	Irwin Shaw	3:
☐	583 11665 5	THE COUNTRY TEAM	Robin Moore	4(
☐	583 11342 7	DYNASTY OF DEATH	Taylor Caldwell	4(
☐	583 11530 6	THE BEATLES	Hunter Davies	4(
☐	583 10437 1	THE MARRIAGE ART	J E Eichenlaub	2:
☐	583 11563 2	OR I'LL DRESS YOU IN MOURNING	Larry Collins & Dominique Lapierre	3:
☐	583 11443 1	THE MAN WHO HAD POWER OVER WOMEN	Gordon M Williams	3(
☐	583 11157 2	THE CAMP	Gordon M Williams	2:
☐	583 11608 6	LOVE IS A WELL-RAPED WORD	Doreen Wayne	3(
☐	583 11600 0	THE BUSINESS OF MURDER	Edgar Lustgarten	2:
☐	583 11338 9	THE JET SET	Burton Wohl	3(

All these books are available at your local bookshop or newsagent; or can be ordered direct from the publisher. Just tick the titles you want and fill in the form below.

Write to **Mayflower Cash Sales, Kernick Rd., Industrial Site, Penryn, Cornwall.**
Please send cheque or postal order value of the cover price plus 4p for postage and packing.

Name..

Address...

....